"FORGIVE ME . . ."

"Tell me about the deep plowing," he urged as they rode toward the east field.

"I . . . I read about it," she said hesitantly. "We'd had such a bad crop, that I decided to try it."

"I see." His voice was noncommittal. "Have you made any other 'decisions'?"

There was the cynicism she had anticipated. Damaris frowned. "I am conducting a small experiment. Why, Richard, do I feel as though I must answer to you? If I fail, it shall be on *my* head. I am weary of your mockery and your condescension!"

He shook his head. "Little could prevent these plants from producing a fine crop. Well done, Damaris. I regret my 'mockery' and 'condescension.' Will you forgive me?"

"If it doesn't happen again," she teased.

His gaze met hers. Mesmerized, she swayed toward him.

He slipped his arms around her.

"Richard . . ."

"Damaris . . ." He lowered his lips to hers.

Tournament of Hearts

CATHLEEN CLARE

AVON BOOKS NEW YORK

TOURNAMENT OF HEARTS is an original publication of Avon Books. This work has never before appeared in book form. This work is a novel. Any similarity to actual persons or events is purely coincidental.

AVON BOOKS
A division of
The Hearst Corporation
1350 Avenue of the Americas
New York, New York 10019

Copyright © 1994 by Catherine Toothman
Published by arrangement with the author
Library of Congress Catalog Card Number: 93-91640
ISBN: 0-380-77432-1

First Avon Books Printing: January 1994

AVON TRADEMARK REG. U.S. PAT. OFF. AND IN OTHER COUNTRIES, MARCA REGISTRADA, HECHO EN U.S.A.

Printed in the U.S.A.

RA 10 9 8 7 6 5 4 3 2 1

For Aunt Luda and Uncle Herb

Chapter 1

Richard Marston, Earl of Delafield, accompanied by his groom and valet, wheeled his new blue-and-gold curricle off the main road and up to the tall, iron gates of Delafield Hall. He looked up fondly at the stone gatehouse. He had missed it. He had missed the whole estate, his family, his friends. He had missed everything about his life in England and everyone, of course, except the woman whose treachery had sent him off on his years of foreign travel. But now he was home again, and until he had seen the great gothic "D" on the gates and the sinister iron falcons perched on the gateposts, he hadn't realized how truly homesick he had been.

"M'lord! Is it really you?" Old Asa, who had been gatekeeper for as long as Richard could remember, spun out of the house on gnarled, bowed legs to fling wide the barrier.

"It is!" He drove inside and pulled up, giving the reins to his groom and stepping down from the conveyance. He extended his hand. "I am glad to see that you are still here, Asa."

"Aye, I'm still among the livin'!" Eyes glowing, the servant pumped His Lordship's hand. "M' rheumatism's worse, but I reckon I can open the gates for a few more years."

"Perhaps I should hire an assistant for you," the earl said with concern. The elderly servant had been kind to him, and to his younger brother too. He

1

didn't like to think of him going out to handle the gates in the worst sort of weather.

"Naw. Thankee anyway, m'lord, but I don't need one." Asa leaned close, lowering his voice. "Got me a woman. She opens the gates on rainy or snowy days, when m' bones are actin' up." He shrugged, rolling his eyes. "Had to marry this one, though. She's right religious."

Richard grinned. "Still a ladies' man, are you?"

"Course I am! A bit of ... uh ... you know ... keeps you healthy." He winked broadly. "Got you a lady yet, m'lord?"

"No, I am not bringing home a new countess."

"Keeping a piece of fluff on the side, mebbe?" Asa chuckled.

"No." Richard pretended ruefulness. "I haven't that either."

" 'Od's teeth, m'lord! Didn't I teach you better'n that, when you was a lad?"

"Yes, Asa, you did. I shall try to improve." He squeezed the old man's shoulder. "But now I had best be on my way. I'm anxious to see Mama and Percy."

"They'll be right happy to see you too, m'lord."

"I shall come visit soon and meet your new wife," Richard said as he hopped into the curricle, took up the reins, and set the team into a smart trot.

"Don't you forget to remedy your problem!" the gatekeeper called after him. "If you don't, your innards'll burst, and then you'll get the gout!"

Waving, Richard laughed. Old Asa certainly hadn't changed. "Do you think he's right, sir?" the groom asked worriedly from his perch behind.

"About what?"

"About innards, m'lord."

Casey, the valet Richard had hired in Venice, when

the man's previous employer had succumbed from an overindulgence of tainted oysters, looked over his shoulder and sniffed. "Don't be absurd, Wesley."

"Asa comes up with some odd ideas." The earl smiled reminiscently. "No, I don't think he is correct in this one."

"God, I hope not! It's been ages since I've had any ... uh ... you know ..."

Casey lifted his nose in stiff disapproval. "Wesley! I'm sure that His Lordship is not interested in your personal exploits. Moreover, your tone of familiarity is to be censured. I cannot comprehend why a man of your appalling disrespect has remained in service." When Wesley fell silent, the valet's nose rose even higher with the satisfaction of it.

Richard sighed. He wondered how a high stickler like Casey would get along in the informal atmosphere of Delafield Hall. The valet was so haughty and dignified that he would probably be uncomfortable with the family's easy relationship between themselves and their retainers. The Delafield servants considered themselves perfectly at home on the estate, as indeed they were. Most of them had come from families who had served there for generations. It was true that some of their actions and statements could be interpreted as impertinent. Just consider old Asa! But Richard knew that they had the family's best interests at heart. Even Wesley, a Londoner, seemed to sense and adapt himself to the Delafield way. Richard hoped that Casey would do so as well. The man was the most capable valet he had ever employed.

Under Casey's ministrations, the earl had evolved from a well-dressed gentleman into a work of art. Even with the harshest conditions of travel, his perfectly tailored clothes were always impeccably clean and unwrinkled, and his boots, spotless and shining. The valet's skill with scissors had turned Richard's unruly, tawny-blond hair into a study of careless elegance. The valet's insistence on frequent manicures kept His Lordship's nails smoothed and properly buffed. But, of course, Casey had good raw material to work with. With his tall, trim figure, brilliant blue eyes, and finely chiseled facial structure, Richard was considered a very handsome man.

The road curved through a thick copse. As they entered it, Richard drew the horses to a slower pace, enjoying the cool forest air and the rich, acrid scent of decaying leaves. As a boy, he had spent many hours playing in these woods. In fact, Asa, when he'd had a woman to manage the gate, had helped him build a treehouse. He wondered if it was still there. He'd have to look.

Grinning, he remembered the time that his younger brother, Percival, and his playmates, two little girls from the neighboring estate, had attacked him in his lofty structure and tried to capture it. They'd lobbed spears made from sharpened branches, and he had returned their fire with his own artillery of sticks and stones. The girls had run away, but Percy had been persistent, until Richard hit him with a large rock. His small brother ran home crying, and the future earl received a spanking as reward for his victory. How simple life had been back then. How complicated it was now.

He settled his face into the cool, aloof expression he had cultivated during his sojourn away from England. Long ago, he had ceased loving Annabelle. He could scarcely recall what she looked like. But would all of society remember the time he had fled the country because of her? Would they whisper about him? Laugh at him? That was the horror that had kept him away from home for so many years.

Annabelle. His first love. Really, she was the only lady he had ever loved, for no one after that unfortunate episode had come near to capturing his heart. Why had Annabelle betrayed him? Why had she given her hand to the loser of the duel? He supposed that he would never know, but it didn't matter now, anyway. He didn't care if he never saw her again.

A movement at the edge of the woods ahead of them suddenly drew his attention from his memories. He heard the clank of metal. What . . . what in heaven's name was that? Richard blinked.

A knight in tarnished armor, astride a gaily caparisoned horse, cantered blissfully out of the forest, crossed the lane, and passed onto the bridle path on the opposite side.

The earl checked the team to a halt and stared openmouthed as the ancient warrior's faded plume disappeared among the trees.

"My God!" Casey exclaimed, exhibiting more excitement than Richard had ever seen him display.

"You saw what I saw?" Richard asked in bewilderment.

"I saw a knight!"

" 'Twas a ghost!" cried the groom.

"Don't be ridiculous, Wesley," the valet snapped, unnerved. "There is no such thing."

"But I saw it!"

Richard shoved the reins into the groom's hands, leaped out of the curricle, and hurried to the spot where the strange incarnation had vanished. "There are hoofprints, Wesley. Ghosts do not leave tracks!"

"You see?" Casey hissed. "You should pay attention to your betters!"

The earl walked a short distance into the copse,

but the knight was gone. He couldn't even hear the clank of the armor. Shaking his head, he returned to the drive.

"It must have been a prank," he guessed, "or someone carrying out the requirements of a wager."

"He didn't even look at us," the valet mused.

"I doubt that knights in armor can turn their heads very well," Richard said. "He probably didn't even see us." After climbing into the vehicle, he snapped the reins and set off again. "I shall find out about him, though. After all, he is on my property."

They broke from the woodlands and entered a vast meadow that bordered the lawns of Delafield Hall. Richard looked at the magnificent, shining stone castle on the rising ground ahead and took a deep breath. Yes, he was home at last! For better or for worse, and within a very short time, he would be walking through the door to greet his family. How long it had been!

"What's that, m'lord?" Wesley asked.

"It's Delafield Hall," Richard said proudly. "I told you it was a castle."

"No, sir. *That*." He pointed off to the side of them.

"They're carpenters, you dolt!" Casey barked. "How many times must I tell you not to attempt to engage His Lordship in trivial chatter?"

Carpenters? Construction on the meadow? No one had the right! He peered more closely.

With the busy beehive of activity, it was difficult to tell exactly what was being built. There seemed to be stands for seating, such as those at a sporting event. And . . . could that be a tiltyard?

Knights. Jousting. Tournaments. What in the hell was happening at Delafield Hall? Richard set his jaw. This was his home. It was supposed to be peaceful and soothing, a haven from the pressures of the outside world. Whatever was going on, he would discover it, discover it soon, and put a period to it! He abruptly started the horses, nearly unseating Casey and Wesley, and raced toward the castle.

"Look at this dress, Damaris." Melissa laid the history volume on top of the opened estate account book and pointed to the picture within. "It would be perfect for the Queen of Beauty to wear to the Delafield Tournament. Do you think that the Misses Rogers could make it?"

Damaris Grayson sighed as the old tome shed particles of leather on the neatly inscribed page. "I wish you would not remind me of that nonsense."

Melissa was shocked. "It isn't nonsense!" she said with consternation. "It shall be fun."

"And expensive."

"Botheration!" She tossed her bright auburn curls and regarded her elder sister with saucy green eyes. "For once, can we forget about expense? We are going to have a good time. You must admit that we have precious few pleasures around here! Besides, Mama says that we may spend as much as we wish."

Damaris stifled a groan. "Mama is not the one who balances the accounts. If she did, she would quickly realize that we haven't the money to spend on dresses that we may only wear once. This whole thing is impractical, Missy."

"Surely you cannot be saying that we should not attend? We would insult the whole Delafield family! Mama won't allow it."

"No, we are neighbors and we must go, especially considering your particular friendship with Percy," she agreed. "But why can't we scour the attic for old fabrics and construct the costumes ourselves?"

"What? Wear made-over dresses!" Missy shrieked.

"In front of all the fine female guests from London? Not me! I would not mortify myself so!"

"But look . . ." Damaris set the history book aside and indicated the figures in the ledger.

"I don't wish to look!" Her younger sister turned away with an impatient swish of her skirts. "I cannot understand all those calculations."

"I shall be happy to explain."

"I *don't want* to understand them," Missy said firmly. "I have better ways to spend my time. Furthermore, I doubt that you could make it clear to me anyway. Your method of interpretation is not the same as mine. For instance, if we are so impoverished that we cannot buy the costumes, how could we afford the new plows that you bought last spring? That doesn't seem logical at all."

"Actually, it's quite elementary." Her sister smiled tolerantly. "Plows help make money; medieval dresses do not."

"They could, and they will! You know how fascinated Percy is by all things medieval! Seeing me dressed in such a fashion might bring him to the sticking point! And you might catch a husband too, Damaris. There will be ever so many gentlemen in attendance. One of them might fall head over heels in love with you!"

Damaris sighed. She wished for only one gentleman to fall in love with her, and he wouldn't be there. The Earl of Delafield had been gone for a very long time, and surely he wouldn't come back to attend this bit of Percy's foolishness. She caught herself. Foolishness? How could she think Percy foolish? *She* was the one who was witless! Here she was at the ripe old age of twenty-one. Why must she hold on to her dreams of Richard Delafield? They were the stuff of childhood.

"I'm serious!" Missy protested. "It might happen! Think of our dresses in terms of an investment ... like the plows."

"Fustian, Missy! That's an absurd comparison. I can already see the improvement that deep plowing has made in the soil. The plants are thicker and healthier. I know that our harvest will be much improved." She sagaciously raised an eyebrow. "But I have never seen a gentleman fall in love just because of a new dress."

"Oh, but they do! Men are attracted to ladies who look their best. Then they fall in love."

Damaris slowly shook her head. "I simply cannot justify it."

"Perhaps it is not your place to do so," Missy murmured slyly. "Mama is the real mistress here. Her decision should be the final one."

Damaris felt a twinge of anxiety in the pit of her stomach at her sister's overt threat. Since their father's illness, it had been terribly hard to control their mother's spending. In the past, Sir Osbert had, somehow, managed to indulge his wife's whims and keep her happy, while still showing a profit on his account books. Of course, he hadn't had to deal with a harvest as poor as the one his daughter had faced last fall. She hoped that, with the new plows, this year would be better, but she couldn't depend on it.

Farming was so uncertain. A skimpy harvest could set one back for years. Even with a bumper crop, the prices could be so low as to make the situation just as critical. When her father became well enough to take up the reins of his estate once more, Damaris wanted everything to be perfect. A debt-ridden property could send Sir Osbert into another apoplexy. The shock and worry might even kill him! Why couldn't Mama and Missy see this and conduct themselves conservatively? Why must they fight her at every turn?

"Please let me explain these figures, Missy," she begged her sister. "If you will only let me show you, I am certain that you will understand. And you can help me convince Mama."

"You are asking the wrong person, Damaris. *I* want a new costume for the Delafield Tournament. I want three of them, in fact. One for the tournament itself, one for the banquet, and one for the ball. That is certainly not asking too much. After all, I did give up my Season this year."

"But if we are careful with our money now, and the harvest is profitable, we might be able to afford your Season next year!" Damaris protested. "Surely that is worth more than three costumes, which you will wear only once."

"No." Missy vehemently shook her head. "There are too many 'ifs' involved in a debut next spring. The tournament is a certainty, and besides, it will be the most talked-about event for years to come. I am going to attend, and I want three dresses. Three *new* dresses."

"Please be reasonable . . ."

"No! Percy will, of course, choose me to be the Queen of Beauty. Can you imagine how I would look in musty old made-over fabric from the attics? In front of the cream of society? How can you even *think* of such a thing?"

Damaris felt her shoulders slumping and determinedly straightened them. She would search every trunk in the attic. If she found enough pretty choices, perhaps she could change Missy's mind. It was worth the effort. At least she would find something she herself could use. It would save that much.

A scurry in the hall announced the return of Lady

Grayson. After several hours spent visiting with the friends, their mother would probably be full of news of the tournament and their neighbors' preparation for it. Damaris prepared herself for another onslaught.

"Are you in here, girls?" Their mama walked briskly through the library door, peeling off her gloves. "Just wait until you hear! My goodness, the entire county is turning inside out in anticipation of the Delafield Tournament!"

Missy flounced over to the sofa and sat down with a bounce of excitement. "Do tell all, Mama! I knew I should have accompanied you!"

"Well, let me see. First, I went to Squire Carter's. The ladies' dresses have already arrived. They ordered them from London, of course."

"Are they pretty? What colors did they choose?"

"La, between them all, they've selected every color of the rainbow! Even the squire has a costume! The gowns are lovely, of course, but I think we can do better." She narrowed her eyes. "Have you searched the history books as I instructed you to do, Melissa?"

"Yes, and I've come up with some perfectly wonderful ideas!"

Damaris glanced down at the engraving in the book on the desk. It was a likeness of Queen Anne Boleyn, and her dress, though impressive, didn't really suit her little sister. It was cut much too suggestively for a girl of Missy's tender years, and it was far too elaborate.

"Our clothing will be absolutely authentic," said Lady Grayson with finality. "The costumes of the squire's wife and daughters seemed to possess too much of a modern influence for my taste. After all, if dear Percy is going to so much trouble to make everything genuine, we can scarcely do less."

"No, indeed!"

Lady Grayson continued on with the description of her afternoon. "After my chat with Matilda Carter, I proceeded to the vicarage. Oh, it is beyond belief!"

"What?" cried Missy.

"Dorothea is to have three new dresses for the tournament! Mrs. White has already purchased the fabrics and engaged the Rogers sisters to construct them!"

Damaris's heart sank. If Dolly White, her sister's best friend, was to have three new costumes, Missy would have to have them as well. Neither her sister, nor their mother, would be able to accept the fact that the vicar allowed the expense, while the Graysons did not. No, it was inevitable that Missy would have her gowns. Still, she might persuade Lady Grayson to use old fabric for her own and Damaris's gowns.

"Naturally," their mother continued, "I went at once to the house of the Misses Rogers and engaged them to sew our costumes. I induced them to begin immediately, for I am a good customer of theirs, and they are well aware of it! I wished to avoid slipshod last-minute work, of course."

"Of course," Missy echoed. "But, Mama, the fabric . . ."

"I've taken care of that." Lady Grayson's green eyes sparkled girlishly. She darted to the door. "Thomas, bring in my parcels!" Turning, she smiled at her daughters. "I know you would have liked to help select the fabrics yourselves, but I was fearful of having to accept second choice. You must certainly consider my judgment to be impeccable, so I went ahead and purchased the materials."

"Mama!" Damaris cried. "We can't afford . . ."

Lady Grayson waved a careless arm. "Of course we can. This is the greatest event this neighborhood has ever witnessed. Guests will be here from all over England. The *best* people! Your papa would not wish us to wear anything but the finest!"

"But . . ."

"Damaris, can you never be satisfied?"

"But, Mama, the expense!" Her hand strayed once again to the ledger.

"Fiddlesticks! We *shall* afford it! Don't you remember that the Rogers sisters accepted produce as part of their payment last fall?"

"Perhaps they would have preferred money," Damaris murmured unhappily.

"Nonsense! They have to eat, don't they?"

Damaris watched with dismay as the footman carried a multitude of parcels into the library. From the sheer number of the packages, she could see that Lady Grayson had, indeed, outdone herself. How would they ever pay for it all? Unless there was a bountiful harvest, they would be forced to make sizable reductions in the everyday budget.

Missy squealed excitedly as she and her mother dived into the bounty. Velvets, brocades, and gold and silver trimmings were quickly strewn across the chairs. Fine, whisper-thin gauze for veils and packages of seed pearls and paste diamonds were exclaimed over. Yes, the Grayson ladies would be top of the trees. *And at great expense.*

"I chose these for you," Lady Grayson said to her younger daughter, pointing out a lovely mint-green velvet, a white brocade, and a shimmering, creamy satin. "They are most suitable for your age. And these, Damaris, are for you." She held up an ice-blue brocade, a gold satin, and a scarlet velvet. "Just think how pretty they will be with your dark hair and blue eyes! Come now, smile for your mama! If worse comes to worst, I can always sell some jewelry."

Damaris forced a grimace.

"Don't you think they're pretty?"

"They are beautiful, Mama, but . . ."

"Now, none of that! We are going to have fun with this. And, remember, do not plan any of your ridiculous crop inspections for tomorrow. We must arrive bright and early at the Rogers sisters' house for consultation."

"Look at this, Mama!" Missy jerked the history book from the desk. "Wouldn't I look perfect in this gown?"

Lady Grayson thoughtfully studied the portrait of the unfortunate Queen Anne. "No, dear, I truly think it is a bit too mature for you." She shifted her gaze to Damaris. "But it would be perfect for your sister."

"Yes, I suppose it would." Missy relinquished her idea with good spirit. "She will be so regal! Mama, if we rinsed Damaris's hair with lemon juice, it would positively glitter! Or if we could get gold dust . . . Did you know that people wore gold dust in their hair? With Damaris's dark hair, the effect would be magnificent!"

"No!" Damaris set her foot down at that. "I absolutely refuse to put gold dust in my hair! Even if something like that would not be so costly, I am sure that it would itch. Furthermore, lemons are expensive. And," she added succinctly, "I will not dress like someone who has been beheaded!"

Chapter 2

I t didn't take long for word of the earl's arrival to spread through Delafield Hall. As soon as Richard had stepped from his curricle, the old, familiar servants, as well as the newer, curious ones, dropped whatever they were doing and dashed out the door to welcome their returning master. More than a few minutes passed before Gilbert, the butler, and Mrs. Evans, the housekeeper, were able to organize the milling staff into a body presentable enough to meet the traveler.

His irritation at the construction in the meadow fading somewhat in the glow of the exuberant reception, Richard realized that it would be some time before he discovered what was happening at the castle. Unless they had been trampled in the rush, his mother and brother would be waiting inside. Before seeing them, he must acknowledge his enthusiastic employees. At Delafield Hall, this was no easy task. The staff was large, and he was expected to greet each one personally.

Accompanied by Gilbert and Mrs. Evans, who introduced the new members to him and kindly silenced the old retainers when they tried to chat overly long, Richard plunged into his duty. At last, after gripping the last hand and receiving the final curtsy, he was free. He rushed inside.

"Dickon!"

"Percy!" He vigorously shook his brother's hand. "Good God, you've grown up!"

"What did you expect, old boy?" the younger man laughed. "The same university student to whom you bid farewell?"

"I suppose I thought everything would be just the same as it was when I left. In six years, much can change." Richard embraced him. "Damme, you're a man!"

The distinct clearing of a throat interrupted any further discourse.

"Mama." Richard hurried into her outstretched arms.

"My dear, dear son." She buried her face in his chest. "You cannot imagine how I have prayed for this day."

He held her close. "It was too long in coming. For me too."

"I hope you will not be leaving soon."

"No, Mama. I've come home to stay."

"Thank God!" Clutching his arms, she took a step backward and gazed at him, her eyes bright with unshed tears. "Let me look at you. My, Dickon! You have become quite the polished gentleman! Not that you weren't always most devastatingly handsome, but now you are absolutely elegant."

"I finally found a competent valet." He grinned.

"If he's the one who trimmed your hair, perhaps you'll lend him to me," said Percy, whose unruly locks were much like his brother's had been.

"Of course," Richard agreed, surreptitiously crossing his fingers and hoping that Casey would comply. The valet's expression had grown more disdainful as each overly ecstatic servant had burst from the Hall.

"Come now." Lady Delafield tucked her arm through that of her elder son and nodded pointedly toward the beaming employees, who were filing back inside. "Let us go to the salon, where we shall have more privacy."

With Percy following, he escorted her up the stairs and into the bright, cheerful room. He glanced around with surprise. "You've redecorated."

"Yes."

The room, which had previously been painted a deep emerald-green, was now a sunny yellow. There was new, modern furniture, upholstered in a gay, floral chintz. Even the pictures on the walls were different. The old oil paintings had been replaced by delicate watercolors. There were oil lamps instead of candlesticks.

"Don't you like it?" his mother asked anxiously.

"Yes," he said slowly.

"Oh, dear. You do not. I can tell," she murmured. "You see, Richard, when your father died, I wanted to make some changes. The memories . . ."

He hastened to reassure her. "It is all right, Mama. The room is lovely. It was just a surprise, that's all."

"I paid for most of it with my own settlement. I refused to use much of your money."

"Mama, it is *all right*." He took her into his arms. "And I *want* you to feel free to spend whatever you wish. Did you make other changes as well?" He could have bitten his tongue, for she began to cry.

"Oh, Dickon, I am sorry. I've redone every room, not with furniture, mind you, but with paint, paper, and fabrics. And Percy . . . well, you shall see what Percy has done with the Great Hall at the proper time, for it is a secret right now. Dear me, it was just that . . . every time I entered a room, I was overset by the memories. They were wonderful ones, of course, but . . . We were such a happy family, weren't we? I was simply unable to face . . ."

"Please, Mama, don't fret. It is all right!" he repeated, giving her his handkerchief. "I'm *glad* you did it. No doubt seeing things the way they used to be would have made me sad too."

The sight of his mother's tears filled Richard with guilt. The air seemed heavy with awkwardness. He glanced at Percy, who shrugged and shook his head.

He drew Lady Delafield to the sofa. "I'm home now, Mama, and everything will be all right. I . . . I have wronged you greatly," he said hesitantly. "I should have come home as soon as I received the news about Papa, but it was too late and . . ."

She laid her fingertips across his lips. "No regrets, son. I know you had your reasons. There will be no more said about it. You are here now, and we are going to be very happy." She blew her nose, shook herself slightly, and smiled. "I believe I would like a glass of ratafia."

"Yes, ma'am. I think a drink would do us all good." He kissed her forehead and stood, suddenly realizing that he didn't know where the spirits were kept.

Percy anticipated, moving to a handsome rosewood sideboard. "Brandy, Dickon?"

"That would be fine." He joined him, pouring the ratafia for his mother.

"You know, you were a real bastard, Dickon," his brother said under his breath.

Richard clenched his teeth. "Thank you, Percy, but I feel guilty enough without your adding to it."

"Just wanted to make sure you were aware of it."

"Believe me, I am."

Percy didn't mince words. "Why didn't you come home when Papa died?" he demanded.

"The news was old when I received it. At the time, it didn't seem to matter."

"It did."

"Can't we speak of it later?" Richard begged.

He knew that Percy was right. It had mattered. But the old earl's demise would have caught the attention of the *ton*. All eyes would have been watching the new earl, and the tongues would have wagged. He hadn't been ready to face it. He took the drinks and returned to the sofa.

"Thank you, dear." The dowager took a hasty sip. "Now Percy, why don't you tell your brother about your grand festivity?"

"I'm not sure he'll want to hear about it."

"Fiddlesticks! Of course he will. He will be just as excited as everyone else!"

Richard nodded encouragingly. "Tell me, Percy."

"Well . . ." His brother flushed. "I'm hosting a medieval tournament."

"What!"

"Percy has become quite respected as a scholar of medieval customs. He thought it might be fun to re-enact a tournament." Lady Delafield explained, moving eagerly to the edge of the sofa. "I must say that I wholeheartedly agree. As do others! Why, all of England is begging for an invitation! Aren't you proud of your brother, Dickon?"

Percy blushed a deeper shade of red. "Oh, Mama."

An unusual event like this would draw the *ton* like bees to blossoms. Richard successfully hid his dismay. "A scholar? I had no idea. Of course I am proud!"

"Mama exaggerates. I'm not *that* well known." His eyes brightened. "But now that you're home to manage the estates, I shall be able to devote more time to my research and writing."

Once again, the pall of guilt settled over Richard. "I'm sorry, I . . ."

The countess pertly smacked his hand. "Don't you *dare* start that again! I shan't have it! Let us talk of the tournament. Percy has had many volunteers to be the knights. And all of our invited guests will wear medieval costume. The public will be welcomed at the tournament and at the ball on the lawn, but we shall have a private medieval banquet."

He shook his head in wonderment. "Unbelievable."

"And you don't like it," Percy stated.

"No, I am quite impressed!" the earl lied. "Well, this tells me that I didn't see a ghost in the woods."

"What are you talking about?" his mother asked.

"A knight in armor crossed the road in front of me."

She nodded. "That would have been Vincent."

"Uncle Vincent is here?" If his mother's eccentric brother was participating, there was sure to be a ferocious muddle!

"You remember Uncle's fascination with all things medieval," Percy explained. "He has come to help with the training of the knights, and he'll participate in the tournament as well."

"Vincent has family armor," the countess said with pride. "As a boy, he was always playing in it."

"Isn't jousting rather dangerous for a man his age?" Richard questioned. "Or a man of any age," he added.

"I am sure that Vincent is quite adept. Oh, dear, Percy! Is it too late to order armor for Richard?"

"I'm afraid so." He frowned. "He can wear mine. I would be honored! After all, he is the Earl of Delafield."

"I wouldn't dream of it!" Richard said hastily. "It would deprive you of firsthand experience."

"Well," Percy said seriously, "firsthand experience might be useful to my research."

"Think no more about it!" The earl took a long drink of his brandy. "But, tell me, have you considered the hazards involved in such an adventure? Those who participate can have little skill at jousting."

"Vincent will handle everything," the dowager countess said with confidence.

"Yes!" her younger son echoed eagerly. "My knights will be arriving, very soon, for proper training. As to any risks, the weapons are designed to break before causing any injury, and the rules are very stringent."

"All will be well." Lady Delafield established, then flinched. "Goodness, Richard! You will not wear armor, or participate in the jousting or the melee, but you will require costuming! I must see to it at once!"

He hid a groan. It was ridiculous. She would attempt to rig him out in some sort of preposterous garb, but at least he wouldn't have to wear a suit of armor. Perhaps, in the spirit of things, and with the guests all clad in medieval attire, it wouldn't be so awful. After the way he'd behaved toward his brother, Percy deserved his thoughtfulness. And he would have to face the *ton* sometime. He might as well get it over with. But why, oh why, hadn't he waited until Christmas to come home?

"So, puss!" Sir Osbert Grayson pushed himself up against the pillows and smiled, eyes twinkling, at his daughter. "That was your day?"

She nodded, sinking into the chair beside his bed. "All day at the account books! But I did take a short walk before coming to see you. Papa, I can almost *hear* the crops growing!"

His smile broadened. "I know what you are saying. I've experienced the same thing myself. When the growing conditions are right, it seems as if the plants ascend before your very eyes." He sighed. "I hope to be up and about within a short time, Damaris."

"Do not be hasty. You must take care."

"I shall." He sighed. "But I do so want to leave this room. I've been confined in bed for so long that I almost do not care what the results might be. I feel stronger, Damaris. I believe that I could get up without difficulty."

"Papa!" Panic rose in her throat. "You must obey the doctor!"

"I am weary of doctors and their potions."

"Nevertheless," she said in her most threatening tone, "you have invested a great amount of time in recovering. You cannot compromise it now. I shall not allow it!"

"You would stop me?"

"Indeed I would!"

A wistful smile played at the corners of his lips. "Poor daughter. I am a sore trial to you. You should be entertaining beaux and dancing the night away. Instead you are managing the estate like a man. It isn't proper."

"Propriety must be defined according to the situation at hand," Damaris said brashly, and drew a short chuckle from him. "Besides, I am learning so very much."

"For what purpose?" He idly picked at the fine embroidered stitches on the coverlet. "Someday you will have a husband who will care for such matters."

Her eyes twinkled. "Perhaps he will not do a good job of it, and I must correct him."

He looked at her with shock, saw that she was

teasing him, and grinned. "Very well, puss. You've chased away my blue devils. I shall remain in bed for a while longer. But do send for Dr. Corey, so that I may consult with him."

"I shall do it first thing tomorrow." She rose. "I must be on my way. 'Tis almost suppertime."

He nodded. "Ask your mama if she is up to receiving a trouncing from me in a game of whist this evening."

"A trouncing!" She laughed. "Really, Papa! Mama's skill at cards is well known."

"I feel lucky."

"All right. I shall deliver the challenge!"

Still giggling, she let herself out of the room and turned down the hall. Sir Osbert's swings of mood were becoming more frequent. It wasn't to be wondered at. He had been bedfast for so long that he must be terribly frustrated. She hoped that Dr. Corey would find him well enough to permit a bit more activity. As the summer progressed, he was sure to become more and more difficult to control. If he did, she would have to be the one to exercise the necessary force to keep him within bounds. No one else would stand up to him.

Always, everything came back to her. Missy and Lady Grayson were only too willing to take on the easy situations. The nasty ones were left to Damaris. Well, most likely, it was for the best. They would make a muddle of anything unpleasant.

She entered her room to freshen up for supper, but instead of immediately performing her ablutions, she drifted across to the window. The green lawn of Grayson Park, with its neatly trimmed boxwoods and flowering beds of perennials, lay before her. Beyond were the rich brown fields, deeply plowed and fertile, their orderly rows of crops marching toward the horizon. Damaris felt a profound sense of satisfaction. When her father was well again, she would miss playing the role of steward. What would her future hold?

Men didn't like managerial wives. But what would that matter? She probably wouldn't marry, for she required a husband who would look upon her as an equal partner. No normal man would be willing to do that. That mate, like Richard Delafield, existed only in her dreams.

No, she would probably remain at Grayson Park for the rest of her life, and one day, she would administer it again. The prospect filled her with loneliness.

After supper, the long summer evening stretched out before Damaris. Lady Grayson had taken up the whist challenge and was ensconced in her husband's room. Melissa had returned to the library to ponder the merits of medieval costumes.

Damaris refused to plunge once more into the accounts. A full day's work on them had been enough. Abruptly, she ordered her horse brought around and went upstairs to change into her riding habit. A short ride would dust the cobwebs from her mind. She would travel cross-country to Delafield Hall to see how work progressed on the tournament field.

She dressed quickly and went outside, telling only the butler where she was going. If Missy knew, she'd want to come too, and it would take a solid hour for her sister to ready herself. Besides, Damaris wished to be alone, with no chatter of gowns or young men.

Cantering across the pasture, her groom loping discreetly behind, she felt a surge of lightheartedness. Riding always lifted her spirits. When she returned home, she knew she would be mentally rested and able to meet the demands of the estate, her parents, and her sister.

She entered a small coppice, threading her way through the trees along the main path to Delafield. Damaris smiled. When she and Melissa were children, this trail had been well traveled. In fact, this woodland itself, and the larger forest on the Delafield property, had been the site of endless games of Robin Hood and King Arthur. Those had been such happy, carefree days!

Damaris and Percy Marston were the same age and had played together long before Missy had grown up enough to unite with them. Richard was older. Once in a while, he had joined them, but usually he avoided them and considered them pests. Poor Richard! They had worshipped him because he could do everything better than they could, but nonetheless, they'd delighted in aggravating him. Usually he was good-natured about his torment, although he had been known to lose his temper. On those occasions, she and Missy had run home as fast as they could, while Richard had caught and thrashed his little brother. His outbursts hadn't hurt his reputation with Damaris. She thought he was wonderful then. She still did.

It had been years since she had seen him. She didn't know the full story of why he left England. It was something to do with a lady who had jilted him, but that was the sum of her knowledge. He would be older now. Despite the image in her dreams, she honestly wondered if she would even recognize him.

Damaris popped her horse over the small, crumbling stone wall that divided Grayson Park from

Delafield Hall. To her right, on rising ground, stood the castle. It had been another wonderful site for children's games of make-believe. Modernized to a comfortable extent, it hadn't been so changed that it had lost all of its narrow winding stairs and secret passageways. It had been ideal for rainy-day activities.

But it was foolish to engage, as she was doing, in maudlin recollections. She had come on this ride to cleanse her mind of cares, not to crowd it with sentimental yesterdays. She directed her attention to the water meadow. The workmen were still hard at their labors, taking advantage of every moment of daylight. She cantered toward them.

As she neared the area, Damaris saw that Percy and another gentleman were present. She giggled. Perhaps this was one of Percy's "knights." They were standing with their backs to her and hadn't heard her approach over the ringing of the hammers. She rode up quite close to them and slowed her horse to a walk.

"Percy?" she called.

He whirled. "Well now! What a pleasant surprise!"

The other man turned more slowly. It took only a brief moment for recognition to dawn, and for her heart to begin pounding almost painfully. He was home!

"Richard?" she breathed.

He didn't reply. He merely stood there, his eyes boring into her. There was curiosity in their blue depths.

"Dickon!" Percy laughed. "Don't you recognize Damaris?"

"Damaris?" he asked uncertainly.

He had forgotten her! How could he have done

that? Especially since he himself had never left her dreams!

"Damaris Grayson," Percy prompted.

Richard sketched a rather formal bow. "I must beg your pardon. You've grown up, Miss Grayson."

"Miss Grayson? Good God, Dickon!" said his brother with disgust. "You need not be so formal. You weren't very formal in the days when you pelted her with stones."

The earl flushed slightly and looked confused. "I did that?"

Damaris's temper flashed. Did he remember nothing of her? And why did he call her Miss Grayson? After years of childhood, there was no need to stand on such convention! What was the matter with him? Did he think himself above her?

"Yes, Lord Delafield," she said coolly, "you did. And you are correct. I *have* grown up. Perhaps it is a pity that the child must become the adult. I am convinced that children are much more spontaneous and sociable. Now if you gentlemen will excuse me, I shall be on my way. The sunshine is fading. Good evening."

Spinning her horse on its haunches, she touched a small spur to its side and galloped across the meadow toward Grayson Park.

Percy stared openmouthed after her. What was wrong with Damaris? Furthermore, what was wrong with Dickon? He'd acted so stiff and ceremonious, causing Damaris to respond with frosty vexation.

"Why did you do that?" he demanded of his brother.

"What did *I* do?" Richard's look of perplexity had changed to one of disquietude.

"You behaved so unfeelingly!"

"I believe that I treated her with the respect that is due a young lady."

"Yes, you did," Percy yielded unwillingly, "but it wasn't proper for the circumstances! Dammit, Dickon! Damaris is an old friend! You conducted yourself as if she were a stranger!"

"She was," the earl said irritably. "She has changed."

"You insulted her!"

"Did I?"

"Yes!"

Richard wiped his hand across his forehead. When he dropped his arm to his side, the lines of annoyance had disappeared from his forehead. "That was not my intention."

"Then you must make amends!"

"Yes, of course. I shall." He thoughtfully studied the retreating horsewoman as she vaulted over the wall and disappeared into the copse. "She is the most beautiful creature I've ever seen," he murmured.

Percy startled. His brother? Damaris? Of course! They were perfect for each other! A tantalizing thought romped playfully through his mind.

It was *his* tournament, but as the Earl of Delafield, Dickon would be the host. His brother would sit on the dais, and at his side would be Damaris, taking the part of the Queen of Beauty. Excellent! They would be thrown together through much of the festivities. And from there . . .

Oh, yes! Dickon and Damaris, earl and countess, husband and wife! Was it possible? His brother needed a wife; his friend should have a husband. Why shouldn't they choose each other?

He would help matters along. Tomorrow he would ride to Grayson Park and asked Damaris to be his Queen. Missy might be disappointed, but she would understand when he explained it to her. Together they would concoct other schemes to forward the match.

"You're right, Dickon. Damaris is perfectly lovely!" Enthusiastically, Percy began to extoll her other virtues.

Chapter 3

"You will do me great honor, Damaris, if you
will consent to be the Queen of Beauty at
my tournament." As if well satisfied with himself,
Percy Marston settled back in his chair and grinned.

What? Damaris's attention had wandered to other
matters, namely the amount of work she had put off
by going to the Rogers house that morning for costume consultation. Then she had been further de-
layed by luncheon, and now by Percy's visit. What
had he said? Why was everyone staring at her?

"I must apologize," she stammered. "I fear I was
woolgathering."

Good-naturedly, he repeated his request.

The atmosphere in the drawing room seemed suddenly hot and stuffy. Damaris looked with horror at
Percy. Queen of Beauty? Oh no, he couldn't mean it!
He couldn't possibly wish her to be the Queen! What
about Missy? She was the logical one to receive that
honor. Indeed, everyone expected it! Was this Percy's
way of telling the girl that he didn't care for her anymore?

She glanced at her sister on the sofa beside her.
Missy had shifted her gaze from her, and now sat
frozen in position, her eyes downcast, her hands
tightly folded. Only the whiteness about her lips be-
lied her turmoil. Her explosion would come later.
Poor Missy! She had counted so heavily on reigning
at the tournament.

Damaris didn't wish to be the Queen. In the light of her daily struggles with the estate, the whole idea of the tournament seemed extravagant, impossibly childish, and probably dangerous for the male participants. If Percy Marston had not been a neighbor and her oldest friend, she would refuse to attend, in spite of what her mother would demand. Given her opinion, for her to be the Queen was utterly absurd! It was unthinkable!

She smiled sweetly at Percy. "I do thank you for the honor, but I really must refuse."

That should do it. Now he would ask Missy. Because he'd asked Damaris first, a certain amount of damage had already been done, but this would go a long way toward mitigating it.

"Come, Damaris," Percy cajoled, "don't be shy. You would be a most suitable Queen."

She shook her head and pointedly eyed Missy. "There are others far more appropriate than I."

He followed the direction of her gaze. "I beg to disagree. The Queen of Beauty should be lovely and stately, and *mature*. I cannot select a young lady who is fresh from the schoolroom."

Missy bit the edge of her lower lip. A light blush tinged her cheekbones. She clenched her hands more firmly together.

"I am sorry," Damaris declared. "I must refuse."

Percy's shoulders slumped. "Well, in that case, I suppose I *could* ask the squire's eldest daughter."

"Certainly not!" Lady Grayson gasped. "Damaris is merely being timid! Once she becomes accustomed to the idea, she will be delighted!"

"Mama . . ." Damaris began.

"Be still, child. I know what is best for you. One's mother always knows best!" she said briskly. "She will do it, Percy."

"Excellent." He grinned with satisfaction.

Missy rose unsteadily. "You must excuse me."

"Missy, I . . ." Percy stood. "I wish a word with you."

"I am feeling rather ill." She didn't pause in her controlled flight from the salon. The door closed a bit noisily behind her.

Percy stared after her with a frown on his handsome face. Turning, he shrugged questioningly. "I . . ."

Lady Grayson waved a fluttering arm of dismissal. "We have been to the dressmaker's today. Standing still for measurement always causes Melissa to be light-headed and nauseated. Do not be concerned."

A soft tap sounded on the door that Missy had just vacated.

"Come in!" Damaris's mama rearranged her skirts and smiled smugly. No doubt she was anticipating the arrival of one of her friends, to whom she could boast about her daughter being the Queen of Beauty.

Damaris's spirits sank. Once the word was out, she'd have no hope of escaping the dubious honor. Everything was just awful. Even if she did not dread being placed on display, she would have to deal with a very hurt and angry sister.

"Good afternoon." Richard Delafield bowed to the group as a footman showed him into the room. He went at once to Lady Grayson and bent over her hand. "How do you do, madam? I can see that you have scarcely changed from when I saw you last. And Damaris." He repeated the gesture. "Won't you forgive me for not recognizing you yesterday? I held the memory of a raggle-taggle little girl, not considering that you might have changed into a comely and charming young lady."

The sleek-tongued viper! He hadn't spoken so

prettily yesterday! She snatched away her hand, which suddenly seemed to burn from his touch. "You are forgiven, Lord Delafield," she murmured coldly.

"Won't you sit down, my lord?" Lady Grayson indicated a chair beside her and leaned forward to pour him a cup of tea. "We were just delighting in Damaris receiving a singular honor."

"Indeed?"

"Yes, but perhaps you already know about it. Percy has chosen Damaris to be his Queen of Beauty."

"No, I did not know." A flash of disapproval passed through his expressive blue eyes. "Congratulations."

He doesn't like it, Damaris instinctively realized. But which didn't he condone? Her being the Queen, or the whole tournament idea?

"Mama," she murmured, "you are being precipitous. I have not yet accepted the request."

"Nonsense! Why must you behave so uncharacteristically timorous? Very well, I have accepted it for you. Your father will be so pleased! He is quite concerned about your lack of ladylike pursuits." She turned to Lord Delafield. "Since my husband's illness, Damaris has managed the estate. It has taken so much of her time that the poor child has been unable to engage in more pleasurable activities. If we had realized that he would be bedfast for so long, we would have employed a steward. Nevertheless, his recovery is now imminent, and Damaris has managed to muddle through."

"Muddle through!" Damaris cried. "I have made improvements! I have purchased the newest equipment for cultivating—"

She halted, mid-sentence. Her mother was favoring her with a mixed expression of shock and warning, Percy was rolling his eyes toward the ceiling, and

Richard was biting back a grin. They were thinking it preposterous that a female, especially a young one, could excel in land management. Not only that, they thought it was laughable.

She wished she could slap that visage of superiority from Richard's face. Who was he to doubt her ability? Hadn't he shirked his responsibility to his own acreage? He could know little of stewardship. She defiantly lifted her chin.

"Forgive me for boring you," she said archly. "Especially you, Lord Delafield! I forget that you have little knowledge of or interest in the latest developments in agriculture. How could you? You have been away for so long."

"Damaris!" wailed her mother. "Such impertinence! You must apologize to His Lordship!"

"Indeed? I was under the impression that I had just done so!" She rose. "Now, if you will excuse me, I have important matters to attend to." Without a backward glance, she swept out of the room.

In the hall, Damaris paused to catch her breath. She *had* been rude. Terribly so. But with his stilted behavior yesterday, and his veiled contempt today, he deserved a setdown. How could she ever have longed for him?

"Collins," she said to a passing footman, "have you seen my sister?"

"In the garden, miss."

"Thank you." She left the house and strode down the brick walk to the rose-covered bower that was Missy's favorite place of refuge. Her sister looked up and saw her coming. Dabbing her eyes with a lacy handkerchief, Missy glared at her.

"Well, Damaris, I suppose that you are extremely pleased with yourself."

"I am not! I find the whole notion utterly ludicrous! I do not wish to be the Queen of Beauty! I do not even want to attend."

"I cannot believe it," Missy scoffed. "Who would not wish to be acknowledged as the fairest lady? It is I who shall not attend. I am absolutely mortified! How can I ever face my friends again? I shall go into seclusion and never again appear in public!"

"Oh, Missy, you know you will not do that! You are excited about the tournament and your new costumes!" She sat down beside her. "Perhaps I can persuade Percy to change his mind."

"Percy has demonstrated what little he thinks of me. It's over, Damaris! What a fool I was . . . dreaming that I might someday be his wife. I shall become a nun."

"I believe that one must be a Catholic before one can become a nun," Damaris said gently.

Missy shrugged. "Then I shall become a Catholic. It cannot be that difficult. Go away, Damaris! I must contemplate my future."

"Missy . . ."

Her sister dramatically folded her hands and bowed her head. "Do not interrupt my prayers."

"Very well." Damaris left her, turning down the path to the outside entrance of the estate office. She seldom used that room; it seemed so stark and impersonal without her father's presence. It was just the place for her to examine her troubled thoughts. There she could indulge in cold logic.

What turmoil she had encountered over the past year! First her father's illness, the poor harvest, and Lady Grayson's lavish spending. Now the farcical situation of the tournament. And Richard.

An uncomfortable lump filled her throat. She had constructed his character from her fantasies. He wasn't like that at all. She could never marry a man like Richard. And he would certainly never ask her to! The dream had ended.

Richard turned down his mother's offer of tea and poured himself a glass of brandy. His visit to Grayson Park had been most unsettling. Once again he had failed with his brother's favored lady. Damaris had not responded to his attempt to charm her. In fact, she had shown all indications of outright dislike! It would make for an awkward situation in the family if Percy married her.

It was obvious that his brother was courting the girl. Last evening, Percy could hardly stop talking about her. And hadn't he made her his Queen of Beauty?

The tournament! What a piece of nonsense! Damaris Grayson had probably encouraged Percy in the whole frivolous concept. It was just like the two of them to conjure up one of their childhood games!

And the way she had tried to make him think her capable of managing an estate! It was a wonder that the Grayson land hadn't gone to wrack and ruin. The little girl who had tagged along after him, her face sticky with cherry tart, could never have gained the knowledge necessary to successfully direct such an enterprise.

Damaris Grayson in the family? Oh, Lord! What would they do? What would *he* do? How would he eliminate that twinge of desire he experienced every time he looked at her?

He downed the brandy. Irritably, he filled his glass again. Damn! It was too bad that she was so lovely . . . and that she was his brother's lady.

From the open window came the unmistakable clank of armor and the clatter of iron-shod hooves in the courtyard. Uncle Vincent must be preparing for his late afternoon ride. But no, the clamor was too great for only one horse and one knight to make. What on earth? Richard exchanged a questioning gaze with his mother and hurriedly crossed the room to look out.

"There are *two* knights, Mama! One of them, of course, must be Uncle Vincent, and the other . . ."

"Fustian!" she said with disappointment. "He wanted to surprise you!" She rose and hastened to join him. Peering outside, she smiled fondly. "Percy's new armor arrived today from London. I was to wait a suitable interval, then take you outside in time to see him gallop across the meadow. No matter! You will appear dazzled, won't you, darling? Please do not spoil his little treat."

"I shall be properly impressed." Richard watched his younger brother stagger awkwardly across the cobblestones. "Mama, has Percy ever worn armor before?"

"No. He refused to borrow Vincent's suit. He wished to wait for his own." She sighed. "I am so distressed that you arrived home too late to have one made yourself."

Percy's high-strung thoroughbred stiffened its forelegs and flung up its head at its master's approach. Rolling its eyes, it pricked its ears so tensely that their tips nearly met. It snorted apprehensively.

"Think of it this way," Richard suggested, interpreting the animal's state of mind. "Because of my prodigality, you will have one son left alive. I had best go out there."

"Please do not! You shall ruin the surprise!"

"There is going to be trouble."

"Oh, surely not. Vincent is there, and the grooms, to assist Percy's mounting."

"I'm not as concerned about his mounting as I am

about his staying on! That horse is not happy with this." He briskly turned away from the window. "I'm going to put a period to this nonsense!"

Lady Delafield caught his arm. "No, you will not. Richard! Your brother is a grown man! He knows what he is doing!"

"He may be of age, but he most certainly does not know what he's about. Enough is enough! His friends may wish to jeopardize themselves, but I will not allow my brother to do so!"

"You cannot control Percy's actions!"

"I can while he resides in my home! I am now the earl, Mama. I can lay down the law!"

She clung to him. "You will only cause hard feelings! Please, Dickon! Percy has put his heart into this event. You must permit him this pleasure."

There was distinct skittering of hooves. Richard turned back to the window to see the jittery thoroughbred shy across the court, dragging a groom with it. The servant managed to stop the horse, but it continued to dance on tiptoe, staring white-eyed at the steel-clad monster. Uncle Vincent took the reins of his own ancient nag and directed his man to go to Percy's assistance. His brother irritably flung back his visor and lurched toward his horse.

"Mama!" Richard said with exasperation. "Don't you realize that Percy could be seriously injured? That horse is terrified of him!"

"Percy will calm him." She caressed his sleeve as if to illustrate. "You must trust your brother."

"This is incredible," he muttered.

With two men holding the straining animal, Percy was able to approach closely. He removed his heavy metal glove and stroked the gelding's neck. The beast stood still, but it was not relaxed. Its forelegs were as rigid as pokers and its back was hunched. Its ears lay tight against its head.

"There now! You see?" asked Lady Delafield. "Percy has gentled him."

"That horse is far from calm, Mama," Richard stated, but another movement had caught his eye. Some distance down the avenue proceeded a dilapidated gig. "Who the hell is that?"

"Do not curse," she reminded him, following his gaze. "Oh! 'Tis the Misses Rogers!"

"Who are they?"

"The local dressmakers. Don't you remember them?"

"Ah, yes." He recalled that, when his mother had needed a new dress and hadn't time to go to London, she had hired the two venerable spinsters. "Are they making your costumes?"

"Lud, no! I had mine made in London! They are for you, Dickon."

"For *me!*"

"Indeed so. Time is wasting. They will construct your tournament attire."

"But they're *women!*" he cried.

"Yes," she agreed pleasantly.

"Women can't sew for a man!"

"I do not see why they can't. Clothes are clothes, whether they are meant for a gentleman or a lady. This is excellent! I am pleased that they are so prompt in answering my summons. But it isn't to be wondered at. We are the ranking family in the district."

"I won't have it!"

"You haven't a choice, Dickon," she said crossly. "I am beginning to believe that you are opposed to your brother's grand event."

"Don't you understand?" he demanded. "They'll

have their hands and their tapes on my ... er ... the private parts of my body!"

"Do not be so squeamish. A dressmaker or a tailor is rather like a physician. Impartial and impassionate. Don't you wish to please me, darling?"

"Yes, ma'am, but ..."

"Then it is settled."

Richard groaned, wishing once again that he had waited a month longer before coming home. This tournament was fast becoming the greatest tangle he had ever witnessed. He returned his attention to Percy.

With the assistance of several inquisitive servants, his brother had managed to hoist himself into the huge medieval saddle. The thoroughbred was standing still, but it was far from tranquil. It was breathing heavily. Its back was arched alarmingly, and its ears continued to be peeled tightly against its head. It frantically champed the bit, pitching saliva onto all those nearby.

Richard watched with steadily growing apprehension. With a groom on each side, surely the animal could be controlled until it became accustomed to its strange rider. They could walk about the courtyard and ... But no! Percy signaled to them, and the men began to unfasten their lead shanks.

"Doesn't he look magnificent?" Lady Delafield clapped her hands with delight. "He sits the beast so straight, so proud! He is the very epitome of a gallant medieval gentleman."

"Mama ..." The rest of his words dried in his mouth. He could only stare impotently as the big horse leaped forward.

Knocked off balance, Percy struggled to retain his seat and lost all pretensions of control. He groped for the flying reins, but the thoroughbred had the bit firmly in its teeth. They thundered down the avenue.

Lady Delafield screamed. "Oh! What are we going to do?"

"Nothing now, dammit!" Whirling, Richard dashed from the room with his mother hard on his heels. When they reached the courtyard, they saw Percy and the horse speeding toward the Rogers gig.

"Oh, my God!" wailed Richard's mother, wringing her hands. "They shall collide! What is wrong with that horse? Can't he see where he is going?"

"He is blinded by fear."

"*Do* something, Dickon!"

He had already started toward the other knightly steed in hopes of chasing Percy down, but he was too late. The horse rushed past them at a gallop. Uncle Vincent was riding to the rescue.

"Thank Heaven!" Lady Delafield wept. "Vincent will save my child!"

"That doddering old fool? Most likely he'll compound the trouble!" Richard set off after them at a run.

The flying thoroughbred managed to avoid a totally disastrous collision with the Rogers vehicle. The horse careened off the side, knocking the carriage up in the air on its opposite wheels. It teetered momentarily, with its occupants shrieking and clinging to its sides, before it returned to the ground. The sisters righted themselves and groped weakly for their smelling salts.

Richard passed Uncle Vincent, whose elderly mount had been unable to hold the pace and had dropped into a wheezing trot.

"Uncle, see to the ladies!" he called.

The knight lifted a feeble hand of assent.

The mishap deflected Percy's horse into the

meadow. There it began to buck. Percy hadn't a chance. He sailed through the air and landed with a spread-eagled thud. The gelding galloped on.

Richard darted to his brother's side. "Percy! Are you all right?"

It seemed as if hours passed before he sat up, removed his helm, and groggily shook his head. "Goddamn."

"Are you injured?" the earl demanded.

"Only my pride." He extended a hand. "Help me up, Dickon."

"Thank God," Richard breathed, then exploded. "That was stupid, Percy! Absolutely, decidedly, unquestionably dim-witted!"

"Don't start in on me, brother," Percy growled angrily. "Just help me up!"

"Any man so brilliant as to trick himself out in a suit of armor should be bright enough to know how to get to his feet!"

"Dickon, you're an ass."

"Perhaps that's better than being a simpleminded fool!" Now that he knew his brother was safe, he lost all grasp of his temper. "This is the most thickheaded stunt I ever saw! Think of the fright you gave Mother! And what about those two old women?"

"The Rogers sisters got in my way! What are they doing here anyway?"

Thinking of the mission of the Misses Rogers made Richard even angrier. "Mother engaged them to sew my abominable costumes for your ridiculous tournament! You see what idiocy you are creating with your ignorant idea!"

Percy began to laugh. "Oh, Dickon! To be measured by the Rogers sisters!"

Thoroughly provoked, the earl let loose a string of

curses and obscenities, all directed at his brother's head.

Percy only laughed harder. "To have them poke and prod you!"

"That will be enough!" Richard snapped.

"What is happening here?" asked an amused voice.

Richard spun around to gaze into the lovely, sparkling eyes of Damaris Grayson, who sat casually on her horse, holding Percy's blowing thoroughbred by its reins.

"I found this horse in our field," she explained.

"Oh, you did, did you?" He remembered how arrogant she had appeared when Percy announced that she was to be the Queen of Beauty. She was probably very proud and pleased with herself. His anger extended to her.

"I had a bit of an accident," Percy informed her, grinning. "And now my ill-begotten brother will not help me up. He is of the opinion that—"

"Take a good look at this potentially hazardous scene, madam," Richard broke in, "and observe what a debacle you will reign over!"

Damaris coldly set her jaw. "I am sure that *I* did not beg for the honor, sir!"

"Perhaps not! But you are lapping it up like a kitten in the cream!" He jerked the thoroughbred's reins from her hand. Starting toward the castle, he glanced back over his shoulder. "Let the *Queen* help you up, Percy!"

"You listen here, Lord Delafield!" Furiously she trotted after him. "This tournament is certainly not *my* idea of pleasure!"

"Get away from me!" He made a violent, cutting motion with his hand.

The sudden gesture spooked her horse. The gelding leaped sideways. Damaris, her mind on the earl instead of her horsemanship, was tossed high and wide. Skirts tangled, she fell at his feet.

Richard stared, transfixed, at her shapely knees, her prettily rounded thighs. "My God," he whispered as he felt his body respond to her allure.

Chapter 4

Damaris stared with horror at Richard, but the earl's eyes did not meet hers. His intent gaze was directed elsewhere. Cheeks burning, she wrenched down her skirt.

"How dare you?" she cried.

"What?" He finally, though rather reluctantly, looked her in the face.

"How dare you frighten my mount, causing me to fall?" Damaris hotly continued. "And then ... then you display the audacity to stand there, admiring the results! How do you know that I am not severely injured?"

His expression assumed a cool composure. "It is obvious, Miss Grayson, that you are not. But do allow me to assist you." Bending, he extended a hand.

Damaris batted it away. "I do not need your assistance!" She scrambled inelegantly to her feet and glared at him. "Furthermore, I have no need for your incivility, your accusations, or your condescension! I have done nothing to earn your displeasure, my lord. Why must you continuously seek to cause me distress?"

"I have done nothing of the sort!"

"You deliberately frightened my horse and caused me to fall!" she charged.

Richard clenched his teeth. "I most certainly did not," he said tightly.

"You did! You fluttered your hand at him!"

"Fluttered . . . If the mere gesture of a hand causes you to fall, Miss Grayson, it would seem that you are vastly overmounted. I suggest that you find a quieter animal. You cannot blame me for your lack of horsemanship."

"Oh," she shrieked. "Oh, how arrogant!"

"Dickon! Damaris!" Percy loudly interrupted. "Won't someone help me up?"

Damaris flicked a quick glance at him before returning to the verbal fray. "If you had not chosen to forget me, Lord Delafield, you would recall that my horsemanship is at least as good as yours!"

"What I remember is a sticky-faced, foolhardy little brat, who refused to accept her place as a female! I can see that little has changed." He eyed her disparagingly. "Oh, perhaps you haven't dipped your fingers in the jam pot, but you are still attempting to prove yourself as capable as a member of the male sex. It won't do, Miss Grayson. It is an impossible dream."

Damaris gasped, staring at him through a sudden blur of tears. "I . . . I . . ." she stuttered.

"Pretending to manage an estate! Riding a horse more suitable for a male!" He indicated the tall thoroughbred, who was nervously chewing grass some distance away from them. "Truly, you should concentrate on perfecting your femininity."

She groped for words. Was that how he saw her, how he'd always seen her? As some sort of defiant Amazon? How wrong he was! She wasn't trying to be a man! She was merely enlarging her horizons and performing up to her capabilities.

"Allow me to inform you, Lord Delafield," she said as coldly as she could, "that I do not *pretend* to manage Grayson Park. I do it quite successfully. Overseeing a property does not require brute power;

it demands an active intelligence. My brain is excellent, and I shall never permit it to rot! Neither does my horse want muscular force. He craves sensitivity and finesse. I believe that you should rethink your ideas about my capabilities. Indeed, about the capabilities of all women! You are far off the mark."

He shook his head. "I don't know what Percy sees in you."

"Percy?" she frowned. "Whatever . . ."

There was a great clank of metal. "Dammit!" Percy shouted. Turning onto all fours, he struggled to stand and collapsed to his knees. "Help me, Dickon!"

"You got yourself into that situation!" Richard exclaimed irritably. "You get yourself out of it!"

"How cruel!" Damaris interjected. "What an ill-tempered, unfeeling beast you are!"

"I? You put him up to this nonsense!"

"I did nothing of the sort!"

"You glory in being the Queen! You are quite a paradox, Miss Grayson. You may not be able to decide whether you wish to be a man or a woman, but there is one common denominator. Power! That is what you want!"

"You are full of fustian!" she snapped.

"Dickon! Damaris!" Lady Delafield, flanked by two grooms, panted up to them. "Why are you shouting? Why aren't you helping Percy? Oh, my dear boy!" She swooped past them and knelt by the fallen knight. "Percy! Speak to your mama!"

Damaris favored Richard with a look of supreme disgust and hastened after her.

"Oh, my darling!" the dowager countess screeched. "Are you dead? Do not tell me you have died! Richard! Richard, *do* something!"

"I'm all right, Mama." Percy managed a meek smile. "I just can't get up."

"Richard! Help your brother up! Why are you standing there arguing with Damaris when your brother needs you? I can scarcely believe it! And why are you quarreling, anyway? I cannot understand it at all!"

"Neither can I," Damaris murmured, grasping Percy's arm and trying to lift him.

Richard tossed the reins of Percy's horse to a groom and stalked forward. He gently elbowed Damaris aside. "This is a case which calls for *brute strength,* the lack of which you must find extremely disappointing, Miss Grayson."

"Why should she feel like that?" Lady Delafield asked wonderingly.

"Well, Mama, apparently Miss Grayson considers herself capable of handling any task." With his fine muscles and superior height, he easily lifted Percy to his feet.

"Oh . . . Well, she is certainly quite talented. I am sure that Damaris could have contrived some solution to this dilemma, but it wasn't necessary, was it?" Lady Delafield smiled, relieved to see that her younger son was alive and standing. "There were plenty of men to assist."

Richard raised an eyebrow and gave Damaris a cavalier grin. "Indeed."

She lifted her chin. "There was, however, a deplorably woodenheaded want of male initiative."

"Due entirely to the shrewish interference of a woman."

"I saw no prior move to—"

"Children! You are spitting at each other like cats and dogs!" the dowager scolded. "Cease it at once!" She slipped her hand through Damaris's arm. "Come, my dear, you may stroll to the castle with me and take refreshment. Richard, assist your brother!"

Damaris's head spun. She'd had enough of her neighbors for today, but there was no way she could politely extricate herself from Lady Delafield's grip. Silently, she walked beside the dowager to the castle, with Richard and Percy clanging along behind, and the grooms bringing up the rear with the horses.

They ascended up the stairs to the salon. Percy remained behind to have his valet free him from his suit of armor, but Richard followed. Damaris was acutely conscious of his footsteps on the stone steps. What would happen next? Would he start up with her again, or allow her to sit in peace? She firmly made up her mind. She would never again permit him to draw her into an argument. It wasn't worth it. He was just too impossible for words! How could she ever have thought that she loved him?

"You were perfectly correct, Vincent!" Lady Delafield said airily to her brother as she entered the bright room. "Percy is uninjured. You cannot imagine my relief!" She shifted her gaze to the two Rogers spinsters. "I do hope that you have escaped affliction as well."

They rose weakly from the sofa, clutching their vinaigrettes. "Yes, my lady," they said in unison, displaying trembling curtsies.

"We were so frightened," offered the elder, "but Sir Vincent proved a great comfort."

"Excellent!" Lady Delafield sank into a yellow silk chair by the window. "Dear Damaris, won't you fetch me a small glass of sherry? Now that I know everyone is all right, I find myself in great need of a restorative."

"Yes, ma'am." Damaris moved to the sideboard, where she knew the wines and liquors were kept, and filled a single glass.

"Nothing for yourself?" Richard asked, coming up

beside her and helping himself to the brandy. "I thought you might like a hefty serving of liquor."

She bit back a retort. "My lord, I much prefer a cup of tea. Thank you, however, for your kind offer." Turning, she hurried to the safety of his mama. Giving the dowager her drink, she helped herself to tea and sat down on the window seat.

"I do hope," Lady Delafield exhorted the Misses Rogers, "that you are not so overset that you cannot measure Richard for his medieval costumes. We haven't much time."

They assured her that they were not.

Damaris tried and failed to hide her smile. So the Rogers women were to construct Richard's tournament clothing? Oh, how priceless! She watched him dolefully glance at them. He hated it! Having the Rogers sisters prod and measure and stick him with pins would be good enough for him!

He caught her in her enjoyment and made a mouth of aversion. Damaris's smile widened, then suddenly faded as she felt an unexpected wave of dismay.

Richard shouldn't have to go through this. He was a man, and Lady Delafield was treating him like a child. He shouldn't have to have the Rogers sisters make his clothes. It would be absolutely mortifying for him. Couldn't another solution be found?

Damaris listened silently as Lady Delafield chattered on and on about the sort of costume she had in mind for her son, with Uncle Vincent adding comments about the authenticity of the ideas. The tournament had certainly turned everyone topsy-turvy. No one could seem to think of anything else. It was perfectly ridiculous.

She eyed Richard to determine his reaction. He was gazing expressionlessly into space, as if he were just as bored with the whole thing as she was. While she watched, she saw the corner of his mouth twitch with distaste. She lowered her gaze.

He obviously hated the tournament. That wasn't surprising. In addition to the cost of the whole festivity, he had probably wished for a peaceful homecoming. No one who'd been away for so long would relish returning to face a house party of such magnitude. But why did he seem to place a portion of the blame on her? It certainly hadn't been her idea. She and Percy might be the best of friends, but she had no influence over him in this regard. How could Richard believe that she did?

"Damaris, dear," Lady Delafield asked sweetly, "won't you refill my glass?"

"Yes, ma'am." She set aside her untouched tea and went to the sideboard. Her heart leaped to her throat when she saw that Richard followed.

He pulled the stopper from the brandy bottle. "I see that my costuming has afforded you much amusement, Miss Grayson."

"At first, it did," she answered honestly. "But now ... Oh, everything is outrageous! Why don't you go to London for your costume?"

"Sympathy from you?" He arched an eyebrow, then shrugged. "Mother fears there isn't time."

"Is there?"

"It doesn't matter. I ... owe it to her."

"Why? Wouldn't she be better satisfied with London-made attire?"

"I don't wish her to worry over it." He set his jaw. "As you, and others, have pointed out, I am lamentably guilty of neglecting my family. I intend to mend my ways."

"My lord, I said nothing of the sort ..." she protested.

"Not in so many words, perhaps, but the thought

was there. Your little comment this morning on my disinterest in the estate?"

"But I didn't mean . . . I'm sure you had good reason!" She stopped and eyed him curiously. "Why *did* you leave England and stay away so long?"

"That, Miss Grayson, is none of your affair." Turning on his heel, he left her.

Thoughtfully, Damaris served Lady Delafield and sat down to drink her tepid tea. My, but Richard was a complex man! But weren't they all? She hadn't yet figured out why Percy had chosen her to be Queen, instead of Melissa. People were so complicated! Managing Grayson Park was easy compared to understanding the humans in her life!

With a sigh, she drained her cup and made her farewells. She would talk, heart to heart, with Percy as soon as it was possible. But right now, the work going on in the north field seemed the most unchallenging occupation.

"Oh, my. Oh, my!" Blushing furiously, the younger Miss Rogers marked the measuring tape with her thumbnail and removed it from Richard's waist, extending it toward her sister, who was recording the numbers. Fearfully, she lowered her eyes for a quick peek at the bottom half of the earl's body. "Oh, my . . ."

"Hips," ordered the elder dressmaker.

"I cannot, Permelia." She timidly shook her head. "I simply cannot!"

"Don't be a goose, Cora."

The frail woman reached out tentatively with talonlike hands and abruptly let them drop to her sides. "I can't."

"You can, and you will." Miss Permelia Rogers exhaled a short breath of exasperation. "We discussed this situation when we received Lady Delafield's summons. We agreed that, as quality modistes, we were impartial to the earl's ... er ... gender. Whether the client is male or female matters nothing to us. We are dispassionate. Hips!"

Miss Cora thrust the tape into her sister's face. "You do it!"

"Cora, you always take the measurements, and I always write them down. That's the way we've done it for years!"

If Richard had not been the subject of their fumbling efforts, he would have laughed. As it was, he could barely control his irritation. Only Percy, seated across the room, his legs draped casually over the arm of the chair, was finding amusement in the impossible scene.

"Hips!" cried Miss Permelia, batting her sister's arm.

"Oh ..." wailed Miss Cora. She staggered to the table, picked up her vinaigrette, and inhaled quickly and deeply. Her head shot backward as if she had been struck.

Percy snickered.

Richard gave his brother a hard frown, but softened his expression for the ladies. "Perhaps I might make a suggestion," he offered. "Couldn't you take the measurements from existing garments?"

The sisters eyed each other, Cora with hope, and Permelia with scowling calculation.

"The costumes wouldn't fit as well," the elder Rogers finally pronounced.

"It doesn't really matter," Richard said kindly. "I shall only wear them once."

"But Lady Delafield might be disappointed in our work!"

"My mother's eyesight is so weak that she will not notice."

"I didn't know that," Percy mused, smirking.

Richard once more sent his brother a frown of warning. "Yes, that's what we'll do. Casey?" he called to his disapproving valet, who had closeted himself in the earl's dressing room. "Fetch me a pair of pantaloons."

"I just don't know," Miss Permelia muttered hesitantly.

"Yes, sister!" Miss Cora frantically encouraged. "It's just the thing to do!" She dropped her voice to a whisper. "After all, we are ladies. How could we measure his . . . his inseam!"

"Furthermore, I insist," Richard said firmly, handing over the garment that Casey had brought him. "I am certain that I shall be delighted with the results."

"I know you will, my lord!" Miss Cora exclaimed.

"All right," Miss Permelia submitted, "but if Her Ladyship is not satisfied with the results . . ."

"I shall take any and all blame," Richard assured her.

The dressmakers gathered their belongings, made their curtsies, and started for the door.

"Do you realize, Permelia?" Miss Cora giggled. "This is the first time we have ever been in a man's chamber!"

"So what? We are indifferent."

"Yes, of course. But he is dreadfully handsome, isn't he?" They closed the door behind them.

Percy chuckled. "Oh, Dickon, what a priceless event! If you could have seen your face . . ."

"Enough, Percy! I don't want to hear another word about it!"

"But it was so vastly amusing!"

Richard shrugged into his coat. "Excellent! I'm glad I afforded you entertainment! This day shall rank as one of the worst in my life."

"Be a sport, Dickon!" his brother chided merrily.

"I'm trying. Oh yes, I'm trying! But between you, your shrewish Queen, Mama, and her dressmakers, it is an extremely difficult challenge to meet!"

"Ah yes." Percy drummed his fingers on his knee and thoughtfully searched Richard's eyes. "What happened between you and Damaris?"

"Her ill temper is what happened!"

"Damaris? She's sweet as sugar!"

"To you, maybe." He strode across the room to the door.

Percy leaped to his feet. "Where are you going?"

"For a walk," Richard said shortly.

"I'll come with you. We'll talk about Damaris. I think you have the wrong impression of her. She—"

"I'd rather be alone." Without a backward glance, he left his brother standing.

Richard sneaked from the castle, avoiding his mother, who was sure to be lurking about in anticipation of questioning him about his costumes. He couldn't believe the turmoil that filled his life. It was just too much for a man to bear. He wished he had stayed in his rented villa in Italy with his voluptuous Roman mistress, who catered to his every need. Life had been far simpler then.

His rapid footsteps took him down the drive, past the busy tournament site, to the woods. After the day's mayhem, the Delafield forest, with its cool calmness, seemed just the place to be. He found himself walking unerringly toward the old rear path to the treehouse. It was long overgrown, but he knew it as well as he knew his own name. Unmindful of the weeds, he turned down it.

The unused trail led deep into the heart of the woodland, where the thick web of interlocking branches shaded out any undergrowth. It was here that the treehouse had been. Richard and old Asa had built the platform high above the ground in one of the hugest trees. He hadn't forgotten. He walked infallibly to the tallest oak.

The steps were still there, weathered boards nailed solidly into the trunk. And the treehouse? Richard leaned his forehead against one of the slabs, but he couldn't look up. The last time he had touched these treads, he had been a boy. He'd been happy, carefree, cherished. His father had been alive. There'd been no Annabelle, no self-imposed exile, no arduous home-coming.

A wave of melancholy washed over him. He blinked back tears. Ashamed of his weakness, he glanced upward.

It was there! Far above his head, the treehouse nestled in its bed of heavy limbs. Its planks were dark with age, and there were inch-wide gaps between them, but it was there! It had survived. Richard threw off his coat and began to climb.

When he reached the top, he realized how foolish he had been. Any one of the steps could have split and sent him tumbling to his death, but they hadn't, and he was here. He reached out to test the platform and found it sturdy. Grinning, he eased over onto it and flopped onto his back, gazing up at the leafy canopy. He was really here!

Richard laughed out loud. What better location to escape the tumult of the tournament preparations? What better spot for a man to go to sort out his perplexities? Certainly no one would look for the Earl of Delafield in a treehouse! Not even Percy, who knew the place as well as he, would think to search for him here. It was the perfect retreat.

Quickly he made plans. After so many years, the treehouse, despite its seeming durability, was bound to have weaknesses. He himself would repair it. He would slip away at night, steal some of Percy's lumber, a saw, and nails, and return in the daytime to renovate the structure. No one would ever know. The project itself would be an escape, and it would be fun.

Cushioning his head on his hands, he closed his eyes. Already he was in a better humor. He didn't feel as disgusted with Percy. He could almost chuckle over the antics of the Rogers sisters. He wasn't as irritated with Miss Grayson.

Damaris. Why did she have such a knack of setting him off? Was it the influence she held over his hapless brother? Or the manner in which she flew in the face of normal feminine behavior? Could it be her propensity for criticizing him? He must find some way to get along with her. After all, it seemed that she would be Percy's wife. She would become an important part of his family.

A tantalizing vision of her shapely legs teased through his mind. Damme, but she was alluring! Thoughts of her delicious attributes could thoroughly muddle a man's mind.

A sweltering heat crept over his body. Richard took a deep breath. He mustn't have these fantasies about his brother's lady! It was wrong. It was unhealthy. She belonged to Percy. And she didn't much like him, anyway.

Chapter 5

"I am beside myself with worry. I am absolutely overset," sputtered Lady Grayson. "What am I going to do?"

Damaris wearily took her seat at the luncheon table. "What is it, Mama?"

"Your sister! She will not leave her room!" She flicked open her napkin and spread it across her lap. "Yesterday I could understand it. The poor girl was so distraught over Percy asking you to be the Queen. But today? This has gone on long enough! What can she be thinking? So Percy has shown his preference for you! There are other fish in the sea."

Her elder daughter sighed. She had spent a long, wakeful night thinking about Missy and Percy . . . and Richard. Try as she might, she could find no reason why Percy should suddenly favor her over her sister. She and Percy were old friends. There was not, nor could there be, any romantic attraction between them. They were more like brother and sister! No, Percy had something else in mind.

"I have thought it over and I cannot believe that he has lost his affection for Missy," she said with conviction.

"Well, you may be correct. He *did* call on her this morning." Lady Grayson peered at the first dish the footman offered her and waved it away.

"Percy was here?" Fustian! She had been so anx-

58

ious to speak with him about this whole predicament. "Why didn't you tell me?"

"Ha! Why should I bother?" her mother asked sourly. "You are seldom at home during farm working hours."

"I was in the library."

"How was I to know?" Lady Grayson pressed her lips into a pale line of disgust. "Melissa, however, refused to see him. She pretended illness."

"If Percy should come again this afternoon, I will be here." She helped herself to a serving of smoked salmon, creamed potatoes, and haricot beans. "I want to talk with him."

"Why?" her mother inquired suspiciously.

"I intend to find out why he selected me instead of Missy."

"Oh, Damaris, you will not refuse to be the Queen, will you?" her parent wailed.

She met her mother's anxious eyes. She had so little in common with the lady. Damaris was more like her father, interested in the outdoors, and favoring practical matters. Lady Grayson was totally the opposite. Her world revolved around gowns and jewelry and social success. This was the first time that Damaris had ever truly delighted her. She could not let her down.

"No, Mama, I shan't disappoint you," she quietly assured her. "I am merely curious as to why I was chosen. Percy cannot have developed a *tendre* for me. He is like a brother to me! There must be some other reason."

"Perhaps he felt that you, as the elder sister, might feel slighted if he did not select you." Even as she said those words, Lady Grayson was shaking her head. "No, no, that cannot be! When you resisted the honor, he began talking of asking that Carter girl.

And remember that he did say he wished to have a more mature Queen. Maybe that's all there is to it."

"Nevertheless, I intend to find out."

"Do be careful! Gentlemen dislike ladies who attempt to pry into their thoughts. He might become angry and deny you the position."

Damaris laughed. "Percy and I have always been frank and forthright with each other. He won't mind my inquisitiveness."

"I am so fearful that you will jeopardize everything!" she fretted.

"I promise that I shall be cautious. In any event, I do hope to ease the situation between Percy and Missy."

Her parent sighed with relief. "Do you realize, Damaris, what a prominent position you will hold at the tournament? All eyes will be upon you! You just might attract the notice of a suitable gentleman. You are one and twenty, and should have been wed long ago."

At her mother's words, a small stab of pain thrust into the pit of her stomach. When she'd had her Season in London, she had been oblivious to the gentlemen who were interested in her. She'd had thoughts for no one but Richard.

Lady Grayson moaned. "I should never have allowed your father to turn down the offers you received. 'Let her grow up a bit more, he said.' Pah! Look at you now. You are fast becoming an old maid!"

"Thank you, Mother," Damaris said dryly, cutting the flaky salmon.

"Well, it's true! You must take advantage of every opportunity offered you at the tournament. You *must*, Damaris. I shall brook no folderols, or obstinate nonsense! I am warning you!"

"Yes, ma'am." She attempted to continue her meal in peace, but Lady Grayson was too high in the boughs to allow it.

"I shall also reproach you for your behavior to Lord Delafield yesterday morning. Such impertinence! I have never been so shocked!"

Damaris gulped an unchewed lump of potatoes. "He was arrogant and obnoxious!"

"He is an earl. A handsome, wealthy bachelor. A prize catch! He can afford to be arrogant and obnoxious. You are a spinster who is fast becoming a fixture on the shelf. You cannot!"

"No, ma'am. I shall take care in the future," she capitulated.

"You must apologize to him," her mother declared with a curt nod of the head.

"That I will not do!"

"But, Damaris, you were so terribly rude! It isn't like you to forget your manners so completely. What can he have thought of us?"

"I don't know, and I don't care!" She savagely stabbed her fork into her beans. "I shall never sit and listen meekly while someone belittles me. He deserved what he got, and more!"

"But he is a *bachelor!*"

"It doesn't matter to me if he is the King of England! He was overbearing, and he required chastisement. I do have my own pride, you know."

"You have too much of it," her mother mourned. "What am I to do with you? How can I make you understand that gentlemen want tender, respectful treatment?"

"In my opinion, people should receive as good, or as bad, as they give," Damaris said with brisk finality. "Mama, may I point out that our luncheon is growing cold?"

"Luncheon!" Lady Grayson eyed her plate with distaste. "Of what use is it to serve a meal in the dining room for only the two of us? No Missy! No Osbert! Oh, I know that your papa is doing his best to recover, but I miss his presence. And as for your sister ... What am I to do? I have never been so overset! My nerves are ragged beyond belief!"

Damaris put down her fork and patted her mother's hand. "Everything will work out."

"I fear not! Missy has never behaved in this manner!" She shoved her plate aside. "I cannot eat."

"Do you wish me to talk with her?" Damaris volunteered.

Lady Grayson considered. "Perhaps it might do some good, but I just don't know. She is rather angry with you." She came to a decision. "Yes, let us try it. Talk with her at once, Damaris, and then you must ride over to Delafield to speak with Percy. You may be able to patch things up."

"Very well, Mother. I'll see Missy, but I do not think I'll go to Delafield today. I didn't sleep well last night, and I'm rather weary. I thought I'd take a nap this afternoon."

"Merciful heavens!" She irritably tossed her napkin onto the table. "You can sleep anytime. This is a serious matter!"

"All right," Damaris relented. "I shall do it."

She returned to her tepid food. It was easier to go along with her mother than it was to resist her. Perhaps that was the way her father felt when Lady Grayson overspent her clothing allowance. There was less strain in juggling the accounts than there was in contradicting his wife.

"Hurry up now, Damaris," the lady urged. "Time is wasting."

"Yes, ma'am," she said obediently, and yawned.

At least she had succeeded in diverting her mother's attention from the matter of her discourtesy to Richard. She would accept being Queen. She would wear the ridiculous medieval fashions. She would assist in smoothing the situation between Missy and Percy. But she would never, *ever* apologize for giving the earl what he so richly deserved.

"Missy?" Damaris tapped lightly on the door. When there was no answer, she turned the knob and found it locked. She knocked again, louder this time. "Missy, it's me. Please let me in. I'd like to speak with you."

"Go away," her sister replied in a muffled voice.

"Please, Missy."

"Go back to your fields, Damaris, and leave me in peace."

"I cannot. We need to talk! Please open the door," she begged.

"No! Go away! We have nothing to converse about."

"Yes, we do! We have a very great deal to discuss!" Damaris choked back her exasperation. A display of anger would serve no good purpose. Whenever people became annoyed, Missy always went to pieces. The girl simply could not bear any form of unpleasantness.

"Please, Missy," she pleaded once more. "Unlock the door."

Her sister loudly blew her nose and did not reply.

Damaris rapped again. "Missy, we must talk! Mama is dreadfully overset by your behavior! And so am I," she added.

"Nothing ever oversets you, Damaris," Missy whined. "You are cold and harsh. You have no gentle feelings."

"That is not true." This situation had affected her immensely. This . . . and Richard. "Open the door!"

"You are wasting your time. I will open to no one."

Gritting her teeth against her rising temper, Damaris spun around and strode purposefully downstairs. In the anteroom to the service area, she retrieved the spare key to her sister's room, tramped back upstairs, and unlocked the door. After stepping in, she closed it solidly behind her.

"Oh, you fiend!" Missy wrenched up from her reclining position on the chaise longue. "I might have known that you would resort to treachery!"

"Well, someone had to do it. You cannot remain locked in your room forever!"

"Why not?" she mourned. "What difference does it make? No one will care. I am worthless; I am nonessential to anyone."

"You are wrong. You know that we all love you very much."

Her sister heaved a great sigh. "All is lost."

Damaris slowly shook her head. Her sister was truly in the midst of a deep fit of the dismals. She still wore her nightrail and dressing gown. Her lovely auburn hair was unbrushed and tangled. Her eyes were red from weeping. On the table beside her was her untouched luncheon tray and a multitude of damp handkerchiefs.

"Missy, this won't do," she said softly. "It isn't worth it."

"Being Queen of the tournament?" She dabbed at her eyes, wincing at their rawness. "Maybe it isn't to you, but it was to me. My life is ruined."

"Oh, come now. It isn't as bad as all that!"

"I have nothing left to look forward to," she moaned.

"That is nonsense!" Damaris pulled up a chair and sat down. "You have your Season to think about."

"Promises," Missy said despondently. "That is all I hear. Promises! Promises, which are always broken. I had counted on Percy, and on being the Queen. It was all I had!"

"I am sorry you feel that way," she sympathized. Missy was so much like Lady Grayson. Social success meant everything to her. "I will personally make sure that there is money enough for your Season. Won't that help make up for this?"

Her sister ignored the offer. "I *loved* Percy, and you have taken him from me!"

"No, I really don't think so. There is more to this than meets the eye. After all, Percy called on you this morning. Not me."

Missy shrugged a dainty shoulder. "It makes no difference. He has demonstrated what he thinks of me."

"I disagree . . ." she began.

"I shall listen no more to your theories, Damaris. I beg you to leave me alone. The very sight of you disturbs me more than I can say!" She flopped back on the chaise and pressed a pillow over her face.

"Very well," Damaris acceded, rising. "I'll go. But won't you allow Mama to come to you? She is so very worried about you."

"All right," she gurgled.

"I'll send her immediately." Damaris left the room, nearly colliding with Lady Grayson, who was waiting in the hall.

"How is she?"

"Bleak, but she will see you." As her mother pushed past her, she caught her arm. "Mama, please try to cheer her up. You mustn't just sit there and commiserate. She looks perfectly ghastly! If she doesn't snap out of this, she is going to make herself ill."

Lady Grayson squared her shoulders. "I shall do my very best, of course. Perhaps I may persuade her to walk in the garden."

"That would be excellent."

Her mother nodded. "Now, Damaris, you must hasten to Delafield Hall!"

"Yes, ma'am." She yawned.

Percy watched his workmen shovel sand from a large wagon onto the tiltyard. The material had come all the way from the coast, and at great expense, but it made a fine base for the event. If a knight fell, he would not be injured because of the hard ground.

He smiled proudly, his vivid imagination picturing how it all would appear on the day of the tournament. Brilliant banners would whip in the breeze. Gaily caparisoned horses would prance nobly onto the field. The sunlight would glint on shining suits of armor. It would be the most magnificent event ever to take place at Delafield Hall.

Best of all, what he would learn would be priceless. How many historians ever had the opportunity to experience personally the era which they studied? It was like going back in time. He would know exactly how a knight felt when he grasped his lance and prepared to charge his opponent. He would have the pleasure of wooing his lady, of wearing her favor, in the gallant and courtly manner of the Middle Ages. He would dance the dances, eat the food . . . Woo his lady? Percy blanched.

Missy must be terribly disturbed by his asking Damaris to be the Queen. If only she would give him the chance to explain! This refusal to see him just wasn't like Missy. She had always been so sweet and gentle, so willing to listen to anything he had to say. No young lady he'd ever known was so content to sit quietly and work her beautiful embroidery while he prattled on about the medieval period. He couldn't lose her! He'd never find another woman who suited him so perfectly.

"Sir?" The foreman of his carpenters startled him from his reverie. "We're missing some lumber."

"What?"

"Some of the boards are gone, sir."

That was strange. Never, in all his years at Delafield Hall, had he known anything to be stolen. The servants and tenants had always been absolutely reliable.

"Are there very many missing?" he inquired.

"No, sir, but we didn't want you to think that we'd taken them."

"I wouldn't think that." Percy frowned. "Will this delay construction?"

The man shook his head. "We had a bit of lumber to spare."

"Good!" he said with heartfelt relief. "But keep an eye on the situation. If someone is sneaking around here at night, pilfering from my brother's estate, I must seek to expose the villain!"

"Yes, sir." The foreman returned to his workmen.

Dammit! Percy kicked at a thick clump of grass. He'd have to remember to tell Dickon to keep watch for any signs of fresh lumber when he made his rounds of the estate. Thievery could not be condoned.

As he turned toward the hall, he spotted Damaris riding across the meadow. Excellent! He needed to speak with her. He hoped she could intercede between him and Missy.

She waved and struck a canter, pulling up in front

of him and hopping down before he had the chance
to assist her. "I'm glad I caught you here, instead of
at the house. I wished to speak privately with you."

"About Missy?" he asked.

She nodded and forged on bluntly. "She is dreadfully overset by your asking me to be the Queen of
the tournament. Why can't we just forget that you
did, and you can select her instead?"

"If she'd given me a chance to explain, she would
understand," he said stubbornly.

"I am not so sure about that. Indeed, Percy, I don't
comprehend it myself. Frankly, I have no wish to be
Queen. The role doesn't suit me."

He set his jaw. He must not allow her to escape.
With all their quarreling, Damaris and Dickon
needed his matchmaking more than ever.

"Why did you choose me?" she probed.

"I told you. I visualize a more mature woman in
the position."

"I do not see that it matters," she contended. "Besides, Missy is prettier. She would make a lovely
Queen."

He could not dispute her. Damaris was beautiful,
but she couldn't hold a candle to her little sister. He
thought of Missy's delicate, dainty comeliness and
felt sick. What if she never spoke to him again? What
would he do? She was the only female he'd ever
want to marry.

"You must reconsider," Damaris declared. "It is the
only thing to be done."

Percy heard the note of resolve in her voice and
wished that he could run. Damaris was going to be
managerial, he could tell. That was her principal
fault. When she set her mind to something, she usually got her way. She was damned headstrong.

He took the reins of her horse and drifted slowly

toward the hall, striving to reach that safe haven before she succeeded in overturning his decision. He had to stand firm. Damaris and Dickon must be thrown together in lengthy enough circumstances for them to discover how perfect they were for each other.

She fell in step beside him. "Percy, are you ignoring me?"

"No, Damaris, I was merely considering, as you asked me to do. I am sorry that my decision has created upheaval, but I cannot go back on it. The Queen must be a mature lady. Besides, if I asked Missy now, she would know that she was my second choice. She would be just as distressed."

"Not for long," she persisted. "Believe me, she would soon snap out of it!"

"If Missy would allow me to see her, she'd soon feel better about the whole thing too."

"Oh, why must you be so determined!"

"I have my reasons."

"What are they?" she cried with aggravation.

"They are complex," he prevaricated. "You wouldn't perceive."

"Try me!"

"They are all tied in with medieval logic." He quickened his pace.

"Balderdash!" she exclaimed.

"It's true," he insisted. "You see, Missy is the younger of the two of you. At a medieval tournament, the Queen was a ranking lady."

"Fustian! In that case, you should have asked your mother."

"There are other factors involved as well."

"I do not understand." She stepped in front of him and stopped, blocking his flight.

"You see?" He smiled triumphantly. "I told you that you wouldn't."

"You are not making any sense!"

"I'll lend you a book on medieval culture. After reading it, Damaris, you'll see what I mean. Come, let's go to the library and fetch it." He tried to ease sideways and around her, but she matched his movement, continuing to prevent him from walking on.

"I don't want to read a book on medieval culture! I haven't the time, nor the inclination! I want you to explain!"

His mind raced. Somehow he must convince her. He must have her on his side.

"Damaris," he began, "with Dickon coming home, things have changed. As the Earl of Delafield, he will preside over the tournament. He will escort the Queen. I . . . I wanted Missy to be *my* lady at the festivities."

"Goodness!" She threw up her hands. "Why didn't you say so in the beginning?"

Percy lowered his gaze. "I find it difficult to reveal my innermost feelings."

"Surely not with me! I've always known that you have a high regard for Missy! Everyone does!"

"I didn't want people to think that I was jealous of my brother," he murmured miserably.

"I would never think that!" She hugged him.

"You're a good friend, Damaris." He grinned. "Will you help me with Missy?"

"Of course!" She sighed. "Oh, my, we do have a dilemma, don't we?"

"If only I could see her, I could explain," he said eagerly. "She would be certain to understand."

"I shall set my mind to it."

"Thank you. I knew I could depend upon you! Let us discuss it over a cup of tea."

"All right," she agreed. "Together we should come up with something that will work."

"I hope we can."

"I know we will!" She took his hand. "Percy?"

"Yes?"

"This means that Richard will be escorting me during the tournament, doesn't it?"

He nodded.

"I see," she whispered, half to herself.

Silently, lost in their own thoughts, they walked toward the castle.

Chapter 6

Richard awakened to a muffled rattle of fire tools. Opening his eyes, he saw a housemaid kneeling on the flagged hearth and deftly positioning kindling and a few larger sticks of wood in the old stone fireplace. A blaze leaped forth. Nodding with satisfaction, the girl sat back on her haunches. With a quick glance toward the door, she thrust her hands forward to the flames.

"Good morning," Richard said.

The maid, startled, bounded to her feet and sketched an awkward curtsy. "Good morning, m'lord."

"It's rather cool, isn't it? Go ahead and warm yourself."

"I'm all right, sir." Busily, she began sweeping the hearth clean of splinters and bits of bark.

"What is your name? I don't believe I remember you."

She paused. "'Tis Ella, m'lord, Ella Farley. I was just a little girl when you went away, but me mam and pap've always been here."

He recognized the name. Her father was his head groom, and her mother, a downstairs maid. Jem Farley had taught him to ride.

Ella finished the fireplace, straightened the tools, and crossed the room to the windows to throw back the drapes. "'Tis nasty weather today, Lord Delafield."

Richard looked out at the heavy gray skies. Rain poured down in a steady stream. There would be no excursions into the fields this morning, nor work on Percy's tournament grounds. He sighed. He'd been waiting for just such a day to closet himself in the library and perform the necessary but dreary chore of examining the estate accounts.

"Me mam says that a day like this chills your bones clear through to the marrow," Ella ventured, "especially in this big old, drafty castle. Why, our own cottage is a lot cozier!"

"I'm glad that it is warm."

"Trouble is, we get drenched on the way to work, but there's nothing to be done about that! Still, I like havin' our own place. More privacy, don't y'know!"

Richard grinned. Now that Ella had overcome her reticence, there seemed to be no end to her chatter. But that was the informal way of most of the Delafield servants.

"I hope it doesn't rain for Lord Percy's doin's," she went on. "That'd be a real mess."

"It certainly would." Her reference to the event sparked his curiosity. "What do the servants think of the tournament, Ella? What do you think?"

"We're real excited, sir. It should be a grand thing to see. Lord Percy says we can sit right up front, and we're going to have costumes."

Richard choked back a groan. Percy was surely sparing no expense in staging his spectacle. He could afford it, but was it really necessary to be so completely authentic?

"It'll be fun," Ella babbled. "Just think of all them knights trying to knock each other off their horses! And the pretty ladies! Miss Grayson will be the perfect Queen. She's sweet as sugar, she is."

Damaris? Sweet? That was certainly not the adjective he would use!

"I wonder what her dress will look like," the servant mused. "Money ain't too plentiful now at the Graysons'."

Aware that he was in the ideal position to take advantage of the harvest of the servants' vast grapevine, he gave his inquisitiveness full rein. "The Graysons are short of money?" he prompted.

"It seems so, m'lord. I've a cousin that works there, and she says they've been hard up ever since Sir Osbert's trouble."

So Damaris thought she could manage an estate? He had always guessed that her claim had been fanciful. Now he knew for certain. She was barely able to muddle along. She was just too proud to admit it and ask for help. Perhaps he and Percy should step in and take over the reins. It would be the neighborly thing to do, especially since his brother had a certain understanding with the young lady. They could begin this afternoon by paying a visit to the Graysons. By then, he would be ready to take a respite from the accounts.

Once again, Richard felt an unexplainable flash of jealousy. Yesterday, he had seen Percy and Damaris cross the meadow together. They had embraced. They had held hands. They were in love.

His spirits plummeted. Percy and Damaris just weren't right for each other. With his nose in a book and his head in the clouds, his brother would allow that overbearing female to trample all over him. He probably wouldn't even realize she was doing it. But maybe he wouldn't care. Damaris Grayson was just as beautiful as she was headstrong. Perhaps that was all that mattered to Percy.

Although it hadn't been his preference, Percy had

done an excellent job administering Delafield Hall, as well as his own estate, which their father had willed the younger son. But if his brother had his choice, he would do nothing but study and write. Therein lay the danger in his wedding Damaris. She would take over the practical and financial side of their life, leaving Percy to indulge in his scholarship. Soon he would be so lost in his dream world that he would lose all touch with reality. He would become as eccentric as Uncle Vincent. The *ton* would laugh.

No, Damaris wasn't the proper lady for Percy. He should marry a gentle, helpless female, who would force him to balance his life with normal, everyday routine. He needed a wife who would lean on him.

And Damaris? That willful woman required a strong, masculine man to control her. Her husband should be firm and very sure of himself.

"Cease your prattle, girl, and go about your duties!" Casey ordered.

Richard wrenched his mind from his reverie.

"A proper housemaid does not stand around gibbering to her betters!" the valet asserted. "His Lordship must be bored beyond belief."

Before the earl could protest, the frightened Ella dashed from the room.

Casey shut the door with his heel and brought the morning tea tray to Richard's bedside. "Such impertinence! Every day I am further astonished at the behavior of many of these servants, sir. The thought of your task in exacting some semblance of discipline in these people is almost more than I can bear."

"I don't mind their gossip," Richard stated. "Sometimes one can learn a great deal from what is being said backstairs."

"I can provide that information, my lord. You need only ask."

"Thank you, Casey. I shall remember that." He slipped out of bed and into his dressing robe, beginning his morning ablutions. "However, I would appreciate your tolerance with the people here. Delafield Hall is a rather relaxed establishment when only the family is in residence. When guests are present, you will find that the staff performs very professionally."

The valet merely shook his head in wonderment and poured the tea.

"I realize that you are unaccustomed to such informality," Richard added, pausing to sip the strong, hot brew. "I hope that you will grow used to it. You are the best valet that I have ever had."

Casey regarded him with a pained expression.

"Is there something else wrong?"

"Well, the castle is rather chilly and damp, but there is little you can do about that." He sniffed. "There is, however, one thing more. My lord, I am *your* valet. Yours, and yours alone. While I do not mind lending a hand when necessary, I am unable to do so on a continuing basis. I cannot properly care for two gentlemen at the same time."

"My brother?" Richard guessed.

"Indeed, sir. Lord Percy is a fine, though singular, gentleman, but he is requiring more and more of my services. I cannot say that I blame him." Casey's nose ascended a trifle higher. "His valet is some sort of . . . of . . . glorified footman!"

The earl smiled. "Perhaps an increase in salary is in order."

"No, my lord. Money will not suffice!" Casey cried, horrified. "I refer to the element of time. There are not enough hours in the day to allow me to care for two gentlemen."

"There aren't?"

"Oh no, sir!" A look of displeasure spread across his thin features. "If I were required to tend both of you, neither you nor your brother would appear to the greatest advantage."

"Well, this is the country. It wouldn't matter so much," Richard said amiably.

Shock replaced the valet's visage of aversion. "I have my honor, my lord, and my reputation. I could not stoop so low! As much as I have enjoyed being in your employ, I fear I cannot condone your looking less than suitably turned out. If that is your preference, I will be forced to tender my resignation."

"Don't do that!"

"I am sorry, my lord."

"Let us discuss other possibilities," Richard quickly suggested. "Perhaps you could train my brother's man."

"Impossible! He is ham-fisted. He irons wrinkles into Lord Percy's shirts. And leaves them there!" Casey gasped. "Besides, I haven't the time to teach another man. Nor do I wish to disclose my secrets."

"What do you suggest?" the earl asked, sitting down on the edge of the bed.

"Another valet. That can be the only solution," his man pronounced.

"Very well. I shall consult with Lord Percy."

"My lord?"

"Yes, Casey, is there something else?" he asked wearily.

"I just might know of a suitable candidate for the post," the valet proclaimed.

"Somehow, I am not surprised."

Casey was undaunted. "The man is my own

brother. At present, he serves an elderly, rather cantankerous gentleman. I believe that he could be tempted away from that position."

"If you approve, then write to him. May I leave the matter in your hands?"

"You certainly may! I shall do it today."

"Good." Richard finished his tea, stood up, and strode toward his dressing room. "Are you sure you have time?" he couldn't help tossing over his shoulder.

Casey was just as quick. "I'll cut short my luncheon," he countered, following his master.

With a neat stroke of the pen, Damaris finished her work on the account books. Now everything was up to date. If her father, who was feeling so much better, asked to see the records, he would be well pleased.

It had been a shock to discover that neither the butler nor the housekeeper was accustomed to keeping up the household tallies, and that Lady Grayson had not performed the chore herself. Sir Osbert had always managed that as well. Damaris shook her head. How had he ever found the time? It was no wonder that his health had suffered. But those days had ended. He had her to help him now. It seemed plain that she was not destined to marry. She would live out her life here.

She leaned back in her chair and closed her eyes, rubbing her temples. Calculating all those figures had given her a headache, but it was a pain of satisfaction. She was proud of her accomplishment.

"Oh, Damaris, here you are!" Lady Grayson called pleasantly from the doorway. "Poor dear, she is struggling so hard to make heads and tails of those fusty old figures!"

She opened her eyes, amazed to see Percy and Richard following her mother into the room.

"We have guests, you see," the lady went on affably.

Damaris resisted the impulse to smooth her hair and straighten her dress. She must look a fright! Why on earth had her mother brought the men in here, without giving her any warning? She didn't mind about Percy, but Richard ... Good heavens, what would he think of her? She sat up and squared her shoulders. She hoped her appearance was not as bad as she thought.

"Good afternoon, gentlemen," she murmured.

They bowed, returning the greeting. She saw the twinkling in Richard's blue eyes. Was he inwardly laughing at her?

Lady Grayson sank down on the sofa. "The dear child is absolutely overwhelmed by the task she is attempting to perform," she moaned, mournfully eyeing Damaris. "I fear it is far too much for her. Such a pity."

"Perhaps I could help," Richard volunteered.

"Would you, my lord?" her mother appealed. "It would be such a comfort to me! You cannot know how hard it has been for us, since my husband's trouble. I am fully aware of my own limitations and wished to engage a steward, but my daughter *would* try it on her own."

"I shall be happy to assist," the earl reiterated, "and I know that Percy will also do all he can."

"Of course." Percy smirked. "My time is rather limited, at present, but after the tournament, I am yours, Lady Grayson! Dickon will fill in admirably until then."

Damaris felt like smacking the grin from her best friend's face. What was he trying to do? He knew full well that she was perfectly capable of managing things!

"Excellent!" Lady Grayson cried. "Perhaps you could begin at once, Lord Delafield. Damaris has been battling those lamentable records all day long. She must have reached her wit's end."

"No, Mother, I—"

"Percy and I shall leave the two of you in peace." The lady quickly rose. "Do not protest, Damaris. His Lordship is being most kind to us."

"But . . ."

"I insist." She hurried toward the door. "After all, they are *my* records. Mine and your father's, that is." With Percy in tow, she left the room.

Richard approached the desk and pulled up a chair beside her. "I really don't mind helping, Miss Grayson. I'm sure that Percy would have stepped in long ago, but sometimes he just doesn't consider practical matters."

"But . . ." she stammered again.

He glanced down at the tidy pages. "Sugar . . . salt . . . These are household accounts!"

"How astute," Damaris said tightly.

He thumbed back through the book until her father's handwriting replaced her own meticulous script. "Gad, you have had to catch up on a great deal! Your housekeeper and butler should have been keeping these up to date, or . . ."

"Or my mother?" she asked cynically. "It seems, my lord, that I am the only one capable of doing it."

He began to scan the figures.

"Lord Delafield." Feeling vastly exposed, she unsuccessfully attempted to take the ledger from him. "You cannot be interested in the administering of a household."

"Numbers are numbers," he muttered.

"Please," she begged, a flush creeping up her neck to her cheeks. If he continued to examine the entries so thoroughly, he would see just how poorly the personal expenditures were budgeted. He would witness how she had juggled accounts to make up for it and would consider her inept. She wished she could angrily object to his study, but all hostility had left her. She could only feel ashamed.

There was a tap at the door. A footman entered, bearing a tray of refreshments. After setting it on the big desk, he withdrew.

"May I pour you a glass of sherry?" she asked Richard, hoping to distract him from his probing. "Or, if you prefer, I shall send for brandy."

"Sherry will be fine," he mumbled.

"There are sandwiches here, and cakes . . ."

"Damaris, please be silent."

She hastily glanced at him, unnerved by his use of her first name. He hadn't seemed to notice. Either he had finally decided to reinstate their childhood informality or he was too wrapped up in those awful figures to realize what he had done. She watched with horror as his index finger seemed to hover, in particular, over those ghastly entries for dress fabric and folderols. It was an absolute nightmare.

Again she tried to divert him. "Richard?" she implored, boldly using his Christian name as well.

"Shh."

He tapped his finger on one distinct notation. Damaris leaned forward to read it. Feathers! She remembered the day her mother had come home with the gay plumage. The price had been exorbitant.

Richard lifted his gaze to meet hers.

Damaris drew a deep breath. "I know what you are thinking, and you are correct."

"Well, I have not yet seen the estate books, so I do not have the full picture."

"No matter. Many of those purchases were extravagant," she bravely told him. "I have cut corners to pay for them."

"You should not do that for unnecessary items!"

"Do you think I don't know that?" Her pride, along with her indignation, came flooding back.

"Apparently not." He raised an expressive eyebrow. "You claim the skill to manage this estate, yet I can see how you exclude necessities to pay for trifles. What do you expect me to think? It's all here in black and white."

"I'm doing the best that I can!"

"You're taking food from the table," he accused.

"No, I am not! I am merely simplifying meals! What do you know of it, anyway?" she snapped.

"My dear, I have lived alone for several years. I have grown quite familiar with running a household. This one, I'll wager, is deprived of essentials. And it's all because of overspending on personal luxuries! It's going to catch up with you."

"I know that!" she shouted.

"Then, for God's sake, do something about it."

"I can't stop it!"

He stared at her. "Can't . . . What? Of course you can!"

It was too much. It was bad enough to fight Lady Grayson's spending habits. It was worse to hear him blame her for them. It wasn't her fault! Damaris burst into tears of humiliation.

"My dear." Richard covered her hand with his. "It isn't so awful as that. I'll help you. We'll set up a budget and . . ."

"I've already done that! You don't understand,"

she sobbed. "It's Mama. I cannot prevent her need-
less spending!"

"I see," he said quietly.

"I've tried to tell her! I've tried to show her the figures!" she cried. "But she will pay me no heed! I'm
trying so hard . . ."

"Poor little girl." He gathered her in his arms,
gently pushing her head to his shoulder.

Mindlessly, she lay against him and wept, damp-
ening his coat and mussing his neckcloth. It was so
soothing to give way to the pent-up strain and allow
her emotion to flow full force. She felt so relieved, so
comforted. Gradually her sobs diminished to snif-
flings. She accepted his handkerchief, wiped her face,
and blew her nose.

"Better now?" he asked.

She nodded. Lifting her head, she realized with
mortification that she was sitting childlike on his lap.
Her cheeks burned.

"How did I get here?" she gasped.

"You crawled right over." He grinned. "Don't be
embarrassed. Percy might not approve, but it made it
ever so much easier for me to comfort you."

What did Percy have to do with it? She couldn't
imagine what difference her friend's opinion made,
but it must matter to Richard. Perhaps he thought
that his brother might question such sudden intimacy, after their previous animosity.

"Percy needn't know." She stood up stiffly,
smoothing her skirts. "I apologize for being a water-
ing pot. I am not usually such a goose."

"You have been under considerable stress."

"Yes," she answered simply and handed him his
drink, taking up her glass and returning to her chair.

"Percy and I are more than willing to assist you,"
he reminded.

With the release of the tension, she found her courage restored. "Percy is so busy, and I know that you also must have much to do. I shall contrive, my lord," she said valiantly.

"My lord?" he questioned lightly. "I seem to remember your calling me Richard."

Again she felt the heat in her cheeks.

"Let us return to our childhood familiarity, Damaris," he urged.

She sipped her wine, avoiding his gaze. "Very well."

"And I *will* help you. You need male assistance, whether you want to admit it or not."

"I can manage."

When he did not reply, she looked surreptitiously toward him. He was doubtfully peering at the open ledger. Damaris set her jaw. He had seen the very worst. He had no idea of the improvements she had made to the property. He thought she was a helpless female. How wrong he was!

Damaris wished she had the will to set him straight, but the remembrance of his embrace entirely nullified her yearning to argue. She remembered how warmly he had held her and how she had succumbed to his cuddling. Despite their differences of opinion, she realized that she was still very much in love with him. No, she corrected herself, she was in love with the image she had created of him. The real Richard Delafield was completely dissimilar. He was dangerous to her very being. She must avoid him.

"I have had enough for today." Reaching forward, she closed the account book. "Let us finish our wine and straighten our attire." She smiled self-consciously. "Then we shall pay a visit to Father. You haven't seen him since your return, and the conversation will please him ever so much."

"All right," he cheerfully acquiesced. "I'll enjoy talking with him too, if he is able."

"Oh, he is greatly improved. Daily I expect the doctor to allow him to be carried downstairs."

"I'm glad to hear that."

"Yes, he does enjoy having company." She proudly lifted her chin. "And if you ask, I am sure that he will teach you to manage an estate, as he has so successfully taught me."

Chapter 7

"**R**ichard Delafield is a fine young man!" Sir Osbert declared with approval as Damaris plumped his pillows and helped him slide down into a prone position in the bed. "I am pleased that you brought him to visit me this afternoon. It certainly brightened my dreary day!"

"I'm glad you enjoyed it, Papa."

"I did indeed. He reminds me of his father," he reflected. "I'll admit that I had my doubts about him when he didn't return to Delafield after my old friend's death, but he must have had his reasons. He doesn't seem the type to shun responsibility. Ah well, what difference? He is here now, and he seems ready to perform his duty."

"After he learns how to manage an estate," Damaris added.

Her father shrugged. "He'll grasp it quickly. I've no doubt of that. He doesn't have the benefit of knowing the more modern practices, however. I'd like to lend him those new treatises we bought, Damaris. He may wish to experiment with some of the ideas. Also, I did take the liberty of inviting him to accompany you one day, so that he may see for himself what we are accomplishing. I hope you don't mind?"

"No," she said stiffly, "but I doubt that he cared much for the thought."

"Why is that?"

"Richard believes that women have no place pursuing matters more challenging than embroidery and child rearing," she said airily.

Sir Osbert chuckled. "Ruffled your feathers, did he? But he is right, you know."

"Papa!" she cried, incensed. "How can you say that? You know what I have achieved! You know that I am perfectly capable of managing this estate!"

"And *you* know how greatly I dislike forcing you to do so. You should be enjoying life, my dear."

"I am!" she insisted, sitting down on the edge of the bed and taking his hand. "I can think of nothing that I would rather be doing!"

His eyes twinkled. "Wouldn't you prefer to spend your time exercising your charms on young Delafield?"

"Certainly not," Damaris proclaimed. "I have far better ways to fill my hours."

" 'Tis a pity. I'd always harbored the hope that the two of you might someday make a match of it. I'd be surprised if the same thought hadn't occurred to Richard's father too, though he never mentioned it directly. A marriage between you would join the estates. It would be a formidable piece of land."

"Indeed it would," she readily agreed, "but that will never happen. Richard doesn't approve of me, and I abhor his condescending manner."

"Condescending? Daughter, isn't that a bit strong? He was very pleasant to me."

"Of course he was. You are a man. He respects you. He considers me to be a helpless, dim-witted ninnyhammer!" she snapped.

Sir Osbert roared with laughter. "The poor fellow has certainly incurred your wrath! I have never seen you wax so emotional over a gentleman! Perhaps my hopes are not dashed after all."

Damaris pursed her lips and eyed him with aggravation. "Anger, Papa, is a long way from love. And, much as I treasure the land, an exceptional parcel of property would never entice me to wed a man whose views were not compatible with mine."

"Nevertheless, I shall continue to watch with great interest!"

"You will waste your time," she said irritably. "Now go to sleep. You have had a long afternoon."

"Damaris!" he called after her as she crossed the room.

"Yes, Papa?" She paused, turning.

"I wish a favor."

"Anything."

"Permit Richard his masculine pride," he quietly advised. "It is very important to a man."

She nodded doubtfully and left the room, striding down the hall toward her bedchamber. Why should she take consideration of the earl's self-esteem, when he had no regard for her own? Shamefully, she thought back on her performance in the library. That tearful breakdown had done nothing to increase his admiration for her strength of purpose. In fact, it had probably further convinced him of her unsuitability to direct even the smallest enterprise. Oh, why had she chosen that moment to surrender to the relentless pressure? He must think her the greatest of incompetents. He had called her a little girl, and she had behaved like one. Good heavens! She had even crawled into his lap!

The memory of it brought the now-familiar warmth flooding to her cheeks. Try as she might, she couldn't banish the recollection from her mind. Richard's embrace had been ... wonderful. Worse still, deep inside, she knew that she wished he would do it again. Why couldn't she persuade herself that her images of him were mere fantasies? He wasn't the man for her. He didn't respect her.

"Oh, Damaris? One moment please! I wish to have a word with you." Lady Grayson beckoned to her from the open door of her room.

She groaned inwardly. No doubt her mother wished to discuss the afternoon's events. That was the last thing she wished to do! Besides, she wasn't in particular charity with her parent. Lady Grayson had been the one who'd begged for Richard's help, left her alone with him, and set the stage for that mortifying scene.

"Mama," she said, hesitating, "I am rather in a hurry. I had planned to take a bath and wash my hair before dinner."

"Only a moment?" she pleaded woefully.

Damaris acquiesced. She entered the room, but she did not sit down. "Do not blame me if I am late for the meal."

"I won't." Lady Grayson blew her nose into a lacy handkerchief. "Especially since you will be my only dining companion."

"Missy has refused again to leave her room?"

Her mother nodded somberly. "I am beside myself with agony. What am I to do? She will not come down for meals, and of course she refused once more to see Percy. You must help me, Damaris."

"I've done all that I can. If she would only see Percy, I'm sure he would explain. But if she persists in being foolish, there is little we can do to prevent it."

"There must be something!"

"Did you assure her that Percy still cares as much for her as he always did?"

"It does no good! She won't believe it!" Lady

Grayson sighed mightily. "Can you think of nothing else?"

"Me?" she cried. "I have already done what I can! You forget, Mama, that Missy is not exactly pleased with me. You have the greater chance of persuading her."

"It oversets me to see her in such a piteous condition!" her mother wailed. "My constitution is not strong enough to witness her decline! I must place the situation in your hands."

"I have an estate to attend to," Damaris objected firmly. "That must be my foremost priority."

"Fustian!" she snapped, sitting up. "Thanks to me, Lord Delafield has kindly agreed to do that! You must concentrate on your sister."

"I will not! The earl has not the knowledge to oversee Grayson Park. I refuse to stand by and watch my efforts destroyed!" She began to pace the floor. "By the way, I did not applaud your giving him carte blanche to pry into our affairs. It was most embarrassing!"

"You are much too sensitive. We have nothing to hide! You do need the help, my dear. You have performed commendably, but you must admit that a man is far more capable."

Damaris ground her teeth. "Nothing to hide? That is certainly wide of the mark! When you begged his assistance, I was working on the household accounts. The first thing he noticed was your immense expenditures for dress materials and folderols. He did not approve."

"What!" Lady Grayson picked up her fan and began to flutter it over her bosom. "I would not have believed the Earl of Delafield to be tightfisted! You are making things up."

"No, I am not," she assured her.

"But his mama is the most finely dressed female in the county!"

"She can afford it. We cannot."

"I still do not believe you, Damaris." The fan began to beat ever more rapidly. "Your father never questioned my bills."

"He took the money away from other needs. That is what I have done."

Damaris's spirits rose, elated by the direction the conversation had taken. Here was her chance to press home two very important points. First, she might motivate her mother into taking a long, hard look at her spending habits. Second, she might eliminate, once and for all, the dreadful threat of Richard's assistance. Eagerly, she halted her pacing and knelt down before her parent.

"Mama, if you insist upon the earl taking charge, he will immediately put a period to your shopping."

"I won't have that!" Lady Grayson gasped. "Would he have us dress in rags?"

"As you can see," Damaris noted wickedly, "he has no business prying into our personal affairs."

"You are correct, my dear. Thank heavens you called it to my attention! Never again must you allow him to examine those papers!"

"I give you my word." Smiling, she rose. "But you must take care to control your spending. Papa likes the earl. If *he* asked him to assist us, we would be powerless to refuse."

"Oh, dear!"

"Indeed! But if you make no new purchases," she warned, "he will assume that you have taken his suggestion, and he will not bother you further."

"I understand. I shall be cautious," her mother whimpered.

"Good! Now I shall leave you and prepare for my bath."

She had almost succeeded in her flight, when Lady Grayson's voice interrupted her at the door.

"Don't forget, Damaris! You must do something about your sister."

"Damn," she muttered under her breath and fled down the hall.

The rain had diminished to a fine drizzle by the time Richard and Percy passed through the gates of Delafield Hall. The journey from Grayson Park had been a strangely silent one. Percy, usually so full of conversation, had been almost morose. Richard assumed that the reason for his brother's depression was the lack of time he'd been able to spend with Damaris. Well, he certainly couldn't blame him for it. Lady Grayson had created that situation, and Percy himself had encouraged it.

It was odd how Lady Grayson had seemed so anxious to whisk Percy away and leave him and Damaris alone together. Perhaps she had merely been worried about the financial state of affairs and was anxious for him to help her daughter straighten out matters. But that didn't seem reasonable. If she was concerned about money, she wouldn't spend so damned much of it on all those unnecessary trifles.

One thing was certain. Damaris certainly hadn't wanted his assistance. In a sense, he couldn't blame her. Exhibiting one's records was like baring one's soul. He himself had felt slightly self-conscious, examining the Grayson books. She had been completely overset. Poor girl. Why couldn't she see that she needed help? He had to admit a certain admiration for her neat, balanced accounts and for the clever method by which she cut corners, but managing an estate and a household was just too much for one young female. The trouble would manifest itself on the land. That was where he would discover her helplessness.

At least they had returned to the first-name basis of their childhood. That should eventually spur on a friendship between them. He hoped Percy would appreciate his efforts.

A small knot formed in the pit of his stomach as he thought of how he had held Damaris on his lap and comforted her. It would be a lie to say that he hadn't derived some enjoyment from it, and that did not stem from the fact that she had finally broken down and behaved like a woman. He had relished it physically. Her body was soft and well formed and ... He banished the thought from his mind. My God, he couldn't allow himself to have those kinds of notions about his future sister-in-law!

The closed carriage rolled to a stop in front of the castle. A footman, carrying an umbrella, hastened to let down the steps and open the door. Percy emerged first and, without waiting for his brother, strode through the shower and into the castle.

Richard shrugged mentally and followed. The younger man must truly be feeling a certain amount of anger toward him. He would have to speak with Percy and ease the situation. But at the door, he heard Percy's voice rising cheerfully. *And there was a great clanking of metal.*

"Hasbrook!" his brother shouted happily. "Is that you in there?"

"It is!" came the exuberant answer.

Percy whirled. "Look, Dickon! It's my best friend, Gerry! Viscount Hasbrook, that is. My knights have begun to arrive!"

Richard stared at the shining armored aberration

on the stairs. Here was another one of the simpletons who thought Percy's scheme would be a grand adventure. He wondered how many other young men in England were so lacking in plain good sense.

Percy's friend paused and flung back his visor. "Are you Percy's brother? You look enough alike!"

He bowed, nodding.

Hasbrook attempted to return the nicety and teetered precariously forward. He balanced himself against the railing and grinned sheepishly. "Pardon me, my lord! I'm not accustomed to this armor yet."

Percy spoke up. "It's taken me ever so long to lose my awkwardness!"

"Have you?" his brother asked dryly.

"Now, Dickon, you just haven't seen me of late. I think I'll put on my armor right now and show you!"

There was a second clanging of steel. Uncle Vincent appeared at the top of the steps. With much greater stability than that displayed by Gerry Hasbrook, he started downward.

"Doesn't he look magnificent?" the elderly gentleman asked, reaching the step on which the younger knight rested. "Dammit, Dickon, I wish there had been time for you to obtain a suit of armor! Perhaps we could attempt to borrow ..."

"No, Uncle!" Richard wildly assured him. "I am perfectly satisfied with my role."

"Doesn't seem right," his relative grumbled, proceeding. "Come along, Gerry. Watch how I move and imitate me. You'll catch on quick enough. You are already doing quite well."

"Thank you, sir, but I doubt I'll ever be as good at it."

"Balderdash! It's just a matter of putting one foot in front of the other."

"And doing it very carefully," Richard added direly.

"I believe you're afraid to wear armor," his brother challenged.

"It's a matter of better sense, Percy, not fear."

"Then prove it!"

"I seem to recall that you proved it yourself when your horse ran off with you and you took that spill in the meadow," Richard murmured.

Percy flushed. "Well, I'm doing better now! You must come and watch my practices. I'm tired of your snickering and your disdainful attitude," he growled bitterly.

Richard glanced with surprise at his brother. First Damaris had accused him of arrogance, and now Percy seemed to agree. Was he really so pretentious? The idea bothered him. He didn't want to be such an obnoxious prig.

"I'd like to speak with you later," he said in an undertone and returned his attention to the wobbling procession on the stairs.

Viscount Hasbrook had once again regained his balance and begun his descent, but he hadn't let go of the banister. Slowly and cautiously, he followed Uncle Vincent's example. With each successful step, his grin widened.

Vincent reached the bottom and pivoted around to admire his pupil's progress. "He'll do," he gloated. "After I helped him put on his armor, and showed that obtuse valet of his how to do it, he began practicing. Walked about for a full hour, he did, before attempting the stairs. Young Gerry has a good head on his shoulders, and a praiseworthy determination."

Percy beamed with pleasure. "You'll find your other students to be just as commendable, Uncle. I chose them with care."

Richard bit back the wry comment that had leaped, unbidden, to his tongue. Damaris and Percy were right! He really was becoming arrogant and derisive. He must examine his ways. He disliked haughtiness and conceit in others. He despised it in himself.

Three steps away from the floor of the hall, Gerry released his grip on the railing. "I think I'm on to it now!"

Pride goeth before a fall, the earl recited to himself, his gaze fixed on the would-be knight.

Unfortunately, the old adage was true. On the next step, the viscount scraped his heel on the riser. With the tumultuous crash of metal meeting stone, he plummeted downward. Richard vaulted aside, but Percy and Uncle Vincent did not react quickly enough. They fell like dominoes as Gerry pitched into them.

Wide-eyed servants rushed to the hall from all directions. Even the cook, clutching her rolling pin, dashed in from the kitchen. Lady Delafield appeared at the top of the stairs.

"What on earth?" she shrieked. "Richard, do something!"

He knelt beside the heaving pile of metal and flesh. "Is anyone hurt?"

Uncle Vincent chuckled. "Almost made it, didn't he?"

"I'll do it next time," Viscount Hasbrook said crossly. "Can't imagine what happened! Steps must be uneven."

Percy wedged himself from under the twisting wreckage, a trickle of blood seeping from his left nostril. "Dammit, Gerry, you bloodied my nose!"

"They're all right, Mama!" Richard called to the dowager.

"Thank heavens! The noise nearly frightened me out of my wits!"

"Will some of you help me get them up?" he asked the group of onlookers and reached for his brother.

Percy extricated his handkerchief, dabbed at his nose, and glared at him. "Go ahead. Say it!"

"Say what?" Richard asked mildly.

"Let us hear one of your famous derogatory comments!"

"I don't know what you're talking about." He extended his hand to help his brother up. "I thought Hasbrook did a very good job of negotiating those stairs. He merely had a bit of bad luck at the last."

Percy regained his feet and eyed him suspiciously. "That's all?"

Richard smiled. "That's all. What did you expect?" He presented his brother with his own fresh handkerchief and bent to help the others.

Chapter 8

Despite the unsettling events of the previous day, Damaris awoke refreshed and willing to meet any problems that might arise. Seeing the brilliant sunshine flooding through her window, she knew that she had slept shamefully late, but she refused to feel guilty about it. There was much to be done today, and the good night's sleep would help her see it through.

Hurrying down the hall on her way to breakfast, she saw a maid with a large tray of food standing at her sister's door and begging admission. A sudden idea struck her. She halted.

"Martha, please take that back to the kitchen."

"But, miss," the girl explained, "I hear her moving around in there. She'll open the door in a moment. She always does."

"There will be no more trays brought to this room. Miss Melissa is quite capable of coming downstairs for her meals. That is an order."

The maid eyed her doubtfully, but slowly obeyed. When she had disappeared through the backstairs door, Damaris tapped again.

"I'm coming!" Missy called from within. "I had trouble finding my dressing robe!" The door swung open. "You!" she cried with dismay.

"There is something we shall settle immediately."

"I don't wish to speak with you!"

98

Missy tried to shut the door, but Damaris had her foot in it. She pushed it open and entered the room.

"I have nothing to say to you, Damaris!"

"Well, I have a great deal to say to you!" She glanced around the room. It looked as if a terrible storm had swept through it. Items of apparel were strewn all over the furniture and floor, as if Missy had thrown out all the contents of her dressing room. A tray of biscuits, bread, and cheese rested on the table by the chaise lounge. At the bedside was a half-eaten box of chocolates. Damaris gathered up all the food and dumped it into the chamber pot.

"What are you doing?" Missy wailed.

"If you wish to eat, you will come to the dining room," she announced severely.

"I am ill! I cannot!"

"Fustian! Your illness is in your mind. What you truly are is ridiculous! And childish. I have had enough of it!"

Missy sniffled. "What difference does it make to you? You hate me!"

"I certainly do not, though God knows why! But I am vastly aggravated with your foolish behavior! You have completely overset Mama. She is pleading constantly for me to do something about you, and that is exactly what I intend to do," she said with a curt nod.

"You are mean and cruel!"

"If I must possess those qualities to bring you to your senses, then so be it." She briefly surveyed her sister's limp, tangled hair and grasped her arm, pulling her into the dressing room.

"What are you going to do to me?" Missy shrieked.

"I am going to comb that mess." She shoved her

onto the chair before her table and mirror and picked up a comb.

"Ouch!" Missy shrilled as Damaris attacked a matted hank. "You're hurting me!"

"You hurt yourself. You are the one who caused this rat's nest."

"I hate you! I hate you! I hate you!"

"So you have said." Damaris eased the fervor of her combing as a large wisp of hair came loose from Missy's scalp.

Her sister saw it in the mirror. "You're pulling my hair out! You're going to make me bald!"

"I can't help it. These huge snarls have already twisted it loose."

"Let me do it!" Missy screeched.

"Gladly." Damaris presented her with the comb. "But I warn you, I shall come to inspect it later. If it is not presentable, I shall do it myself. I might even bring scissors!"

The girl gasped. "Oh, you are a monster!"

"Think what you will. I am acting in your own best interest." Damaris began her retreat. "I shall also order a bath for you. And I'll send someone to clean up this squalor!"

After leaving the room, she continued down the hall to her mother's chamber and knocked lightly on the door. At her parent's bidding, she entered and approached the bed, where Lady Grayson lay propped up on an abundance of pillows, her breakfast tray on her lap.

"Good morning, Mama," she greeted. "You will be happy to know that I have begun restoring Missy from her doldrums."

"Thank God!" She clapped her hands excitedly. "I knew you would think of something, my dear!"

"Yes, I have, but I will require your support."

"Anything!"

"I have given the order that no food be brought to Missy's room. You must confirm this by giving your own direction to the housekeeper."

"Oh, dear," Lady Grayson murmured dubiously. "I do not know if that will work. If she has no nourishment, she will lose her energy and slide into a steeper decline."

"Please trust me. Missy does not have the willpower to deprive herself for long. I would not be surprised if she appeared for dinner!"

"Well . . . all right. We shall try it, but only for a short while. I will not permit her to starve."

"Of course not!" Damaris assured her. "Just do not give in prematurely to her pleas. On second thought, it might be better if you didn't even visit her room today."

"But she will be bored!" Lady Grayson protested. "I entertain her with all the latest news!"

"Exactly. She has been fed and amused in her self-imposed exile. Now it is time to make it distasteful."

"It might work," her mother mused.

"I know it will." Damaris started toward the door. "Don't forget that Dr. Corey is to see Papa this morning."

"I remember. I shall be ready to hear his report. Oh, I *do* hope that it is a good one!"

"So do I."

Damaris hurried on to the breakfast room. Consuming her meal, she mulled over what the day might bring. Missy's emergence from seclusion? Official word of Sir Osbert's improvement? A visit from Richard?

The toast stuck in her throat. Hastily she washed it down with a swallow of tea. She must avoid him. Her mother, fearful of his opinion of her spending, would not prevent her escape. Her father, approving of him, was a different matter. The situation might become difficult.

At all costs, she must elude his presence. It was common sense. He was dangerous to her well-being. So why must she feel such great longing to see him again? Couldn't her logic prevail? A sensation of warmth spread through her veins as she remembered sitting on his lap, his arms securely around her. It wasn't just comfort. She wanted something else, something she refused to name even to herself.

Why must she be caught in this turmoil of warring emotions? Hadn't she enough to worry about? Damaris threw down her napkin and got up from the table. She had work to do. With Dr. Corey expected at any time, she couldn't stray far from the house, but that was all right. There was much she could do in the nearby area.

But oh, Richard had been so sweet when he had held her. He hadn't been arrogant then. With a heart-wrenching sigh, she set her mind to agricultural affairs.

Richard tossed down his hammer, skipped the last two plank steps, and dropped lithely to the ground. Wiping his arm across his face to clear the perspiration from his eyes, he stared upward to the rotting platform in the tree. He had finished the steps. Tomorrow he would begin work on its rebuilding. He had done enough for today. From the position of the sun, he could tell that it was almost noon. He would barely have time to make himself presentable for lunch.

He gathered up his tools and stashed them in the hollow of a neighboring oak. Grinning, he reached for his pristine white shirt, which was draped across a bush. If a stranger saw him now, stripped to the waist and damp with dirty sweat, he would never guess that he was the exalted Earl of Delafield.

As he picked up the garment, he heard a rustle in the underbrush. Richard froze. An animal? Someone prying in the woods? Surely it couldn't be Percy. He probably never came here anymore. Slowly, he turned toward the direction of the sound.

Old Asa, the gatekeeper, emerged from a little-used path through the timber. "It's me, m'lord."

"Asa! What are you doing here?" Richard relaxed. "I wouldn't have expected to see you in the woods."

"Oh, I have m' good days when I can get out and about. I like to come here. And remember." He looked up at the treehouse. "Fixin' 'er up, are you?"

He nodded. "You'll keep my secret, won't you?"

"I will." He pulled on the first step, testing its strength. "Don't suppose people'd understand why the earl wanted to mend his old treehouse."

"I doubt that they would." Richard shrugged, peering upward. "I'm not so sure I comprehend it myself."

Asa chuckled. "Sometimes a man just needs to act like a boy, m'lord. Nothin' wrong with it. Wife might not understand, but then, you ain't got one of them."

"No."

"Only way a man can get by actin' like a boy is when he plays with his son. But you ain't got that either, not one you can claim at least."

Richard laughed. "I don't have one of any sort! I do believe I'll have to remedy that soon, however. Delafield Hall needs an heir."

"True. We go on and on, don't we? Always wanted my son to end up gatekeeper," he said slyly.

"I didn't know you had a son!"

Asa winked. "Man who thinks he's his papa don't know it either."

"You rogue! Now you'll have me guessing."

"Maybe I'll tell you someday, m'lord." He studied Richard's appearance. "What you need is a swim in the stream."

"That is exactly what I had in mind," he agreed.

The old man smiled sheepishly. "Care if I walk with you?"

"I'd be glad of the company."

They set off along the path through the woods. Although Percy was missing from it, the trek revived many of Richard's memories. They had spent many hours splashing in the deep hole where the brook curved. Sometimes Asa had even dived into the cold water. Those days were certainly gone now. But his elderly friend was right. Sometimes a man did need to be a boy, he thought as they arrived at the streamside.

"Sure you won't join me, Asa?" he asked, stripping down to his undergarment.

"Go 'long with you!" The gatekeeper plopped down on the bank. "But I wish I could."

Richard plunged into the refreshing water and dived down to the bottom. Strange, it didn't seem as deep as it had been when he was a lad, but it was enough to serve the purpose. He wondered, surfacing, if Percy might like to join him sometime.

"It feels good!" he called to Asa, who waved in return. Suddenly he didn't care if he was late to luncheon. Lady Delafield might scold, but it would be worth it. And Cook would be willing to serve him a bite.

He swam awhile longer, before he remembered that he had other things to do today. That afternoon he had planned to call again at Grayson Park. Invigorated, he climbed up the bank.

"I have to be leaving, Asa."

The old man nodded. "Grown-up. Responsibilities."

"Yes. That's the way of it." He paused for a few minutes, sunning himself partially dry. "Let's visit the creek again, someday. I'll bring a picnic lunch."

"I'd like that, m'lord. We can talk about the old times."

Richard began pulling on his clothes. Maybe Percy would like to come too. No, he was too busy with his tournament and he'd have to bring Hasbrook. Damaris? She was too occupied with pretending to run an estate. He laughed inwardly. He'd have to ask Missy, who was of the age to be afraid of insects, but would probably accept because he was a wealthy, titled gentleman.

"M'lord?" Asa broke the silence. "You need a woman."

"Yes, I'll have to begin searching for a wife." He sighed. "Grown-up responsibilities, right?"

"You can do that, but you need a woman in the meantime," he advised. "Remember what I taught you?"

Richard grinned. "My insides will burst, and I'll come down with the gout."

"That's right, and don't you forget it!"

"I won't." He slung his coat over his shoulder. "Coming with me?"

"Naw. Think I'll stay here a bit longer. Rememberin'."

He left the sunny little stream bank and walked quickly through the woods and across the meadow to Delafield Hall. Skirting the castle to avoid being seen in his disarray, he approached from the rear. He opened the kitchen door.

"M'lord!" Cook startled, fluttering her hands excitably before she executed a plump bow. Two of her kitchen girls ran into each other. The scullery maid resoundingly dropped an iron pot.

"I'm sorry," Richard said apologetically, "I didn't intend to frighten you. I missed luncheon. I thought you might fix me a bite."

"Oh, Lord Delafield!" The aged retainer looked him up and down. "You aren't late. They've waited for you."

"Waited!"

"Well, sir, you *are* the earl."

"My God, I'd forgotten! Look at me. I'll have to change!" Frantically, he dashed from the kitchen to the backstairs, leaving Cook and her minions gazing in wonderment.

With only a brief tap on the door, Lady Grayson burst into Damaris's room. "My dear! You should see your papa! Gibson has carried him downstairs, and he is seated in the drawing room. Oh, what a wonderful day!"

"Yes, it is." Happily, Damaris began drawing on her riding boots. "I shall be along, as soon as I am dressed, to congratulate him."

Her mother clapped her hands. "I am so glad that Dr. Corey has allowed him to leave his room, and when he gets his new wheeled chair, he will be able to take himself around on every level surface!"

"It is truly marvelous."

"Indeed, but we do have one problem." Lady Grayson glanced uneasily at her daughter. "He will wonder why Melissa has not come down to witness his accomplishment. I thought I might stop by her chamber to tell her and maybe persuade . . ."

"No!" Damaris cried. "Mama, we have gone this far. We cannot soften now!"

"But her absence will worry your father!"

She sighed. "Then tell him the truth. Now that he is up and about, we can no longer conceal our little dilemmas from him. His spirits should have risen sufficiently to accept the news."

"If you are certain," her mother murmured doubtfully. "Very well, I shall tell him the whole of it." She moved toward the door. "Do hurry, dear. Your father is most anxious to see you."

"I shall only be a few more minutes."

Damaris quickly completed her toilette and descended the stairs. She would have a pleasant chat with Sir Osbert and then ride out to inspect the fields. After the rainy day, she was impatient to see how the crops were doing. The new deep plowing should allow for much more moisture to be absorbed. She hoped the roots weren't waterlogged.

"A fine day, Miss Damaris!" the butler greeted her.

"It certainly is." She laid her hat, gloves, and crop on the hall table. "Will you have my horse brought around? I'll visit awhile with Papa, then I'll be going out."

"Yes, miss." He threw open the drawing room door.

"Papa!" she called out, hastening in, "this is a happy sight!" She stopped dead in her tracks as the Earl of Delafield rose, bowing. "I'm sorry," she mumbled, a catch in her voice. "I did not realize that you had a guest."

"Come right in, Damaris," Sir Osbert greeted, eyes twinkling. "Richard and I have nothing private. In fact, we've been expecting you!"

"Very well, but only for a moment." Nodding to the earl, she advanced uncertainly into the room. "As you can see, I am going out."

"That will wait," Lady Grayson directed. "Come have a cup of tea."

"No, thank you, Mama." She sank down uneasily on the edge of a chair. "And my business will not wait. I have a great deal to accomplish this afternoon."

"Checking the crops?" Sir Osbert guessed.

"Yes, Papa."

"I wish I could go with you," he said wistfully, then smiled. "But I am determined to be satisfied with my progress for now. Perhaps Richard would like to accompany you."

Damaris cast a fleeting glance at the earl. "I am sure that he has far too much to do."

"No, I don't," he swiftly denied. "I am most anxious to see the effects of the deep plowing that Sir Osbert has been telling me about."

"Go along with you then!" Sir Osbert commanded before Damaris could reply. "I shall be keenly awaiting a report."

"All right." Damaris rose and rudely whisked out of the room, leaving Richard to make his farewells and catch up to her as best he could.

As luck would have it, she was forced to wait for her horse. She stood on the front steps, restlessly tapping her crop on her knee. What a tangle! Here she was, thrust into his company once more. How could she battle her conflicting emotions when she was so frequently in his presence?

"Somehow, I have reached the conclusion that you did not wish me to come along," Richard said into her ear.

She struggled to regain her manners. "It is not that.

It is just that I am so preoccupied that I fear I shall be poor company."

"I understand. I know you have a great deal on your mind. I shall try not to distract you."

She eyed him suspiciously. Was he being cynical? Or did he truly mean what he said? Her heart skipped a beat. Good heavens, he was handsome! How could she concentrate on the crops? Indeed he was a distraction!

Richard assisted her mounting and swung onto his own waiting animal. "Pay me no heed. Pretend that I am not here."

Damaris couldn't help laughing. "That is impossible, sir."

Her stomach fluttered. Being alone with him, with the exception of her groom who followed at a discreet distance, violently brought back that tender, compelling feeling of being held in his arms. Goodness, how would she get through the afternoon?

"Tell me about the deep plowing," he urged as they rode toward the east field.

"I . . . I read about it," she said hesitantly. "We'd had such a bad crop that I decided to try it."

"With your father's approval."

"No! Papa was still too ill to be disturbed with something like that. It . . . it was my decision."

"I see." His voice was noncommittal. "Have you made any other 'decisions'?"

There, at last, was the cynicism she had anticipated. Damaris frowned. "I am conducting a small experiment with cover crops. Of course, it is too soon to ascertain the results. Why, Richard, do I feel as though I must answer to you?"

"I don't know. Do you?"

"Yes I do, and I don't like it one bit! This is not *your* land. If I fail, it shall be on *my* head! I am weary of your mockery and your condescension!" Kicking her horse to a canter, she ended the conversation.

When she reached the east field, she drew back to a walk and skirted the perimeter, ignoring Richard and studying the oat crop. She sighed with relief. No one could fault these plants. They were healthy and sturdy, with not a spindly one among them. The heavy rain had only done them good. They looked as though they'd grown overnight.

Damaris dismounted. Removing her glove, she plunged her hand into the earth. It was still very wet, but thank God it had not compacted. From the corner of her eye, she saw Richard do the same. Did he really know what he was looking for?

"The drainage is superb," he mused. "The deep plowing allows the soil to absorb a great deal of moisture without becoming oversaturated."

"And it permits the roots to expand easily," she added.

"I must initiate this practice at Delafield."

Damaris smiled proudly. "Perhaps you'd best delay your opinion until we witness a harvest."

He shook his head. "Little could prevent these plants from producing a fine crop. Well done, Damaris."

She caught her breath. "You are surprised?"

"Yes, I am." Richard grinned ruefully. "I regret my 'mockery' and 'condescension.' Will you forgive me?"

"If it doesn't happen again," she teased.

They led their horses to the shade of a nearby copse. Demaris's heart soared. He had complimented her, applauded her efforts! He had even apologized. Had he truly changed his opinion of her ability?

"I must apologize too," she said affably. "I have been rude and hostile."

"I deserved it."

"I shall not agree to your taking all the blame!"

His gaze met hers. Mesmerized, she swayed toward him. He slipped his arms around her.

"Richard . . ."

"Damaris . . ." He lowered his lips to hers.

She melted against him, lifting her hands to his neck, touching his soft, thick hair. Knees dissolving to water, she kissed him back. Before any semblance of coherence left her thoughts, she realized that her perennial dream had come true.

Richard broke the kiss suddenly. He stepped back, removing her hands from his neck. There was a mixture of alarm and guilt shadowing his blue eyes.

"I'm sorry," he breathed. "That should never have happened."

She stared at him in confusion.

"I shouldn't have done that."

"No, Richard, I . . ."

"Do not take the blame upon yourself." He quickly changed the subject. "Damaris? Would you like to go on a picnic? By the stream where we used to play?"

"Yes! I'd love it! But as to . . ."

"I'll ask Percy, and old Asa, of course. Do you think Missy would like to come? Also, we'll have to include Hasbrook, Percy's friend, who has already arrived for the tournament."

It was on the tip of her tongue to tell him that she'd rather picnic alone with him, but he turned and began leading his horse from the trees.

"Let us inspect the rest of your fields now!" he called over his shoulder.

Damaris trailed behind. What had happened? What had gone wrong? He had been kissing her most sweetly and then he had stopped so abruptly. Could it be that he was still in love with the lady who'd caused his exile? Did they have some sort of new understanding? Or was there someone else? Or some*thing* else! He had admired the results of her plowing experiment. She had taught him a lesson in the underestimation of female capability. Hadn't her mother always preached that men did not crave women who challenged them? She had certainly done that! Had it been worth it?

Merciful heavens, there could be so many reasons! Later, when she wasn't so dazed, she would visualize them all and try to think of something to do. The dream would not go away. She seemed destined to love him, no matter how he acted. Biting back tears, she followed him from the copse.

Chapter 9

Missy had not come down for the previous evening's meal; nor, Damaris was certain, had any nourishment been carried to her room. The single-minded girl had gone without food for one solid day. By now, she was probably growing very hungry, and her mother would be beside herself with apprehension. Damaris felt a small measure of guilt as she plunged hungrily into her breakfast, but she remained determined. Her sister could not hold out much longer.

Thoughtfully, she nibbled a slice of crisp bacon. Setting her mind to the problem of Missy was far preferable to thinking about Richard. Last night, for what seemed like hours, she had explored possible reasons for his unsettling reaction to the kiss, but she had reached no conclusions. Finally, emotionally exhausted, she'd fallen into a deep slumber. The sleep, at least, had been good for her. She was rested and refreshed and ready to meet the challenges of the day.

The breakfast room door opened, and Lady Grayson bustled in.

"Mama!" Damaris half rose, fearing trouble. Her mother never came down to breakfast unless there was some great crisis.

"Missy isn't here," the lady moaned with anguish. "Oh, how I'd prayed that my darling had come down this morning!"

"I'm sorry, Mama." Damaris sat down and uncomfortably picked up her fork.

"No, you aren't." Missy stood framed in the doorway. "You are not sorry at all, Damaris."

"My lamb!" Lady Grayson cried, rushing to throw her arms around her younger daughter. "My sweet, dear child! Oh, how thin you've become!"

Damaris muffled a snort, remembering the box of chocolates she had disposed of.

Her sister weakly reclined her head on her mother's shoulder. "I'm starving," she whined.

"Of course you are!" Lady Grayson snapped her fingers at a hovering footman. "Fetch ham, bacon, and eggs. Bring everything you can. And hurry up with it!" She helped the languishing girl to a seat at the table. "My poor baby, can you wait just a little while longer?"

Missy covetously peered at her sister's meal.

Smiling wryly, Damaris heaped a slice of toast with strawberry jam and offered it to her.

The famished young lady almost snatched it from her hand. "I shall not thank you, for you owe it to me," she mumbled, eating ravenously. "You are the cause of my near starvation, Damaris. I know that Mama would not do such a thing."

"Oh, dear." Lady Grayson wrung her hands together. "Please, girls, we must let bygones be bygones. Damaris did what she thought was best."

"She is bossy and cruel." Missy sniffed. "What she did was unnecessary. I was ready to leave my room anyway. I was bored with it all."

Damaris raised an eyebrow, but held back the skeptical comment that had immediately come to mind. Her sister had left her seclusion and apparently meant to return to family life. There was no benefit in antagonizing her. She wished, however, that the girl had abandoned her animosity toward her. It was terribly uncomfortable.

The footman returned with a heaping plate for Missy and the usual tea and toast for Lady Grayson. As he quietly took his leave, the young lady began to eat with gusto. Damaris exchanged a glance of satisfaction with her parent.

"Now that Melissa has recovered," her mother announced, "we must plan a visit to the Rogers house. Our gowns should be ready for a first fitting."

Missy shrugged. "I have little interest in Percy's tournament, Mama," she said between bites. "My appearance is of small concern."

"But darling, I have assured you that Percy sincerely does care for you. Isn't that true, Damaris?"

"Yes it is. He only asked me to be Queen so he would have you all to himself. With Richard back, Percy was afraid that he would get to spend no time with you if you were made Queen. That Richard would monopolize your attention as head of the tournament." Her heart made a strange, tiny thump. Richard would escort her. She wondered what he thought of that.

"I truly don't care," Missy said flippantly. "And please do not include me in this discussion. I cannot eat and talk at the same time."

"Very well." Lady Grayson sighed and turned her attention to her elder daughter. "You will be escorted by Richard. I do hope you make the most of that."

"What do you mean?" Damaris asked suspiciously.

"He is, after all, a most eligible bachelor." Her eyes twinkled. "I would not be averse to such a match!"

Damaris eyed her with curiosity. Her mother had brought up the earl's name, not she. She could take advantage of the lady's penchant for gossip without raising undue interest.

"Tell me, Mama, about the affair that caused Richard to leave the country."

"Do you know that I have *never* discovered the entire truth behind that misfortune!"

"Tell me what you do know," she prompted.

Lady Grayson wrinkled her forehead with thought. "The young lady's name was Annabelle Leigh. She was from an excellent family, though they were not particularly wealthy. Her father was a baron, I believe."

"Go on," Damaris urged.

"I'm trying!" She took a sip of tea. "Richard was very young and just a viscount at the time. He had a comfortable income, but one would not have considered him rich. His papa was still alive, you see."

Damaris resisted the impulse to beg her mother to hasten, as she paused in her story to munch a bite of toast.

"Richard was head over heels in love with Annabelle. Everyone thought she was in love with him too, and expected a match to be announced any day. But suddenly the Marquess of Kelford appeared on the scene. I do not know what precipitated the incident, but next we heard that he and Richard had fought a duel, in which the marquess was wounded. Sources say that Annabelle took the side of Kelford and berated Richard dreadfully. It broke his heart and he fled the country. A sad tale, is it not? But Richard was so very young. He has probably forgotten her completely by now."

Damaris almost feared to ask her next question. "What happened to Annabelle?"

"She married Kelford. I believe she is a widow now. He was a great deal older than she."

A hard, painful knot formed in the pit of her stomach. It was the memory of Annabelle that had disturbed Richard. He loved her still, and he knew she was a widow, probably ripe for remarriage. That was why he had withdrawn his kiss so abruptly. He had succumbed to the pleasure of the moment, and then had thought better of it.

"What is wrong, Damaris?" Lady Grayson asked anxiously. "You look so strangely pale!"

"Do I?"

"Is it because of Annabelle?" she pried, instantly alert. "If you care for Richard, I wouldn't give her a second thought. Even as a young lady, she was the coldest, most calculating flirt I have ever seen! No intelligent, mature gentleman would fall for her wiles."

"The Marquess of Kelford did."

"Fustian! He was a bawdy old fool in his dotage." Anxiously, she leaned forward. "I would like to see a match between you and Richard Delafield, and I know your father would."

"Mama, please!" Damaris shook her head.

Missy, her hunger sated, stared avidly at them both. In her excitement, she forgot her quarrel with her sister and reverted to staunch family loyalty. "If Damaris wants him, this Annabelle could never challenge her," she declared. "Damaris is worth ten of her!"

"That is true!" Lady Grayson cried happily.

"Furthermore," the girl continued, "Damaris must be younger, which is a distinct advantage. What does Annabelle look like, Mama?"

"As a debutante, she was very beautiful," she admitted. "She had blond hair, and her eyes were the loveliest shade of blue. Of course, she dressed in the first stare of fashion."

Missy studied her elder sister. "There are possibilities for improvement. Mama, Damaris must have new clothes."

"No!" Damaris protested. "We cannot afford it! Mother, remember our discussion of finances? Richard would not be impressed by further spending."

"How does he know what your wardrobe already contains?"

"No," she repeated flatly. "I will not be a party to it."

Missy's chin rose irritably. "She's right. Why does she need to attach another gentleman? She already has Percy."

"Percy loves *you!*" Damaris exclaimed. "Why will you not believe us?"

Her sister placed her napkin on the table and stood up. "I see no sign of his regard. I am going to visit Papa. He is the only man who will ever love me!" Rigidly, she walked from the room.

"Wait!" Lady Grayson leaped to her feet as the door snapped shut. "Oh, dear, I thought she was coming round."

"She will." Damaris smiled ruefully. "A few moments in Percy's company will cure her completely."

"You must ride at once to Delafield," her mother commanded. "Advise Percy to call today. He must come immediately. I can scarcely bear much more of this!" Fluttering her hands, she rushed after Melissa.

Damaris finished her tepid tea and poured herself a fresh, hot cup. She was disappointed that Missy had regressed to her former aggravation with her, but at least it had served the purpose of removing attention from her and Richard. She must take care that the mortifying subject did not arise again.

Annabelle Leigh. Annabelle Kelford. *Lady* Kelford. The widow was probably tremendously wealthy, extravagantly dressed, and full of practiced wiles. Damaris could be no competition to her, except that she was *here*. She was in Richard's company on practically a daily basis. She had the advantage in that. But there was that other difficulty, the one of their clashing attitudes.

She swallowed her tea and got up from the table. At least one thing had gone her way that morning. Missy had emerged from cover. It would be only a matter of time before her sister had returned to normal. Missy never could carry a grudge for long. Papa would be pleased, and Mama would be positively overjoyed. Damaris smiled. She was happy too, because she had the perfect excuse to ride to Delafield Hall. Her heart throbbing with anticipation, she hastened to dress for the outing.

"Percy!" Richard stepped from the library into the hall. "Might I have a word with you?"

His brother and Lord Hasbrook hesitated on the stairs. "I'm rather busy, Dickon. Uncle Vincent is expecting us for practice. We're to be in the paddock at ten o'clock."

"It won't take long, and it's rather important." Now that he had made up his mind to have a heart-to-heart talk with the younger man, Richard didn't want to put it off. It was best to have it over and done with. He couldn't bear his guilt a moment longer.

"All right," Percy acceded, detaching himself and returning downstairs. "But make it quick. I don't want to miss anything."

Richard stepped back to allow his brother to precede him into the room. He wasn't happy about having a time constraint placed on such a grave matter, but it made little difference. When Percy heard his confession, he'd probably plant him a facer and leave immediately. It didn't take long to flatten a man who refused to fight back. Percy would be on time for his lesson.

Grimly, Richard shut the door and advanced into the room. This wasn't easy. Admissions never were.

"I am not certain how to tell you this," he slowly began.

Percy flashed him a look of alarm. "You best not have canceled my tournament!"

"Of course not. I wouldn't do that! No, this is a much more serious issue." He sat down on the edge of the desk. He'd had his speech all planned. Now that he was ready to deliver it, the words had fled from his memory. Frowning, he idly swung his leg, staring at the gleaming toe of his boot and trying to formulate his revelation.

"What's the matter, Dickon?" Percy asked quietly.

It was terrible. What sort of man would attempt lovemaking with his own brother's intended wife? It was beyond all integrity! He was base. He was wicked. He was the most despicable beast on the earth! But her lips had been so soft, so rosy, so inviting, and he had ached to possess them.

"Dickon?"

He had wanted her. He *still* wanted her, despite their differences of opinion and despite his brother's prior claim. How could he ask Percy for forgiveness when he wasn't penitent?

Percy sighed noisily. "I wish you'd get on with it. I have things to do."

"This isn't easy," Richard declared. "I can't think of a good way to tell you."

"Why don't you just spill it, Dickon, and save us both the torment?"

"Are you sure?"

"Yes I'm sure!" Percy exclaimed. "Come on, brother. Spare us the agony!"

"All right." He drew a deep breath and said with a rush, "I kissed Damaris."

"Good!" his brother cried. "I was wondering when you would finally appreciate her worth!"

"You don't understand." Bleakly, Richard slipped off the desk and began to pace the floor. "It wasn't a brotherly kiss."

"I should hope not!"

Intent on his own confession, Richard did not heed Percy's reaction. "I *wanted* her, and not as a sister." He gritted his teeth. "I wanted to seduce her, Percy."

"Did you succeed?" he asked mildly.

"Certainly not!" Richard said with shock. "I may be the lowest form of being in the world, but I wouldn't stoop to those depths!"

Percy chuckled.

"You must believe me in that. I even managed to break off the kiss before it grew too warm." His strides increased, taking him rapidly back and forth across the library. "I'm sorry, Percy! I just couldn't help myself. I was too weak to resist. Can you ever forgive me?"

His brother got up from his chair and caught up with him, grasping his shoulders and bringing him to a halt. "Dickon, what the hell are you talking about?"

"Dammit, Percy, it was hard enough to tell you the first time! Must I do it again? I kissed Damaris!"

"And I am glad of it! Why in God's name do you think that you have to apologize to me? Damaris would be the perfect lady for you. I approve whole-heartedly!"

Richard stared at him numbly. "You do?"

"Yes!"

"But ..." He shook his head. "Do you care for her?"

"I love her!"

Richard groaned.

"Next to you, Dickon, she's the best friend I ever had."

His heart leaped to his throat. "Friend?"

Percy began to laugh. "Now I see! Have you had the impression that Damaris and I were something more than friends?"

"Yes." Excitement poured through his veins. Percy and Damaris were friends, nothing more. She was available! He could . . . He could court her.

"Brother?" Percy clapped him on the shoulder. "I can't think of anyone else whom I would prefer to have for a sister-in-law."

Richard grinned. "I can't believe that I was such a damned chucklehead. Damaris probably imagines me to be the greatest fool she's ever known."

"You can make up for it." His brother winked. "And you weren't far off the mark. I *am* entranced by a Grayson lady, but my interest lies with Melissa. Unfortunately, she isn't very happy with me just now," he added dismally.

"Why not?"

"She is disturbed that I chose Damaris to be the Queen of the tournament."

"Why did you?"

"It's a long story." Percy glanced at the clock on the mantel. "I have to go, Dickon. We can speak of our ladies later. Why don't you come and watch Gerry and me?"

"Maybe I will," he considered. It was good to be at ease again with his brother. He didn't want to jeopardize it by laughing at his knightly efforts or being sarcastic.

"I'll expect you." Percy hesitated at the door and

chuckled. "You might just see how much fun this will be!"

"All right! I'll be there!" He laughed. "Good luck, younger brother, and *do be careful.*"

"I will." Percy hurried on his way.

Richard dropped into his desk chair and heaved a great sigh of relief. It was over. He was in charity with his brother, and he could give full rein to exploring his feelings for Damaris. He felt like shouting with exhilaration. Who would have ever expected the dreaded interview to end so happily?

Having followed the shortcut through the woods, Damaris rode across the lawn toward Delafield Hall. She had taken great care with her appearance that morning. Instead of wearing her normal workaday riding attire, she had put on her good habit of deep, lustrous amber. She'd even worn its matching plumed hat. She looked fine, but she hoped that she wouldn't seem unusually overdressed. That might make Richard suspicious.

As she drew near the castle, she saw him emerge through the front door. He caught sight of her and waved. Nerves tingling with hope, she moved her horse into a trot.

"I was just thinking of you," he greeted as she came to a halt.

"Were you?" She hoped for further enlightenment, but he said no more.

A groom took the horse's reins, and Richard slipped his arms around her waist to help her down. She laid her hands on his broad shoulders. Dear Lord, she thought as her heartbeat quickened. She could scarcely touch him without becoming breathless. As he set her on the ground, she smiled up at him.

"I hope that your thoughts about me were pleasant ones," she told him.

"They were." His hands lingered at her waist. "I was on my way to watch Percy and his friend practicing. Would you care to accompany me?"

"Yes, I'd like that." She took his arm and strolled toward the stable.

"You look lovely today, Damaris."

She gazed at him from the corner of her eye and saw that she had his rapt attention. Her spirits soared. "Thank you," she murmured.

"I'm not sure what to expect from this practice session," he went on. "It seems as though many of these ventures end in disaster. I hope that all goes well, and that I ... that I can control my *arrogance*." He grinned self-consciously.

Damaris laughed. "Improving your image, my lord?"

"I'm trying," he said sincerely. "Lately, it seems as though I am constantly being proved wrong in many of my convictions."

She shot him a quick glance.

"If you don't know it by now, I do sincerely respect what you are doing at Grayson Park."

"Thank you," she breathed.

"Yesterday," he began, and paused. "We'll talk of that later," he hurriedly amended as they neared the paddock where two knights in armor approached their steeds. "Let's give Percy and Hasbrook our attention now."

"All right."

They reached the stoutly fenced training enclosure, where Uncle Vincent stood shouting orders and gesturing. Several grooms held the fidgeting horses as Percy and Gerry Hasbrook clanged toward them. A highly charged atmosphere of excitement prevailed.

Damaris could see it in the choppy motions of Richard's uncle, the rolling of the horses' eyes, and the determined set of the knights' shoulders. She crossed her fingers.

Percy awkwardly ascended the mounting block and flung his leg across his horse's back. The animal quivered slightly, but remained composed. They edged forward into a walk.

"Well done," Richard approved. "The horse is growing accustomed to it."

Viscount Hasbrook was next to try his luck. He settled himself into the saddle. His horse, much calmer than Percy's, merely looked around curiously at him. It refused to move.

"Come on, Gerry!" Percy called. "Watch this!"

He broke into a slow trot, circling the paddock. His horse, though restlessly tossing its head now and then, cooperated. As he passed Richard and Damaris, he flung them a smile of triumph and pushed the animal into a canter.

"I hope he does not think to show off," she said, tightly clutching Richard's arm.

He covered her hand with his and squeezed gently. "There is nothing we can do about it."

"Giddap, you bacon-brained sapskull!" Gerry Hasbrook cried, drumming his horse's sides with his heels. The gelding took several reluctant steps forward, then stopped once more. Turning its head, it sniffed the viscount's toe.

Damaris giggled.

"Don't do that, my dear," Richard begged, his body shaking with pent-up humor. "You're going to cause me to laugh, and then Percy will accuse me of mockery. Remember? I'm trying to reform."

"But it is funny!"

"I know, I know." He half turned. "Come, let us go to the house."

"Wait, Richard." She tugged his arm. "Look!"

The knees and haunches of Hasbrook's horse began to tremble. Very slowly, the gelding sank down. Finally with a grunt and a crash of steel, it rolled over.

"Goddamn!" the viscount yelled. "Somebody help me!"

Damaris burst into laughter.

"*Come on.*" Richard grasped her hand and dragged her out of sight behind the stable.

"Oh, how can you keep from laughing?"

"I can't." He released his own hilarity and joined her, leaning against the wall and laughing until their mirth was satiated.

"My goodness!" Regaining her constraint, Damaris removed her handkerchief to wipe her eyes and blow her nose. "They are going to make cakes of themselves."

"Indeed." His merriment had died and he was looking deeply into her eyes.

"Richard?" she breathed, her body alive with fluttering anticipation.

"Yesterday . . ." he ventured, then broke off. "Let us finish what we began yesterday."

Lifting her chin, he lowered his lips to hers.

Chapter 10

Damaris laughed out loud.

She was living in a dream. Nothing around her appeared normal. The leaves on the trees and the path before her were blurred. Even the chirping of the birds and the tickling of the little breeze on her face seemed lost in a fog. She was in love, thoroughly, wonderfully, dazzlingly, truly in love. She loosened her reins and let her horse pick its way. Thank goodness it would take her home, for she certainly hadn't the faculty to do it herself.

Richard had kissed her. He hadn't done it the way he had the day before. It hadn't ended prematurely. He had kissed her slowly and deeply, locking her in his embrace and thoroughly exploring her mouth. Dear God, she had never been kissed that way before! The few furtive little pecks she had received in the past were as nothing compared to this. Just thinking about it made her body throb with unfamiliar longing.

It must have been improper. Anything that felt so marvelous just had to be indelicate. He had been a gentleman about it. He hadn't fondled her in any of the wrong places, and with the exception of her hat, he hadn't tried to remove her clothes, but shameful though it might be even to admit it, she had wished he would. Neither had she been alone in this strange new desire. Richard had wanted her too. He had held her so closely that she had no doubt of that.

She sighed. When her mother had advised her on the facts of life, she had referred to marital duty, not pleasure, and Damaris had believed her. She didn't anymore. Inherently she knew that anything Richard would do to her would be absolutely delightful.

Mentally she shook herself. She was leaping too far into the future. He hadn't asked her to marry him. Not yet.

The horse left the woods. Instinctively she drew in the reins and guided it around the planted field. She was oblivious to the fine, healthy crops, which had been so all-important just a short time ago. All she could think about was Richard, and the kiss.

When he lifted his lips from hers, he had continued to hold her tenderly in his embrace. She'd laid her head against his chest, listening to his heartbeat and feeling his feathery kisses on her hair. They didn't speak. Somehow, words weren't necessary. Finally, he had replaced her hat, and they'd walked to the castle.

Damaris wondered how she'd ever gotten through the polite visit with his mama. Her mind had been in a daze, but she'd managed to sip her tea and keep up some semblance of conversation. It had been difficult to refrain from merely sitting silently and gazing at Richard, but she had succeeded. Lady Delafield had cast several curious glances at both of them, but if she thought that something was strange about their behavior, she hadn't raised an inquiry. When Percy, Uncle Vincent, and Lord Hasbrook came in, Percy had smirked rather knowingly, but that was all. Her report of Missy's recovery had channeled his thoughts in other directions.

Percy and Lord Hasbrook would be calling that afternoon. Would Richard come with them? Damaris panicked. He hadn't said whether he would or not! What could that mean?

She mustn't jump to conclusions. He might have business to attend. She, of all people, should understand that, but just in case, she must be ready. She eased her horse into a canter. Goodness! It was almost lunchtime! She must freshen up and change her clothes and make herself as attractive as she could. She must hurry.

Pulling up in front of the house, she slipped down before the groom advanced to assist her. She entered the hall and began skipping up the steps.

"Damaris!" Lady Grayson, descending, met her on the steps. "You look so flushed! What have you been doing?"

Kissing Richard, she wanted to cry out, but she held her tongue. "Nothing, Mama. I rode to Delafield Hall, as you requested."

"Your face is so glowing." She narrowed her eyes. "Do not tell me that you removed your hat and have been burned by the sun!"

"No, ma'am, but it is hot, and I hurried. It is probably due to exertion."

"Hm. Very well. I assume you spoke with Percy?" her mother inquired.

"Yes! I watched him practice for the tournament. He and his friend, Lord Hasbrook, will be calling this afternoon." Damaris edged past her.

"Excellent! Damaris!" Lady Grayson caught her arm. "Don't rush off so quickly. I have not finished speaking with you."

She stopped.

"Was anyone else present at Delafield Hall?"

"Oh, yes, the entire family was at home," she said airily.

"I am speaking of Richard. Will he be calling today too?"

"I don't know, Mama," she candidly answered.

"Damaris." Lady Grayson clicked her tongue and shook her head. "Did you not attempt to entice him? Flirt with him a little?"

She could feel the warmth of the color rising to her cheeks. "No, Mama, I did not flirt."

"For shame!" she scolded. "How do you expect to attract him?"

"Perhaps . . ." Damaris stammered, choking back a giggle. "Perhaps he will respond to other things."

"Such as?" her mother demanded.

"I don't know," she said quickly. "Please, Mama, I must freshen up for lunch. I am going to be late."

"Go along then." Lady Grayson waved her away. "But if Richard comes to call, you must not let the time slip by without showing him that you are interested in him."

"I won't." This time the giggle burst forth. Blushing, Damaris fled up the steps.

"Silly girl," her mother muttered, continuing down the stairs. "First she is mannish and stubborn. Then she becomes a regular goose! How on earth will she ever trap a gentleman?"

Damaris groaned inwardly at the artificial atmosphere that Lady Grayson had insisted on contriving in the salon. Knowing in advance that callers were to be expected, her mother had concocted the sort of domestic scene that she imagined young gentlemen might admire. It did not occur to her that Richard and Percy were far too familiar with the Grayson household to be unaware of the laughable falsity in her setting. Nor did she take into consideration that idleness in the middle of the day was out-of-character for her elder daughter. Furthermore, she had not kept in mind that the cozy salon, used mainly in the winter, received the brunt of the afternoon sun. A quiet, genteel gathering was the image she wished to present. Too many times did visitors catch the Graysons at rackshamble sixes and sevens. Today they would be prepared.

With frustration, Damaris plunged her needle into a horrible piece of fancywork and listened to her father's voice drone on, as he read aloud from what must be the most boring novel ever written. This was ridiculous. Her father never read aloud. In fact, the only items he read at all were newspapers and agricultural treatises. And her sewing? It was awful! She could mend well enough, but she hadn't the talent or patience for the exquisite stitchery her mama and Missy could perform. Seeing her thus, Richard would laugh until he burst. She affixed her needle in the fabric and set it aside, folding it so that her handiwork wasn't revealed.

"Damaris, pick up your sewing," Lady Grayson ordered.

She grimaced. "Mama, you know I am deficient in this sort of thing."

"Nonsense. Young ladies are expected to while away their time with needlecraft."

"But I do so poorly! They will laugh."

As if to prove her correct, Missy snickered. "She is right, Mama. You should see the tree she is attempting to embroider. It looks like a medieval mace!"

"That will be enough, Melissa," Lady Grayson gently chided. "*Pick it up, Damaris.*"

"Yes, ma'am." When the callers arrived, perhaps she could quickly hide the thing.

"I would rather go to my room," Missy announced. "I am not altogether sure that I want to see Percy."

"You shall not! After all, you must see him sooner or later," her mother proclaimed.

"I'd rather it be later."

Further dissension was ended by the arrival of the visitors. Damaris's pulse quickened when she saw Richard. He looked so handsome in his pale leather breeches, shining black boots, and coat of deep blue superfine. But most of all, she noticed his lips. Unable to halt her involuntary flush, she wondered if he too was thinking of hers and of their kiss. Hurriedly, she set aside the needlework and rose for the greetings and introductions.

Lady Grayson expertly guided the earl away from Sir Osbert and seated him beside Damaris. She paired young Hasbrook with her husband, leaving the way clear for Percy to make his peace with Missy. Satisfied, she sat down and returned to her needlework.

"I thought that you might be outside this afternoon," Richard observed.

"No," Damaris replied uncomfortably, suddenly at a loss for how to continue the conversation. The mood seemed so formal and stiff. She couldn't chat and be at ease in an awkward situation such as this.

"You probably wish to spend time with your father, now that he may come downstairs."

"Yes. That's it," she agreed.

"No estate projects to oversee?"

She glanced at him swiftly. Was he going to start *that* again? She was relieved to see that his expression was merely one of friendly interest.

"I have some workmen replacing planks on the bridge," she told him. "Did you come that way?"

He shook his head. "We rode through the woods." Idly, he picked up the piece of handiwork.

Damaris cringed inside. Why hadn't she stuffed that ghastly thing under the cushions? Mortified, she saw a grin tug at the corners of his mouth.

"Yours?" Richard asked.

She nodded miserably.

"It's ... It's ..."

"It's hideous!" She snatched it away and threw it on the floor, hearing her mother's sharp intake of breath.

"I suppose that one cannot be proficient at everything," Richard observed.

Damaris glimpsed the humor twinkling in his eyes and laughed. "Well, I certainly am not adept at stitchery!"

He joined in her merriment. "Your own accomplishment is much more valuable."

"Truly?" Smile fading, she almost held her breath.

"To me, it is."

Happiness flooded over her. Once again, he had acknowledged that he had changed his mind about her. The future could bring nothing but good. She could almost thank her mother for making her exhibit that terrible needlework. It had helped prove that he admired her for what she was.

Damaris could not, however, show gratitude to Lady Grayson for the setting she had devised. The room was stuffy and airless. Tiny droplets of perspiration were already beading on her forehead. She watched Richard surreptitiously slip a finger into the neck of his cravat, loosening it.

"Mama will soon be serving refreshments," she said impulsively, "but would you rather go outside instead?"

"I'd love it."

"She won't like it. She wishes me to sit inside like a proper lady," she admitted boldly.

"I shall take full responsibility for the excuses. I'm stifling." He stood up and extended his hand to her, drawing her to her feet. "Lady Grayson, Sir Osbert? Won't you excuse us? I've asked Damaris to show me the bridge that is being repaired."

Lady Grayson looked confused. "But I've lemonade and . . ."

Sir Osbert overruled her. "A fine idea! The workmen should be observed now and then."

Damaris took Richard's arm as he whisked her from the room before more protests could be raised.

"A grand escape," she said with relief, descending the front steps. "Poor Mama. She does favor that salon. It is a pleasant room in the winter, but in the summer, the heat is outside of enough."

They strolled down the drive, her hand tucked securely in the crook of Richard's arm. It was a beautiful day. The sky was so very blue, the grass so green, the air so sweet. Everything seemed to be at its best. She had been with Richard in the morning, and now in the afternoon. Could anything be better?

"Isn't it strange?" he mused. "As a boy, I would never have imagined escorting you on an afternoon walk."

"Oh?" she asked with mock annoyance. "Whom would you have chosen?"

"No one." He grinned. "I hated girls."

She tilted her head. "Do you despise them still?"

"I think not." He lifted her hand to his lips, lightly kissed her fingertips, and returned it to his arm. "Little boys are notoriously simpleminded."

"I don't think so! I envied you so much. Especially your treehouse! La, how I wanted a treehouse of my own, but Mama said no."

"Damaris, what would you think if—" He broke off, shaking his head. "Never mind, you'd think it was foolishness." He doubled his stride.

"What, Richard?" she pried, half skipping.

"Nothing important. It was just something about that treehouse."

They reached the bridge. The workmen took the opportunity of their visit to withdraw to the shade of a tree and take a short rest. Damaris sat down on the edge of the bank and allowed Richard to make an inspection of the planking on top and the underpinning beneath. The heat was making her so lethargic. It was nice to have someone to help oversee.

Richard ducked out from under the bridge, brushing sawdust from his shoulders. "Don't you want to see?"

"No. I trust you."

"You do?" He teasingly wrinkled his brow in wonder. "I can scarcely believe it."

"I shouldn't have accused you of being incapable of managing an estate," she confessed. "I wish you would forget it."

"You were right, in part." He extended his hand and lifted her to her feet. "I do have a lot to learn."

"We have some books of the new agricultural methods. Would you like to borrow them?"

"Yes. Thank you." They started back toward the house. "Since your father is so greatly improved, I doubt that you will need my help on the account books. Not that you needed it anyway."

"No. Papa will probably take over now." She smiled, remembering the scene in the library. "I had a talk with Mama about her spending."

"Did you have success?"

She shrugged. "Only until another bauble catches

her eye. I don't know how Papa manages things so well."

"Perhaps she doesn't goad him as much as she does you."

"That could be true."

It was strange what a difference a short time made. She had been so mortified when he had examined the Grayson Park ledgers. Now their new intimacy had changed everything. She could discuss matters very comfortably with him. Damaris was sorry when they arrived at the house and saw that her mother and Missy were bidding farewell to a damp Percy and Lord Hasbrook. Richard joined the young men.

"I'll see you soon," he promised her, mounting his horse.

"I shall send over a servant with the box of books."

"Thank you." With an affable nod, he rode away.

Damaris climbed the steps.

"Did you have a pleasant chat, my dear?" Lady Grayson queried her.

"Yes, we did."

"Excellent!"

"I know I had a marvelous time," Missy breathed longingly.

"Did you make your peace with Percy?" Damaris asked.

"Percy?" She sighed. "Who is Percy? I am far more interested in Lord Hasbrook. Isn't he magnificent?"

"You cannot . . ." Damaris began, but Missy had already drifted into the house. She eyed her mother questioningly.

"I fear your sister has developed a *tendre* for the viscount," Lady Grayson explained. "Ah, well. At least it will bring her from the doldrums. And he *is* a very eligible young man."

"Oh, no," she moaned.

"And after all," her mother chirped, fluttering her hands, "he is a viscount. Percy has no title at all!" Turning, she dashed after her younger daughter.

There were two strange coaches pulled up in front of Delafield Hall when the trio of gentlemen arrived from Grayson Park. Trunks were being unloaded, indicating that the occupants meant to stay. Richard frowned, knowing that his quiet life was soon to be undone and that he would have to play the host. Percy's friend, Gerry Hasbrook, hadn't disrupted his routine, for the two younger men stayed much on their own. This would probably be different.

"Oh, I know who that is," Percy volunteered. "It's Cousin Helen, come early for the tournament. She doesn't usually travel with two carriages though. Perhaps she felt she needed more baggage. Do you remember her, Dickon?"

"Vaguely." He dismounted and tossed his reins to a waiting servant. "Will she be annoying?"

"No. Cousin Helen's sweet as sugar. Wouldn't harm a flea. That's her problem. She allows everyone to walk all over her. Do you recall that obnoxious husband of hers?"

"Not really."

"Well, thank goodness he's dead. If he were here, he'd have had the whole house up at arms." He grinned crookedly at Richard as they entered the castle. "You needn't worry about your tranquillity being overset, Dickon. You won't even know that Cousin Helen is in the house!"

"I'm glad of that. I have a lot to accomplish before the tournament."

The butler and footmen took their hats, gloves, and riding crops. "The ladies are in the drawing room, sir, waiting for refreshments to be served."

"Thank you. We'll join them." Richard, leading the way, was a full stride ahead of Percy and Gerry Hasbrook when he entered the room. He stopped dead in his tracks, his ready smile fading to a look of shock.

"Richard!" Annabelle cried, leaping up off the sofa. "How wonderful it is to see you!"

He barely had time to witness the pained expression on his mother's face before his former love scurried across the room to greet him. She sank into a deep curtsy.

"Oh, Richard, how long it has been!"

She extended both hands to him, causing him, for politeness' sake, to reach out to her. Her fingers laced through his, squeezing gently as she rose. He covertly tried to disengage her grip, but she wouldn't allow it. She lifted her hands toward his mouth, compelling him to kiss them, and making it look as if he had instigated it himself. He complied, performing the gesture without touching her skin.

"How do you do, Lady Kelford?"

"So formal, Richard?" She released a practiced peal of tinkling laughter. "One would think that we were scarcely more than strangers!"

Lady Delafield glanced at them, frowned slightly, and turned her attention to her other guest.

"As you say, it has been a long time." Richard tried to extricate his hands, but the wench held them captive. He couldn't jerk free without making a scene. In desperation, he slipped his thumbs into her palms and dug her with his nails.

Annabelle blinked in surprise and released him.

"Allow me to present my brother, Percy, and Lord Hasbrook."

She greeted them properly, but her eyes never left him. She linked her arm through his. "Come, Richard, and greet dear Helen. Then won't you pour me a glass of wine? My throat is parched from that dusty journey!"

Mind racing, he performed the niceties to his cousin. How could Annabelle have been invited here? Lady Delafield would never have done it. But she was here, and there was nothing he could do about it. Surely she didn't mean to stay for the tournament! How could he live under the same roof with her for that long? What about Damaris?

"The wine, Richard?" Annabelle softly reminded him.

He escorted her to a chair, but she refused to sit, accompanying him to the sideboard where the spirits were kept. Her grip was possessive, almost feral. Richard looked down at her hand, half expecting to see a keen set of claws piercing his flesh. That was almost the case. Her beautifully manicured nails were long, pointed, and feline.

"You act as though you are not happy to see me." She pouted.

"Under the circumstances, it would have been best if you had not come here," he said coolly.

Her clench increased in intensity. "Perhaps you are not entirely aware of those *circumstances*."

"Let me go, Annabelle. I can't pour the drinks."

"I'm sorry. It is just that I am so exhilarated from being in your company once more." She unlatched her grip, smoothing his sleeve. "Richard, we must talk," she purred.

"We have nothing to talk about." He poured her a glass of sherry. For himself, he chose brandy, a very hefty amount of it.

"You shouldn't have come here," he repeated. "It will make things awkward for us, and for everyone else too."

"You are not fully aware of the events surrounding our last meeting. If you were, you would not say that."

"It was a long time ago. I am not really interested." He looked past her, hoping to see Percy and Hasbrook coming to the rescue, but the two were still chatting with his damnable Cousin Helen.

"I don't accept that," Annabelle whispered in a low, honeyed voice.

"I'm sorry. It is the truth." He stepped away from her. "Please excuse me. I must speak to my man about some pressing estate problems."

Before she could delay him any longer, Richard hurried away, made feeble excuses to his mother and the rest of the company, and then practically ran from the room. Damn the woman! He glanced back at her. Smiling superciliously, Annabelle stood by the sideboard, like a cat lurking for its prey.

Chapter 11

The next morning, Richard was surprised to see his mother seated at the breakfast table. Lady Delafield was in the habit of taking her breakfast in her chamber and remaining closeted there until late morning. For her to exert herself to come downstairs at such an early hour was most unusual, but Richard could guess the reason behind her actions. She was worried about Annabelle's presence at Delafield Hall. And she was concerned over what might happen between the beautiful widow and him.

He greeted her and took his seat, waiting until he was served and the footman had departed before beginning the inevitable conversation. Wishing he could prolong the interval of silence, he took a sip of tea.

"Richard?" Lady Delafield took the initiative and valiantly plunged straight into the subject that both of them dreaded. "What are we going to do about That Woman?"

He shook his head. "I don't know," he said wearily. "Why is she here in the first place? I know you would never have invited her."

"It was Helen and her cursed kindness! It seems that she has befriended That Woman and felt sorry that she was being left out of all the excitement of the tournament. This event is the talk of the *ton*, you know. Everyone wants to attend."

"It wasn't proper for Cousin Helen to invite a guest to someone else's home," he growled irritably.

"That is true, but she did it." She sighed. "What could I do when they appeared on the doorstep? In all politeness, I couldn't drive them away."

"No." He scarcely tasted the bite of ham he put in his mouth. "I cannot believe that Cousin Helen could be so dim-witted."

"She'd probably forgotten all about the scandal."

"Perhaps. But others won't. This will bring it up again." He shuddered inwardly as he thought of his name being dragged once more through the gossip mill. "There will be all manner of speculation. I had hoped to make my return to England as unnoteworthy as possible."

"You fret overmuch about gossip. We shall ride through it, as we did before."

"As *you* did before. Remember?" he asked darkly. "I ran."

"Don't be so hard on yourself, Dickon," she begged. "You were very young. And you will not run now. Will you?" she weakly entreated, visibly holding her breath.

He grinned crookedly. "Along about three o'clock this morning, I did consider it! But no, Mama, I shall stand my ground against the scandalmongers. I've come home to stay."

Lady Delafield exhaled with a moan of relief. "Then let us explore the ways in which we shall face this dilemma," she suggested hopefully.

"All right."

"First, I fear I must ask you this." She painfully eyed him. "Do you still care for That Woman?"

Richard took a deep breath. "No. Any feeling I had for her is gone."

"I am so relieved," his mother said with heartfelt fervor. "I just can't like her, darling. I never could."

"She has lost her charm."

"She never had any!"

He laughed cynically. "Come now, Mama. When I knew her, she was the toast of London. She was sweet, amiable, and lovely."

"She was not," she disagreed, her voice dripping with distaste. "She was cold, calculating, and cruel."

"At the time, you liked the idea of having Annabelle as a daughter-in-law," he reminded her, defensive of his former feelings.

Lady Delafield bristled. "I most certainly did not! Neither did your father, for that matter. But what could we do? You thought yourself so deeply in love with her. We could not risk alienating our son. We could only sit back and hope that you would come to your senses."

"But I did not, did I?" Richard thoughtfully chewed a forkful of creamy eggs.

"You have now, and that is the only thing that is important. Remember that, Dickon, and do not fall once more for her trickery. Mark my words, she is intent on becoming the next Lady Delafield, and she will stop at nothing to achieve her goal."

He grinned. "Shall I lock my door at night?"

His mother clicked her tongue. "You may find that amusing, but there is a very distinct possibility that she might attempt an overt compromise. She will try anything! I watched her at work last night. Those slyly alluring ways! That indecently low-cut dress! Before the evening was ended, she practically had the three of you young men eating out of her hand!"

"Fustian, Mama! We were merely enjoying the scenery!" This time his laugh was genuine.

"You were ogling her like a trio of tomcats eyeing

a tender morsel of meat," she accused severely. "And That Woman deliberately continued her disgusting little practice of leaning forward to tempt you further. Even Percy, for heaven's sake ... even Percy, whose mind, half the time, is in the clouds, could not keep his eyes off her!"

"Mama," he chuckled, "if an interesting view is offered, a man is going to look."

"I know that!" she snapped. "I also know that the entire male sex is a passel of fools to be taken in so easily!"

"We weren't taken in," Richard protested, eyes twinkling. "The exhibition was free."

"You gave her the satisfaction of holding your interest. This constitutes encouragement."

"Very well, Mama," he conceded. "The next time, I won't look."

"That is best. Ignore her completely!"

He couldn't help teasing her. "Even if she strips stark naked and dances on the table?"

"Richard! For shame!"

"I'm sorry. I couldn't resist. I promise that I shall ignore and avoid Annabelle as much as possible."

"For the moment, that is all I can think of to do," she advised. "Perhaps if she receives none of your attention, she will become bored and leave. But you must take caution that she does not entrap you. Lock your door at night."

"If it will ease your mind," he consented.

"It will. Oh, dear." She slowly shook her head. "Think of poor Damaris."

He paused with his fork halfway to his mouth. "What about Damaris?"

"I could not help noticing that you seem to have developed an ... interest ... in her." Lady Delafield inquisitively watched his face for his reaction to her words. "Am I correct?"

"Perhaps," he said evenly. Had Percy told her? Or did it show that plainly?

"Now there . . ." she mulled. "Now there would be an ideal wife for you! I would be delighted, even though her mama can be a regular ninnyhammer."

"It's early times yet, Mama." He ate the forkful of ham.

"I wonder what Damaris will think of That Woman's presence here?" she murmured worriedly.

"Why should she think anything of it?"

"If she does not remember who Annabelle is, Lady Grayson will, and she will tell her. Perhaps you should speak with Damaris about it."

"That I will not do." He finished his meal and arranged his flatware on his plate. "I will not discuss past loves with Damaris. She'd think me ridiculous! In fact, she would probably decide that Annabelle was very much on my mind. No, if I am to ignore Annabelle in her presence, I shall ignore her in thoughts and conversation too. The least said, the best."

"I am not so sure . . ."

"I am! I will not discuss Annabelle with Damaris. Right now, it's just too personal."

"But, Dickon—" she began, and broke off as the door opened and Percy and Lord Hasbrook entered the breakfast room. "We shall speak of this again," she vowed and smilingly greeted her younger son and his friend.

Richard folded his napkin and laid it on the table. "If you will excuse me, I have an appointment with the steward."

"Of course, dear boy." Lady Delafield waved him

on his way. "But remember, we still have matters to discuss at your earliest convenience."

"Dickon?" Percy halted him. "When you finish with the steward, will you allow me a bit of your time? I'd like your opinion on the matter of the tilt-yard."

"All right," he agreed genially. "Shall I meet you there? In an hour and a half?"

His brother nodded. "I'll be there."

Richard left the room and strode down the hall in the direction of the estate office, pushing all thoughts of Annabelle and her intrigues from his mind. At present, he had more important affairs to consider. Today, he and his steward were going to make plans to purchase the new plows that Damaris had recommended.

"Will you come riding with me?" Her younger sister, already attired in her fetching blue habit, caught up with Damaris as she walked toward the stable.

"I'll be happy to, Missy, if you'll consent to make the west pasture our destination. We're renewing some fence there today, and I'd like to be on the scene."

The young lady's eyes clouded with disappointment. "No, I'd rather not go there. I wanted to ride to Delafield to see the tournament grounds, and I don't want to go alone, with only a groom to accompany me."

"I'm sorry. This afternoon, perhaps?" Damaris continued on her way.

"But I am ready now!" Missy skipped along beside her. "Besides, we have an appointment with the Rogers sisters later this afternoon. Didn't you remember?"

"No, I did not." She smiled pensively. There was a

time when she would have dreaded being pinned and tucked into her tournament attire. With the advent of Richard's regard, that had certainly changed. Now she looked forward to dressing prettily as she sat beside him on the dais.

"Wouldn't you rather go to Delafield than to that old pasture?" Missy wheedled.

Of course she would. If she went with Missy to Delafield, she might see Richard. But, disappointing though it might be to miss the merest moment in his presence, she must not allow her new emotions to interfere with her responsibility. Since her father had been permitted to go downstairs, he had improved by leaps and bounds. Yesterday, he had informed her that he was ready and willing to help keep the account books up to date. He still depended on her, however, for anything that needed to be done outside.

"Ride with me, Damaris," her sister insisted. "You can go to the pasture before the Rogers sisters come this afternoon."

She hesitated, wavering. "I really shouldn't, and I am not dressed for visiting."

"We aren't making a formal call. We'll ride only as far as the tournament grounds. You look fine for that! Please, Damaris. I don't want to go alone. My riding skills are poor. I might need assistance."

"That is one of the reasons for taking a groom." She glanced suspiciously at her sister. "Why are you so anxious for me to accompany you? You've been acting as if you despise me."

"If you must know, I am still piqued with you! But not so badly as before. I wish you to go with me because I imagine that there are numerous workmen at the site. I would feel less self-conscious if another female is present."

Damaris made up her mind. "All right, but we shall make it a short visit. Then I'll ride out to the pasture and be back in time for the dress fitting. On one condition."

"What is that?"

"You will explain to Mama why I am not at lunch."

"That's fair," Missy genially agreed. "I can handle Mama."

They continued to the stable, mounted their horses, and rode down the driveway, the groom following a lengthy distance behind.

"We'll go through the woods," Damaris announced, turning across the lawn.

"Oh, let's go by the road," Missy whined. "There might be spiders in the trees. Low branches might muss my hat and hair."

"There are no low branches. I ride through here all the time. It's quicker."

"I don't like the woods. They're full of bugs."

Damaris drew rein. "If you wish me to go, we'll take the shortest route possible."

"All right," her sister grumbled.

She struck a trot, left the parkland, and skirted a field, entering the woods.

"Slow down!" Missy cried. "This is outside of enough!"

"Baby!" Damaris called over her shoulder. "You used to ride your pony at top speed through here!"

"Times have changed! Stop, Damaris, or I shall tell Mama. And Papa too!"

At that moment, Missy's mare kicked up in a series of bucks. Adroitly, the girl braced herself in the saddle, snapping back on the reins and neatly bringing the horse out of it.

"I thought your riding skills were poor!" Damaris taunted appreciatively and pulled up.

Missy grinned. "It is best to cultivate frailty. Men adore a lady's physical failings. It makes them feel ever so much more superior."

"If it works for you, continue to do it, by all means!" She laughed. *She* would certainly never do so. To pretend to be frightened by insects, or branches, or a speedier gait would be positively abhorrent. But she hadn't her sister's sweet and dainty looks. If she were so petite and delicate, that sort of behavior might be entrancing to someone. She didn't think, however, that such fragility would appeal to a man like Richard. He liked *her*. He liked her just as she was.

In deference to Missy's fine appearance, Damaris proceeded more slowly through the trees. She was glad she had agreed to come on this outing, and not just for the sake of seeing Richard. It had given her a chance to ease the hard feelings with her sister.

When they left the coppice, Missy rode up abreast of her. "I do hope that the gentlemen will be present."

"Don't be disappointed if they are not," Damaris cautioned. "They may be practicing in the paddock."

"Oh, dear. I hope not!" She glanced wistfully at the castle. "If they are, might we ride past on our way home?"

"I truly haven't the time. If we went to the castle, we would be invited in for tea." She saw the regret written plainly on her sister's face. Once again, she faltered. Missy and Percy needed time together to mend their upheaval. She should assist them.

"Very well," she acquiesced, hoping that it would not be necessary.

Luckily, it was not. When they arrived at the work

site, Percy and Lord Hasbrook emerged from under the stands and made a beeline toward them. Missy gaily waved her crop.

"What a nice surprise!" Percy cried, hurrying to the young lady's side.

"Indeed it is!" Lord Hasbrook somehow edged him out and claimed the honor of helping Missy dismount.

The girl laid her hands on Hasbrook's shoulders and coyly smiled at him. Percy frowned slightly and stepped back.

"I am so anxious to see the tournament grounds," Missy said in a charmingly breathless voice. She took her time in descending, allowing Lord Hasbrook the maximum opportunity to hold her waist. Alighting, she gazed up at him in the same worshipful manner as Damaris had seen her do with Percy so very often. She slipped her arm through his.

"Won't you give me a tour?" she asked sweetly.

Percy glowered, but there was little he could do. Missy had chosen his friend as her escort. When they set off toward the tiltyard, he doggedly followed, completely forgetting Damaris in his indignation.

The groom helped Damaris down and took the reins of the horses as she worriedly hastened after the threesome. What was Missy doing? How could she treat Percy so? She had been attracted to Lord Hasbrook, but it hadn't occurred to Damaris that her sister would actually act on her fascination with the young viscount. Good heavens, she'd always loved Percy!

And what of Lord Hasbrook? What kind of man was he? No honorable gentleman would seek to steal his best friend's lady! He must not realize that Percy and Missy had somewhat of an understanding. He seemed like a fine young man. She hoped that someone would quickly warn him off. She herself would tell Missy exactly what she thought of her disgraceful conduct!

She caught up with them as Percy was gallantly attempting to explain the purpose of the various structures, but Missy was paying him no heed at all.

"From what part of the country do you come, my lord?" She tilted her head and looked up at Hasbrook, fluttering her eyelashes.

Damaris nearly groaned aloud.

"Shropshire, Miss Melissa," he answered, drinking in her attention as if it were the sweetest wine.

"I have heard that it is very beautiful there," Missy warbled.

"It is. Perhaps you may visit it sometime and see for yourself."

"I would dearly love to. I have always longed for travel," she proclaimed, her voice soft with yearning. "Geography was ever my favorite subject."

"Mine too!" Lord Hasbrook eagerly agreed.

Damaris bit back a disparaging remark. Until this moment, Missy had probably never imagined that a place named Shropshire existed. Furthermore, geography had been the girl's downfall. She doubted that her sister could locate London on a map. What a piece of nonsense!

"Shropshire." Missy sighed. "What a delightful environ."

"That is the tiltyard," Percy announced loudly, pointing.

"What?" The girl stared at him as if he had suddenly appeared from nowhere.

"The tiltyard!" Percy scowled.

"Oh, yes ... the tournament. It had slipped my mind." She batted her lashes at Lord Hasbrook. "Will you be participating, my lord?"

"Of course." He made a slight bow.

"He certainly will." Percy ground his teeth. "Hasbrook and I will be challenging each other."

Missy gasped. "It sounds so dangerous!"

"It is," Percy spat, glaring at his friend.

Missy patted Hasbrook's sleeve. "Perhaps you will carry my favor, my lord."

"I . . . I would be most honored!" he stammered.

Percy squared his shoulders and took a menacing step forward, but Damaris quickly intervened. "Come, gentlemen, show us where the activities will take place."

"I'll show you where Hasbrook will eat the dust!" He stalked off in the direction of the tiltyard.

"It is Percy who will find himself on the ground," Lord Hasbrook boasted as they strolled after him. "If I am wearing your favor, Miss Melissa, I cannot lose!"

I will wring her neck, Damaris thought. Didn't Missy know what she was creating? The two friends were already at swords' points with each other! If her sister did not cease her goading, there would be a fight right then and there! Percy was furious, and Lord Hasbrook was showing signs of irritation.

"I didn't realize that we had guests!"

Hearing the earl's voice, Damaris was flooded with relief. She whirled. "Richard, thank God! You—" She froze.

On his arm was the most beautiful woman she had ever seen. The lady was blond, petite, and very, very feminine. Her complexion was flawless and her features, perfection itself. It was unimaginable that one single female could possess every attribute of loveliness. If someone had told Damaris that such a creature existed, she would never have believed it.

Richard's introduction pierced her state of shock. "Damaris, this is Lady Kelford."

Lady Kelford! The infamous Annabelle! Throat contracting, she made an awkward curtsy.

"How do you do?" the beauty whispered in a honeyeyed voice.

She murmured a routine response. Annabelle! Why had she come to Delafield Hall? She looked at the lady's hand, lying so softly and familiarly on Richard's arm, and knew the reason. Annabelle and Richard. Their love had not been forgotten through the years. It was just as strong as ever.

A sickness settled deep in the pit of her stomach. She meant nothing to Richard. He had merely dallied with her while awaiting his love's arrival. Or perhaps he had used his skilled lovemaking to pay her back for her earlier treatment of him. Whatever it was made no difference now. Her hopes were dashed, and her heart was broken. How could she have been so foolish? Hadn't she known from the start that he had despised her?

Damaris bravely lifted her chin. "I hope you enjoy your stay in our neighborhood, Lady Kelford. Percy is showing my sister the tournament site. Come. Shall we catch up with them?" Stiffly, she smiled.

Chapter 12

❧◦❧

The presence of Annabelle Kelford at least had the effect of silencing Missy. As soon as her sister laid eyes on the beautiful widow, she ceased her frantic flirtations and machinations. Instead, she intently studied the older woman, as if it were possible for some of Annabelle's London polish to rub off on her.

Damaris was too miserable to care what Missy did now. Why had she allowed herself to be talked into coming to Delafield this morning? She looked positively frumpy in her old brown habit. It was outdated and worn, and would have been cut up for rags long ago if she had not decided that it would be perfect for estate work. Gad, next to Annabelle, she looked like a bumpkin!

The widow was dressed in a gown of yellow muslin so thin and fine that it could have been drawn through the circle of the smallest lady's ring. On her fair, modish curls, she wore a straw hat with delicate saffron roses and streaming ribbons. She shaded herself with a perfectly matching parasol, which she twirled and tilted coquettishly to great advantage.

Damaris was glad that Missy looked pretty, so that the Grayson name was somewhat redeemed. Though her sister's habit was country-made and lacked the superior style of one crafted by a fashionable modiste, it was tasteful and attractive. And Missy's dewy-fresh, youthful face made her serious competition to an older lady, a fact that Annabelle was most likely aware of.

The widow scanned Missy up and down and returned her attention to Damaris. "The two of you are so different. I would never have guessed that you are sisters!"

"Yes, we are different," Damaris said tightly. "It is said that Missy resembles our mother, and I, our father."

Annabelle's gaze hovered over her faded brown habit. "I see," she murmured with bored condescension.

"Let's continue around the tournament field," Percy interrupted.

"Be patient, my dear," Annabelle trilled. "We are conversing. But do not fear. I shall see everything. I am already most impressed with what I have seen thus far. How lucky I caught up with Richard as he was leaving the house! I was most anxious to view the site."

Percy eyed her sullenly but did not make a comment.

"Are you excited about the tournament, Miss Grayson?" she asked.

"I'm sure that it will be most interesting," Damaris replied.

"Damaris is to be the Queen," Percy announced smugly.

"*You?*" Annabelle arched a thin eyebrow and stared at her.

"Won't she make a lovely Queen?" Richard commented hastily.

"Oh, of course." She smiled doubtfully. "Have you a queenly dress to wear, Miss Grayson?" she asked, slightly mockingly.

"Annabelle," Richard warned.

"Our costumes are in the process of being made," Missy interjected. "They shall be of absolutely authentic design."

"How nice. Mine were made in London by my modiste. I cautioned her to consult scholars." She turned her attention to Richard. "I hope that you will like them, dear."

"Lord Delafield will have short time to notice them," Missy said nastily, "since he will be escorting Damaris."

Annabelle barely concealed her sharp intake of breath, covering it with a brittle smile. "I am sure she will not claim his full attention. You would not permit that, would you, dear?" She gazed soulfully up at Richard.

Damaris could bear no more. "Come, Missy, we must go. I have a great deal to accomplish today. Good day to you." She flicked her glance over them all and turned on her heel, starting toward the horses, without even waiting for her sister to follow.

"One moment, Damaris!" Richard called after her.

She reached her horse. "Help me up, Furman," she ordered the groom.

"Miss, the earl . . ."

"Help me up!"

He moved uncomfortably to obey, legging her up into the saddle.

She tried to draw up the reins, but there was an iron hold on them.

"Damaris?" Richard said.

"You must excuse me, Lord Delafield. I did not realize it was so late. We are renewing fence in the west pasture, and I have a lot to do," she stated coldly.

"We must talk."

"Indeed? I can think of nothing I have to say." She

tried to turn her horse, but he retained control. "Let go of my reins!"

"Damaris . . ."

She smacked him across the knuckles with her riding crop. When his hand sprang open with the surprise of it, she quickly spun her horse on its haunches and galloped off, leaving Missy to catch up as best she could. She had reached the trees before she heard the hooves of her sister's mare hard on her heels. She drew down to a walk.

"Damaris!" Missy cried breathlessly. "I saw what you did! You should have seen his face!"

"Pure anger, no doubt."

"No! It was unhappiness!" she gasped.

"Poor little Dickon had his hand slapped," Damaris muttered scornfully. "That should teach him to keep it out of the jam pot."

Missy's face twisted with confusion. "The jam pot? Whatever do you mean?"

Visions of Richard's kiss floated through her head. He had toyed with her. She meant nothing to him. She was merely an amusing substitute while he waited for his beloved Annabelle to arrive. She set her jaw.

"Never you mind," she said sharply.

"But Damaris, I think he likes you better than that Annabelle woman," her sister insisted.

"He has a strange way of showing it. She was hanging all over him, Missy, and he was doing nothing to prevent it!"

"I am not so sure. You should have seen how frantic he was to extricate himself from her clutches to follow you. She had him trapped. I am certain of it!"

"Men do not become ensnared unless they wish to be. She has won him again. How could she not?" She sighed. "She is so very beautiful."

"She is also a perfect bitch!"

"Missy! I cannot believe that you would say such a vulgar word!"

The girl shrugged. "Well, it is most applicable, is it not?"

Damaris smiled grimly. "I suppose it is, but it certainly isn't becoming to you. By the way, your behavior with Percy was not pleasing either," she chided. "You treated him most cruelly. What are you attempting to do? Turn him away?"

"It is not your right to criticize me!" Missy cried, incensed.

"I told you that for your own good."

"For your information, dear sister, I happen to prefer Lord Hasbrook," she avowed spitefully.

"You do not even know him! How can you say that?"

"Percy has done me great injury."

"Fustian!" Damaris shook her head. "Surely you cannot continue to dwell on that matter of the Queen."

Missy ground her teeth. "Being the Queen was important to me. I shall never forget it!"

"Did you ask Percy about it?"

"No! And if you think I shall deign to do such a thing, you are far off the mark!" she snapped.

"You tell Percy that you will be the Queen. Inform him that I have relinquished my throne to you," Damaris hissed disparagingly. "I shall not attend the tournament."

"Mama will never allow it!"

"Mama cannot force me." She kicked her horse into a gallop and sped through the woods, leaving Missy behind.

It was final. She had made up her mind, and no one would change it. After all, she hadn't wanted to be the Queen in the first place. The arrival of Lady Kelford had given her an excuse that even her mother would understand. She would not be the Queen. She would not even show her face at the tournament. In fact, she would avoid Delafield property entirely, and she would particularly dodge the hypocritical earl. Let Annabelle be the precious Queen! Damaris Grayson would not be set up as a fool.

At the edge of the copse, she pulled up and waited for Missy. "As you must remember, you agreed to inform Mama that I shall not be present at luncheon," she reminded. "I am going to see to the fencing."

Her sister nodded curtly. "Don't forget the dress fittings."

"I shall not attend that either. Since I am not going to the tournament, I do not require costuming. The fabrics may be restyled as gowns for you or Mama. I have an estate to administer. I have no need for fine clothing."

"You are beetle-headed, Damaris!"

Damaris ignored her. She gestured to the footman, who was looking perplexed at his ladies' division of destinations. "Go with Miss Melissa, Furman," she directed. "I do not need your protection. I am much too old, shabby, and unattractive to be accosted by anyone!" Quickly, she rode off toward the west pasture.

Before it was time for the workmen's midday meal, Damaris, accompanied by the man she had chosen to oversee the project, rode along a portion of the fence line and marked the rotted boards and posts for replacement. With the sun rising high overhead, it was hot work. Rivulets of perspiration trickled down her back between her shoulder blades, beaded on her face, and soaked her bodice. She wished she could remove her jacket and go about in her shirt as the men did, but that action, even from an independent lady such as she, would have been much too scandalous to her employees. She endured in silence, dabbing at her face with her handkerchief and looking forward to the end of the day when she could have a long soak in cool bathwater. This was just another inequity for the female gender, she thought. Even when a woman had the courage to rise to a challenge, she must be made to suffer for it because of stuffy, impractical social mores.

At least, her discomfort and the task to be accomplished took her mind away from Richard and Annabelle. But it did not soothe her rumbling stomach. Damaris was hungry. While the men ate, she sat under a large oak tree and tried not to notice their meat pies, cheeses, and bread. Here was another social injustice. Though each man might be willing to share, he could not offer his mistress a portion of his lunch. And it would shock them if she begged. Finally, to avoid staring at the mouth-watering morsels, she returned to the fence, leading her horse and chalking the portions to be replaced.

She had worked her way to the far end of the pasture when she suddenly spied a horse and rider in the distance. Richard! She instantly recognized him by the set of his shoulders and the graceful manner in which he rode his gelding. Good heavens! What was he doing here? Even if she were not determined to avoid him, she couldn't allow him to see her in the damp, sweat-soaked habit. She must escape.

Hurriedly, she mounted her horse. Turning the animal toward the fence, she popped over it and dashed for home. The workmen knew what they were doing. They could get along without her for now. She could return later. Glancing back over her shoulder, she saw that Richard had seen her and was following at a ground-eating gallop. Damn! At that pace, there was an excellent chance that he would catch up to her. Wildly, she urged her horse to greater speed.

She was still in the lead when the house loomed in sight. Riding at a madcap gait across the lawn, she circled the building and drew up at the rear entrance. She leaped off her horse and tossed the reins to a lounging kitchen boy.

"Take him to the stable!" she gasped breathlessly and darted through the servants' entrance.

Inside, she took the backstairs two at a time and ran into her room. After slamming the door, she leaned weakly against it and snapped the lock. With any luck at all, Richard would take the hint and go home.

It was not to be. After the interval it took him to dismount, enter the house, and ask for her, she heard footsteps in the hall. Someone knocked on her door.

Damaris held her ragged breath.

The knob jiggled. "Damaris! Open this door at once!" Lady Grayson ordered.

She did not reply.

"Damaris! The servants saw you, so I know that you are in there! Do not behave like your sister. Open this door! You have a caller."

She groaned. Why hadn't she rushed up the steps to the attic? Or she could have hidden in the back-yard privy!

Lady Grayson rapped once more. "Damaris! Richard is here."

"I do not wish to see him!" she shouted back.

"Open this door or I shall fetch the key!"

Cursing her ill luck, Damaris unlocked the door

and jerked it open. "I do not wish to see him," she repeated firmly.

Lady Grayson entered the room. "What is the matter with you? Richard has come calling. Of course you will see him!"

"No, I will not. Look at me, Mama. I am pig-dirty!"

Nose twitching, her mother frowned her disapproval. "Such an expression," she scolded. "I shall order a bath. Perhaps he will not mind waiting."

"I refuse to see him," she insisted, "and there is no sense in ordering a bath, for I must return to the fields. I came home only to escape him. I hate him."

"Nonsense! And despite this visit, you must clean up anyway, so as to be ready when the Rogers sisters arrive for the dress fittings."

"I shall not be fitted. I do not plan to attend the tournament."

"Damaris!" Lady Grayson sputtered. "You must attend! You are the Queen!"

"I have relinquished that repulsive position to Missy," she proclaimed determinedly. "Didn't she tell you?"

"Yes, she enlightened me on the morning's events."

"Then you will know why I refuse to see Richard and why I will not go to the tournament."

"Because of Lady Kelford?" Lady Grayson somberly eyed her. "I believe that you are being too hasty."

"No, I am not." Damaris swished irritably across the room and, oblivious of her dusty skirt, sat down on the bed. "Mama, if you had been at Delafield this morning, you would understand."

Her mother sighed. "Very well. I shall tell Richard that you are unable to see him at present. But you will not go back to the field before you and I have had a discussion of this matter."

"You will accomplish nothing by it. My mind is made up," Damaris warned, but she was much too relieved by Lady Grayson's agreement to send Richard away to quarrel over it. "I will wait for you here, and I'll listen to what you have to say."

"Sensible girl," her mother approved. "I shall return shortly." After leaving the room, she closed the door behind her.

Before Lady Grayson came back, a parade of servants bearing a tub and bathwater arrived. Though Damaris knew she was compromising her ability to forgo the dress fitting, she was just too hot and sticky to resist. She dismissed the hovering maid, undressed, and lowered herself into the scented, tepid water, preparing for a long, reviving soak.

Oh, but the water felt marvelous! All would have been perfect if her mother had sent up refreshment to accompany this respite, but even though her stomach continued to protest its emptiness, she was much too relaxed to get out of the tub and ring for food herself. She smiled sardonically. Even with her strong streak of stubbornness, she couldn't have lasted as long as Missy had without nourishment. Trying to ignore the hunger pangs and carefully blocking all thoughts of Richard and Annabelle from her mind, she sank down up to her neck and closed her eyes.

"Damaris?"

There was movement in her chamber. Damaris sat up. Goodness, she must have dozed!

"Are you still in that bath?" Lady Grayson appeared at the dressing room door. "Get out of there at once!" She snapped her fingers. "Jane? Assist my daughter."

A maid replaced her mother in the doorway.

Oh, dear, Damaris thought. Now she would have to have pointed conversation with her parent. There would be a verbal struggle. Lady Grayson would insist that she attend the tournament, and Damaris would assert that she would not. In the end . . .

"I am not yet finished, Mama," she announced.

"Of course you are! You have been in the water so long that your skin will be puckered!"

"In a little while."

"Now, Damaris!" her mother ordered.

The delicious odor of cinnamon cakes wafted through the doorway. Her mouth watered, and her stomach rumbled. Food! Lady Grayson had come accompanied by a tea tray. It wasn't fair.

"Come, Damaris," her mother called invitingly. "I thought you might be hungry, since you had no luncheon." She paused. "Um, um. My, but these morsels are delectable!"

It was outside of enough! The repast was certainly worth whatever disagreement might ensue. Damaris scrambled from the tub and gave herself up to the ministrations of the maid.

Hoping against hope that Annabelle had tucked herself away for an afternoon nap, Richard entered Delafield Hall. Dammit all! What an awful day it had been! First, Annabelle had lain in wait and captured him when he left the castle to meet Percy at the tournament ground. Then had come that dreadful scene when the widow had conducted herself as a perfect witch, and Damaris had hit him with her crop. Finally, after he'd cried off from luncheon and gone to seek her, Damaris had run from him and then refused to see him. What a muddle! Furthermore, from the looks of things, his brother hadn't fared much better.

Poor Percy! That teasing Missy had draped herself all over Hasbrook and absolutely ignored him. His brother must be floundering in the depths of despair. He must find him and talk with him. One of them should have a word with Gerry Hasbrook too, and warn him of the situation. Most likely, the viscount had no idea that he was overstepping his bounds. No man would try to steal his best friend's lady.

"My lord?" the butler intoned, taking his hat, gloves, and whip. "I am to inform you that Lady Delafield requires your immediate presence in her salon."

"Thank you, Gilbert." He hesitated. "I'm sorry, but I must ask you if the Lady Kelford is present, for if she is . . ."

The man smiled knowingly. "She is within her chamber, sir."

Richard nodded and proceeded to the stairs.

"My lord?"

He turned.

"I and my staff are constantly aware of the location of all family members and guests, if you ever have need of that knowledge."

The earl grinned. "I see that you understand my predicament."

Gilbert's eyes twinkled. "Indeed so."

Richard climbed the steps and presented himself in his mother's salon, barely able to stifle a groan as he saw who awaited him. Gilbert should have warned him of these guests as well! They were nearly as unwelcome as Annabelle.

"Good afternoon," he greeted the Rogers sisters, bowing.

"Richard!" Lady Delafield cried. "I had nearly despaired of your arriving in time! We must make haste! The Rogerses are expected momentarily at Grayson Park!"

"One of your costumes is almost finished," Percy clarified, rising from his seat beside her on the sofa.

"Go to your room and put it on at once," their mother commanded, "and then return. I am anxious to see it! Any further fitting can be accomplished here."

Well, at least he would avoid the ignominy of having those women in his bedchamber. Also, it would serve to take his brother's mind from his troubles. The young man seemed excited.

"Come on." Percy picked up the carefully folded garment. "I'm impatient to see it too!"

The two left the room and walked down the hall to Richard's bedroom. While Casey pulled off his boots and assisted his master in his undressing, Percy spread out the ensemble.

"Dammit, it's a dress!" Richard frowned, staring at it with frank distaste.

"You dunce! It's a doublet! You know how medieval men dressed!"

"Gad, Percy, it . . ."

"You agreed to this, Dickon." His brother held up a delicately knitted pair of hose. "Put these on first."

Richard moaned. "Do you realize how I am going to look?"

"Of course! I have a similar costume for the ball. You'll look like a fine medieval gentleman."

His face pinched with outraged disapproval, Casey moved to help. "It is obscene," he muttered. "Lascivious and indecent."

Richard dropped helplessly into a chair. Together, he and his valet managed to pull on the tight hose. He stood and yanked them up the rest of the way.

"My lord, I feel . . ." Casey stared at him with

glowering distaste. "My lord, I feel that I . . . may be forced . . . to terminate . . . my employment," he stuttered with shock. "I am mortified. Humiliated! Everyone will know that you are my gentleman and will blame *me* for this abomination!" he finished with a rush. Clutching his head as if to keep it from exploding, he ran out of the room.

"What the hell . . ." Richard began.

"Oh, Dickon!" Percy burst into laughter. "You do not look as I do! Your hosiery . . . well, it is a bit too tight!"

He swiveled slowly and gazed aghast into the mirror. "My God!"

The hosiery fitted him like a second skin, molding lewdly to his form, exhibiting his private parts like trophies on display and leaving nothing to the imagination of the onlooker.

Wiping tears of hilarity from his eyes, his brother picked up the doublet. "Let us hope that this is long enough to cover your . . . er . . ." He broke into fresh gales.

"This isn't funny!" Richard snapped. "If I have to wear this, I won't attend your cursed tournament!"

"I think we can do something with it. Maybe we can stretch the hose." Between guffaws, Percy managed to attire his brother in the doublet. "There! That isn't so bad."

"I hate this! Why in the hell did you have to come up with such a brainless idea?"

"Now, Dickon," he soothed. "You'll be fine. Oh, just wait . . . just wait until Annabelle sees you! Her pursuit will become even more ardent!" At this new thought, he fell back in a chair, covered his eyes, and howled.

Chapter 13

Damaris wrote the current date beside the entry for the butcher's bill in the household ledger book. Gazing thoughtfully at it, she put down her pen. Two weeks to the day had crawled by since that bleak day she had met Annabelle Kelford at Delafield. It didn't seem possible, yet before her was the cold evidence in black and white. She had passed two whole weeks of mundane estate routine and sheer boredom, punctuated only by several narrow escapes when Richard had come to call. People said that time healed grief, but she wondered if they were wrong. After fourteen days, her aching heart was just as raw as it had been on the day she'd seen Richard and Annabelle together.

Up to a point, her mother had been sympathetic, but not knowing the full extent of her daughter's feelings toward the earl, she tended to be irritable at Damaris's avoidance of social contacts. But other than clicking her tongue and scolding when Damaris refused to see Richard, Lady Grayson left her alone. The matron seemed to be well enough satisfied to have bullied her elder daughter into tolerating the fittings for the tournament costumes. Besides, Missy was providing her with enough to think about.

Many guests had already settled in at Delafield Hall, and Percy's entire contingent of knights had arrived to practice for the tournament, adding an excess of interesting bachelors to the community. Of all the eligible young ladies in the neighborhood, Missy seemed to have captured their greatest attention. It was quite a triumph for the girl, and it had gone to her head. Though she exhibited a decided preference for Lord Hasbrook, she flirted gaily with all of them, except Percy, whom she continued to treat as if he were the plague itself.

Damaris could not accept the fact that her sister had fallen so easily out of love with her old friend. Neither could she believe Missy capable of harboring a grudge for so very long. She'd tried to talk with her about it, but had only succeeded in making Missy angry with her. The girl had called her a busybody and had told her to stay away from her and to tend to her own business. After that, Damaris had avoided her, which was just as well for her own peace of mind. It always saddened her to watch Missy dally with her beaux while Percy morosely looked on.

The horrid tournament had ruined everything. Damaris wondered if Percy realized how much his event had affected all of their lives. Was he sorry that he had ever conceived the idea?

If it hadn't been for the tournament, Richard might have fallen in love with her. Perhaps it hadn't been merely a dalliance. Maybe he'd experienced a true regard for her that just hadn't had time to grow strong enough to overcome his feelings for his old love.

If it hadn't been for the tournament, Percy and Missy would still be carrying on their romance. By now, he might have asked for her hand. He'd seemed on the verge of it.

One thing was certain, Damaris thought as she closed the ledger with an aggravated snap. If it hadn't been for the tournament, there wouldn't have been such a drain on the household expenses.

She stood up and stretched her back. There was no point in musing on what might have been. She would take a stroll in the garden to clear the cobwebs from her mind, then she'd have a nice chat with her father, unless that dastardly Richard was visiting him as he so frequently did.

As she entered the hall, she heard the sound of male laughter emanating from the drawing room. Obviously, Missy was entertaining her beaux. Damaris left the house by the side door to escape being seen. She walked quickly toward the rose garden, hoping that Lady Grayson wouldn't glimpse her through the window and notice that she had neglected to wear her hat. As she passed through the arch of the boxwood hedge, she spied a familiar figure.

"Percy! What are you doing out here?"

Her old friend arose from a stone bench. "Hullo, Damaris. I just wanted to be alone for a while."

"Oh." She turned to leave.

"No, wait! I'd like your company!" He strode toward her. "Shall we walk?"

She nodded, falling in step beside him and waiting for him to initiate the conversation.

"It just makes me angry as hell!" he burst out, then eyed her sheepishly. "Pardon my expression."

"It's all right." She smiled sympathetically. "Since when have we stood on ceremony?"

"Thank you, Damaris. You are the best of friends. In fact, I suppose that you're my *only* friend, excepting Dickon of course. That damned Hasbrook certainly isn't, and neither are the others, though they aren't quite as false. Oh, well." He shrugged. "Can't blame 'em. Who could resist her?"

Damaris sighed. "Who indeed?"

"She seems to care a lot for Gerry. Maybe I should

be happy for them, but I'm not that noble. I just can't understand what happened. She was miffed because I didn't choose her to be the Queen, but it has to be more than that. Missy's been annoyed with me before, but she's never done anything like this."

She agreed and let him ramble on, making only polite remarks at the expected intervals. He needed a soundboard, not an adviser. She listened with only half an ear, until his comment brought her to rapt attention.

"And furthermore, I don't understand what happened to you and Dickon! I thought you were developing a *tendre* for each other."

"I can explain it in one word," she murmured sadly. "Annabelle."

"You're wrong, you know. Dickon doesn't care for Annabelle."

"He has a strange way of showing it."

He shook his head. "You're far off the mark."

"I am not!" she protested. "You saw how closely he held her!"

"She was holding on to *him*, Damaris. Dickon detests her. He dodges her whenever he can."

Her heart made a hopeful little leap. "Are you certain?"

"Would I lie to you?" he demanded.

"No," she answered slowly. "You would not do so, knowingly."

"Then believe me! He has no regard whatsoever for Annabelle Kelford. Whatever he felt in the past is finished now, and has been finished for a very long time."

She tried to ignore the hopeful throbbing in her veins. She must not leave herself open to additional pain. She'd survived the past two weeks. Surely sometime the wound would heal. She must not expose it to further punishment.

"Let us ride at once to Delafield," Percy urged. "Find out for yourself!"

Damaris flushed. "I could not do that."

"Why not? You used to visit frequently!"

"Things have changed," she said firmly. "I cannot do it now."

"Then permit me to go home and fetch Dickon," he zealously proposed.

"No! That would be too embarrassing!" She gasped. "I must think about this first. I must do the right thing."

"Why waste time in thought?" he cried with exasperation. "For God's sake, Damaris, don't you know whether or not you care for my brother?"

Cheeks burning, she bent her head, fixing her gaze on a full-blown crimson rose. Merciful heavens, she thought, my face must be as red as that flower.

"Damaris," Percy repeated, "don't you know?"

"I . . . I . . ." She swallowed, but the lump in her throat remained.

"Dickon is in love with you."

"How can you be certain of that?" she wailed.

"Because he told me!" He grasped her shoulders. "Look at me, Damaris."

Reluctantly, she lifted her chin.

"My brother loves you," he said distinctly and confidently.

"But he never told me," she whispered.

"If you would cease running and hiding from him, he might get the chance! What do you expect him to do? Chase after you, shouting his innermost feelings for all to hear? Dammit all anyway! You Grayson ladies are the absolute worst at allowing a man to explain himself!" He threw up his hands in aggravation. "A pox on you all!"

Damaris's temper flared defensively. "You are exaggerating."

"I most surely am not!" Percy spat out. "You and Missy have peas for brains!"

"Missy and I?" she shrieked. "I'll have you know, Percy Marston, that if it wasn't for your damned tournament, we wouldn't be in this muddle today!"

"*My tournament!* You're blaming me for your feather brains?"

"If you hadn't selected me to be the Queen, you wouldn't be in this tangle with Missy," she caustically reminded him.

"And if she had used a tenth of her miniscule brain, she'd have allowed me to justify my logic in doing so! I had good reasons, and she'd have understood them!" he ranted. "But no! She chose to take offense! To be hurt! To be pitiful! I swear, a woman is nothing but a bag full of stupid, snarled emotions, with no common sense whatsoever, and you Grayson ladies are among the worst!"

"Well, I certainly take exception to that!" Damaris shrilled. "Who has been running this estate?"

"I'm tired of your damned estate!" Percy growled.

"Good! Then get off it!"

"Why don't you just see if you can throw me off?" he challenged.

"Maybe I will!" She glared at him, saw the twinkle in his blue eyes, and burst out laughing.

Percy followed suit. Taking her in his arms, he held her while they both shook with merriment. "Dammit, Damaris, we sounded like we did years ago!"

"Fighting like cats and dogs! But we always made up." She laid her head against his chest. "Oh, Percy, what are we going to do about all this?"

"The solution to your problem, dearest friend, is simple. I am going to to tell Dickon that you are just as much in love with him as he is with you."

She trembled. "Will he believe you?"

"Yes, dear, he will." He gave her an encouraging squeeze. "As to my dilemma, I suppose that I must prove to Missy that I am the better man. Perhaps I'll do it on the jousting field. Like the knights of old!"

She smiled understandingly at his wishful fantasy. "I hope you will have all the best of success."

"I'll need it," he acknowledged.

Hand in hand, they started back to the house.

When he arrived home from Grayson Park, Percy slipped away from his guests and hurried to his bedroom. He locked the door to ward off inquisitive intrusion. Then, sitting down at his desk, he withdrew pen and paper, and began to write. He had conceived this plan some days ago, but had postponed its implementation until the time was ripe. Now was that moment.

"Darling Richard," he began, in what he hoped would appear to be a feminine hand. *"I love you with all my heart. Please meet me tonight in the grove, at dusk. Damaris."*

Smiling, he sealed it and wrote a similar note from Richard to Damaris. That should do it! The two lovers would probably catch on to him, but by then it wouldn't matter. Right now, his brother and his friend needed action as well as words. The romantic grove in the twilight hour should provide the perfect atmosphere for a thoroughly head-spinning kiss. Satisfied with himself, he took the letters downstairs and dispatched a footman to deliver Damaris's, then went in search of Dickon and found him hiding in the library.

"Hurry! Close the door!" Richard hissed as he entered. "Annabelle has been hot on my trail all afternoon long, and I want her to think that I am still busy with the steward."

"An unpleasant situation."

"She seems to have heightened her determination. I'm having my difficulties escaping her."

"Be cautious, brother," he warned. "La Belle has claws."

"Don't I know it!"

Percy nonchalantly tossed Richard's note onto the desk. "I've been at Grayson Park. Damaris asked me to give this to you."

"Damaris?" He reached for it, almost hesitantly.

Percy knew he should leave his brother alone to read the missive, but he couldn't resist watching his face. Richard must have scanned it several times, his grin expanding with each perusal.

"Good news?" Percy interrupted.

Richard gave him a long and rather wistful look. "It's the best news I've had in a very long time," he said softly.

"Going to tell me?" Percy prompted eagerly.

"Not yet. Soon." Tucking the message into his coat, Richard reached for the bottle of brandy and two glasses. "Little brother, let us have a drink together. Suffice it to say that I feel like celebrating!"

Heart thumping with happiness, Damaris reread the note from Richard. Percy had been as good as his word. He'd spoken with Richard, and here was the result. *I love you with all my heart. Please meet me tonight in the grove ...* She touched the letter to her lips and secreted it in the hidden drawer of her bedroom desk.

Meet me at dusk. That might require some planning.

Since Sir Osbert had his new wheeled chair, he spent longer and longer periods of time downstairs. Lately he had begun joining his wife and daughters in the salon after the evening meal, soliciting Damaris, in particular, for a game of chess. She would have to plead a headache and steal away very quietly from the house.

Arising, she went to her dressing room to prepare for dinner. No, she thought with a giggle. She was preparing herself for Richard! This was the gown she would wear to meet him in the grove. She chose one of her most feminine garments. It was constructed of thin rose muslin and trimmed with burgundy ribbons. The styling was simple, so that she should not call attention to herself at the dinner table, but it was flattering and dreamy enough for a tryst with a lover.

Damaris laughed to herself. Who would have believed that the time would come when she was more interested in her appearance than in the management of the estate? But the grove was meant for romance, not practicality, and she must look the part.

As she took the dress from her wardrobe and laid it across a chair, she caught sight of the tournament costumes that had been delivered that day. Thank heavens she had bowed to her mother's wishes and had them completed! The event would begin with a banquet tomorrow. As the Queen, she would sit beside Richard. Suddenly, she was very glad that Percy had selected her for the honor.

Her lighthearted mood was so obvious that even the maid commented on it.

"Miss Damaris, you look so pretty and happy tonight." She beamed as she twisted up her mistress's hair.

"I hope I am not overdressed."

"Oh, no, miss. You're just perfect for a warm evening."

Warm. She thought of Richard's kisses and blushed gently. Yes, he would surely kiss her tonight!

She got up from the dressing table. "Don't wait for me tonight. I shall be playing chess with Papa, and the game is apt to go on rather late."

"Thank you, miss. I'll lay out your night rail." She began tidying the room.

Damaris hurried downstairs, meeting her family in the salon just before dinner was served.

"How lovely you look, my dear!" Lady Grayson acknowledged, while Sir Osbert nodded his approval.

"You look as if you are going somewhere special," Missy said flatly.

Damaris laughed. "It is a very warm night, and this is my coolest gown."

"We should expect you to be practical." Her sister fluttered past her as a footman wheeled Sir Osbert toward the dining room.

Damaris had expected the meal to drag on and on, with the clock ticking out the interminable minutes, but it proceeded at a reasonable pace. Luckily, Lady Grayson had called at Squire Carter's home that afternoon and was possessed of all the latest gossip, so she monopolized the conversation. It was a blessing. Damaris could think of little but Richard. As dusk grew near, she became fidgety.

"What is wrong with you?" her mother interrupted her monologue to ask.

"I am getting a headache," she answered weakly. "The heat, no doubt."

"You should not have spent the afternoon in the fields," the lady chided. "Do you wish to be excused?"

"Please. If I may?"

"Indeed so. Go to bed, Damaris." She waved her hands toward the door. "You must be fit for the banquet tomorrow. I shall not tolerate illness then!"

"No, ma'am." She laid down her napkin and rose. "I'm sorry about our chess game, Papa."

"Another time." He chuckled. "I want you at your best whenever I trounce you!"

She fled from the room and up the stairs. After pausing at her chamber to gather up her shawl, she tiptoed carefully down the back steps. Holding her breath in hopes that no servant would see her, she slipped out the rear door.

She knew the way to the grove as well as she knew the back of her own hand, but because she must be cautious to escape detection, she couldn't reach her destination as speedily as she might have wished. Stealthily, she glided from shadow to shadow, suppressing the guilty urge to giggle, until she reached the edge of the woods. Just a short distance now! She set off rapidly down the path, alert for any fallen branch or rough spot that might trip her up. It wouldn't do to reach the glade with torn gown and skinned knees!

The picturesque trysting place was a short distance down a secondary path from this main shortcut to Delafield Hall. The trail was rather overgrown, and she had some difficulty finding it in the fading light. La, despite the rising moon, it was getting dark in the woods! She was going to be late. Surely Richard would wait for her! She accelerated her pace.

Bathed in moonlight, the grove lay just ahead. Happily, she burst from the fringe of the densely grown coppice and faltered, frozen to the spot. Richard was there, but he was not alone. Annabelle was in his arms. They were kissing!

"No!" The word seemed to wrench from the very depths of her soul. For one horrible moment, Damaris met Richard's eyes. Whirling, she ran.

Chapter 14

"**S**top it!" With a frantic glance in the direction in which Damaris had fled, Richard tugged at Annabelle's arms, locked firmly around his neck.

"My darling, if you will give me a chance!" She laced her fingers tightly, resisting his force with all her might. "What were you doing? Meeting a serving girl for a brief interval of pleasure?"

"No." He struggled with her, wincing as her sharp thumbnail stabbed his neck.

"It isn't necessary!" Annabelle cried, ignoring his reply. "Heed me, love. I have been married! I am no longer a tender, untouched maiden! I have no qualms about providing for your needs!"

"Let me go!" Tossing to the winds all chivalrous scruples of handling the opposite sex with gentleness, he yanked her free and shoved her away from him. As Annabelle reeled backward, he dashed to the edge of the grove and listened.

Damaris was gone. He couldn't even hear her running footsteps in the underbrush. His mind raced.

He couldn't catch her on foot. With the honeycomb of paths in the woods, he wouldn't know which one she had chosen to lead her back to Grayson Park. Then, too, she might have hidden, along the way, to restore her composure.

He couldn't ride over to the Grayson estate. It was much too late to make a call. Besides, such a frantic visit would call attention to their clandestine tête-à-tête. Her parents would be angry with her, and him too. No matter how good-natured Sir Osbert might be, he would have a dim opinion of this night's work. He might punish Damaris and forbid Richard to set foot on Grayson land.

He must wait until morning to make amends. Would Damaris believe his explanation of how Annabelle had secretly followed him and thrown herself in his arms just as Damaris had reached the glade? In his mind's eye, he saw her pallid, stricken face. Her wrenching sob of protest rang in his ears. He felt sick all over.

"Richard," Annabelle moaned.

"What is it?" he snapped, spinning on his heel.

"You have caused me injury," she whimpered.

"I? For God's sake! Whatever distress you are experiencing, you caused yourself!"

"You must help me," she wept. "I am hurt."

He stared at her with loathing. She had fallen when he'd pushed her, and she still lay on the mossy carpet of the grove. Her skirt was rumpled up around her shapely thighs. There was a rip in the underarm seam of her fashionable spencer. She looked thoroughly manhandled.

He studied her more closely. One slipper was missing and, oh, hell! Her ankle was rapidly swelling!

"It hurts," she sniveled.

Woodenly, he walked toward her, feeling sorry for both himself and her, and mortified by the violent force he'd exerted in repelling the lady. She had compelled him to do it, but that didn't matter. He had totally disregarded the ethical code of a gentleman.

"I'm sorry, Annabelle." He knelt down beside her and gave her his handkerchief.

"Do not fret, Richard. I shall always forgive you,

no matter what you do." She wrenched upward to a sitting position. "I know I caught you in a most indelicate situation. You were embarrassed. You were not yourself."

"Let us not speak of it."

"No. Never again!"

He touched her hot, pulpy ankle. It was terribly swollen. In just that short space of time, it had distended so greatly that it was nearly the size of her delectable calf.

Annabelle winced as he probed more deeply. "Is it broken?"

"I don't know. I hope not. I'm afraid to investigate any further. We need a doctor."

"Don't leave me alone in the woods!" she wailed.

"No, I won't do that," he soothed. "I'll carry you back to the Hall."

"Poor Richard." She reached out to stroke his cheek. "I am such a bother."

He clenched his jaw at her touch, but resisted the urge to bat her hand away. He had done her enough damage this night. He forced himself to smile.

"Let me find your slipper."

He found it, half hidden under a loose chunk of moss. When she had plunged backward, she must have caught her foot in the substance. The impetus of his push had kept her falling, twisting her ankle. He picked up the flimsy footgear and brushed it off. Returning, he handed it to her.

"Hold on to this." Pulling down her skirt to a more genteel position, he slipped his arms under her knees and shoulders and easily lifted her up. Annabelle dropped the slipper into her lap and put her arms around him.

"I could never have wished for this accident to oc-

cur," she whispered, "but I cannot deny my joy at
having you hold me thus."

He groaned inwardly. "Am I hurting you?"

"Oh, no. Even the pain from my ankle is better like
this." She laid her head against his chest and cuddled
closer.

He trod slowly and carefully from the woods. With
Annabelle in his arms, it was difficult to see the foot-
ing just ahead. Moreover, he was distracted by the
movement of her fingers through his hair.

"Annabelle, please don't do that. I can't concentrate on where I am going."

She laughed with naughty merriment, but ceased
her caresses. "We shall never forget this evening,
Richard, not for as long as we live!"

That was damned true, and he and Annabelle were
not the only ones who would remember. He thought
of Damaris. Most likely, she was home by now, and
probably ensconced in her bedchamber. Was she
weeping? Was she angry? A deep pain lodged in the
pit of his stomach. Would she understand and believe him? And if she did not, would she ... ever ...
forgive him?

They left the woods and entered the meadow. With
the castle almost overflowing with guests, it seemed
as if a light glowed from every window. He walked
more quickly.

"It won't be much longer," he reassured Annabelle.
"We're almost there."

"I am fine." She giggled suddenly. "Goodness,
Richard, think of all those guests who will witness
this. We'll be the talk of the *ton!*"

He stiffened.

She must have felt the tenseness in his shoulders.
"Do not be overset, love. They all remember our previous scandal and will expect nothing more from

us." She laughed lightly. "Our shocking compromise tonight will provide a most suitable end to our fairy tale."

Compromise? End to a fairy tale? He drew a huge breath. "What in the hell are you talking about?"

"Our marriage, of course! I would love to have a grand festivity for the occasion, but in light of what has happened tonight, it probably would be best if we wed immediately."

Richard halted. "Annabelle," he said slowly, "I am not sure that ours would be the most successful match."

"Nonsense!" She laughed lightly. "Once you loved me to distraction!"

"Times change. *People* change."

"But not us. Besides, it doesn't matter, for I am thoroughly compromised. I wish, however, that my ruin had been more gratifying." Playfully, she tugged at his ear.

"Don't do that."

His heart sank to his toes. It couldn't be true. Surely her slinking after him and throwing herself at him didn't constitute a compromise! Annabelle had previously shattered his life. Must she do it again?

He had to talk with Percy, and he must speak with his mother. If everyone believed he had ruined Annabelle, his failure to marry her would bring down another scandal upon the family. He couldn't allow that to happen again.

Disheartened, he trudged up to the castle and knocked on the door with his foot. It was opened by an astonished footman, behind whom stood the butler. Gilbert stared at him, his mouth pressed in an unhappy, tense line of disapproval.

"Fetch a doctor," Richard ordered with a faint

shrug and started toward the stairs. "And Lady Delafield, too," he added.

"I don't like that ill-natured butler," Annabelle said as he carried her up the steps. "I wish him fired."

"He is a loyal old retainer."

"I don't care. I want him gone immediately. If I am to be the mistress of this ancient pile of stones, I must have the respect of my servants," she said with haughty resonance. "He treats me with disparagement."

Was she already beginning the reorganization of his household? He visualized spending the rest of his life with Annabelle. He would be miserable.

Lady Delafield, with several guests trailing behind her, rushed into Annabelle's room as he was laying her on the bed. She surveyed the situation with a glance. A look of distaste crossed her face.

Gladly relinquishing Annabelle to the care of the ladies, Richard quietly withdrew to his bedchamber. It wasn't long before Percy came tapping on the door, and then Lady Delafield. They gazed helplessly at each other.

The dowager broke the silence. "The tale That Woman is spouting is utterly impossible, isn't it, Richard? Surely you did not slip away into the woods with her?"

"She followed me." He flicked a glance at Percy. "I was going to meet Damaris." Hurriedly he told them the entire story, ending with, "Annabelle considers herself compromised. Can that really be true, Mama?"

"Some of our guests are already offering her their best wishes for the upcoming nuptials," she declared uncomfortably.

"Then consider it done," he said bitterly. "I will not

cause this family to become the butt of scandal once more."

"I don't care about any gossip!" Percy shouted. "They can talk about us all they want! You can't sacrifice yourself, Dickon, not with the feelings you have for Damaris."

"I agree," his mother seconded. "I do not want That Woman to be my daughter-in-law!"

He shook his head. "I see no way out of it. I won't allow any more dirt to be thrown on the family name."

"To hell with the family name!" Percy cried. "You'd be wretched if you married Annabelle! And what about Damaris?"

"She probably wouldn't have me now, and I certainly don't want her name dragged through the mud. Please support me in this. Perhaps it won't be so bad."

Percy ground his teeth. "Don't do it, Dickon. Annabelle is a veritable shrew!"

"You could never be happy with her," Lady Delafield urged. "Never mind the gossip. We shall ride it out. This marriage must not take place!"

"I see no honorable way out," Richard contended and grinned crookedly. "Besides, if it becomes too ghastly, I can always travel."

"Run away? That is your practice, isn't it, Dickon?" his brother snapped.

"Dammit! I am trying to do what is honorable!"

Percy uttered a vile obscenity.

"The same back to you," Richard countered.

"Enough!" shrieked Lady Delafield. "We shall not make a decision tonight. Until we give more thought to the matter, we shall make no comment to anyone! Furthermore, we shall not affirm any mention of marriage. If you love me, Richard, you will agree."

"Unfair tactics, Mama!"

"I am quite aware of that, thank you, and I do not care!" She threw her arms around her elder son. "My darling, I am going to think of *some way* to get you out of this!"

"Very well, Mama. I will do as you say, and I wish you the best of success." He hugged her. "But I see no way out that will not bring forth disgrace and scandal," he said sadly.

Unmindful of covering her deceit and thinking only of reaching her bedroom in the shortest possible time, Damaris ran through the front door of her home and loudly slammed it behind her, acutely startling a drowsy footman who stood nearby.

"Miss Damaris!" he blared out with shock, staring openmouthed at her rumpled appearance and tear-streaked face.

She caught herself, looking around with dismay. Now her parents would surely discover her clandestine activity. As if the horrible scene in the grove hadn't been enough for one evening, she would have to face Sir Osbert and Lady Grayson too.

"Shh," she began, but the door to the salon had already sprung open.

"What is happening?" cried her mother, sticking her head out. "Damaris! What on earth are you doing?"

"I . . . I went out for a walk," she stammered.

"Walking? It is dark!" She suspiciously narrowed her eyes. "What about your headache?"

"I . . . er . . . I thought the cool night air might help."

"You've been crying!"

Damaris lowered her gaze.

"Do not lie to me, young lady!" Her mother stood

back from the door and motioned imperiously. "You will come in here and explain yourself!"

"Yes, ma'am." Miserably, she obeyed.

Telling her parents and Missy everything that had happened was not as difficult as she had anticipated. The awful story in minute detail came pouring out, along with a deluge of tears. When she had finished, she collapsed on the sofa, covering her face with her hands.

"Oh, I am so humiliated!" she sobbed. "That must have been his answer to me! When Percy told him I loved him, he determined to show me how he felt. How could Percy have been so wrong?"

"Your reputation is surely destroyed," Missy observed. "That Lady Kelford will tell all who will listen. She is probably laughing about it right now."

"That is why I will not go to the tournament," Damaris declared.

Lady Grayson pressed a glass of sherry into her hand and gave her another handkerchief. "You *must* go to the tournament. You are the Queen!"

"I don't care." Damaris wiped her eyes, blew her nose, and took a gulp of sherry. "I refuse to go."

"I cannot bear it!" her mother wailed.

"Let Missy be the Queen, or, better still, Annabelle. I won't do it."

"But . . ."

"I'm sorry, Mama. I know how much emphasis you have placed on my being the Queen, but surely you can see how mortifying it would be for me."

"No, I can't!" Bursting into tears, Lady Grayson rushed from the room.

"See to your mama, Missy," Sir Osbert requested. "I wish to speak with Damaris alone."

"Yes, Papa." The girl followed more slowly.

"And now, Damaris," he said kindly, "we do have a tangle, haven't we?"

"If you can call it such."

"I must say that I find something strange about the whole situation. It isn't like Richard to do this."

Damaris sighed. "I saw them with my own eyes."

"Things are not always as they seem."

She firmly shook her head. "If you had been present, you would have no doubt. Papa, I must beg you never again to receive Lord Delafield in this house."

"Damaris, he is a neighbor," Sir Osbert reminded.

"He has done me great harm!"

"So it may appear at present, but I am not convinced. If Richard comes to Grayson Hall, we must allow him the opportunity to explain." He smiled grimly. "Of course, we do have his written declaration of regard. I could hold him to it, Damaris, and claim compromise."

"No!" she gasped. "If he does not want me, I would never force him to marry me!"

"I did not think so," he said gently. "You have a great deal more pride than that."

"We must forever shun him," she asserted emphatically.

"Let us table that thought for the moment. I wish to discuss your attendance at the tournament."

"Papa! Surely you cannot expect me to go! Not after what has happened!" she shrilled. "If I were to attend, I would be forced to take my place as Queen! I would be escorted by Richard! It is intolerable!"

"You have given your word to Percy."

"I don't care!"

"Daughter, do you wish to play the part of a liar? Your honor is at stake. *Our* honor," he prompted gently.

"Oh, Papa, do not do this to me," she beseeched. "It would be so very arduous for me!"

"I have never known you to turn away from a challenge."

"This is different!"

He peered at her intently, an arousing glint of defiance in his eyes. "Pride, Damaris. It is a matter of pride."

Pride. Why must he place the matter in that context? Oh, yes, she had her pride. She had an abundance of it. She bravely lifted her chin.

"Very well, Papa," she murmured quietly. "I shall strive to uphold the family honor."

He nodded curtly. "I am proud of you. As always."

"I will attend the tournament," she reiterated, "and I shall reign as Queen, *if* you will agree to deny Richard Delafield the distinction of ever entering this house again."

He cleared his throat. "Done. Won't you please inform your mother of this development?" He smiled wistfully. "Before her tears soak through the floor and rain down upon us all!"

Percy walked sadly down the hall to his chamber. This was all his fault. His little deception had ruined everything. Oh, why had he penned those notes? Because of him, Damaris was hurt to the core, and Dickon was in a hell of a tangle.

He paused at his door. He should go back and confess to his brother. He should get down on his knees and beg his forgiveness. Dickon and Annabelle! It was insupportable!

He gripped the doorknob as if it were a lifeline. He couldn't do it right now. If he told Dickon what he'd done, he would be certain to break down and cry.

Tomorrow. Things might look brighter tomorrow.

In the morning, he would gather together Dickon and their mother and make his confession.

As he opened the door, Gerry Hasbrook came ambling down the hall.

" 'Lo, Percy. They say Lady Kelford's injury isn't bad at all. Ankle's not broken."

"I wish her neck was," Percy snapped. "Yours too, for that matter."

"Mine? What'd I do?"

Percy entered his bedroom and banged the door shut in his best friend's face. Dammit all! Why must he be battered by such misfortune? Tomorrow, his tournament festivities would begin. His elaborate plans would reach fruition. He should be happily looking forward to it. Instead, he was faced with what must be the most horrid tangle in the history of Delafield Hall. Spying his suit of armor, which he'd proudly displayed on a special stand of his own design, he let fly a vicious kick and sent it all clanging to the floor.

"God help us all!" a strange voice yelped from his dressing room.

"Who's there?" Percy cried with alarm.

" 'Tis I." A thin, dark fellow emerged, bowing exquisitely.

"Who are you?" he demanded. "What are you doing in my chamber?"

"I am Godfrey Casey, sir. Lord Delafield has hired me as your new valet. I arrived this evening." His nose twitched. "My employment, of course, must be considered probationary at present."

"That is true," Percy agreed. "My brother would never force me to accept a man of whom I did not approve."

"Indeed so." The nose ascended a notch higher.

"Nor could I accept the position of caring for a man of whom *I* did not approve!"

Percy eyed him suspiciously. "Casey," he mused. "Would you happen to be a relative of Lord Delafield's valet?"

"His brother, sir."

"I might have known." He sighed. "Well, you may begin by helping me prepare for bed."

"I do not know how it will be possible for you to do that, sir," the valet pondered.

Percy glanced at the bed to see if something had happened to it during the last few hours. "Why not?"

"Since my arrival, I have been tidying your clothing. I find dressing robes, but no further nighttime apparel. Therefore, you must wait, sir, until I locate your nightshirts," he proclaimed.

"Oh, that! No problem there! I don't use 'em."

The valet discharged a strangulated gasp. "You don't use them?"

"No." Percy shrugged. "Why attempt to sleep in something that nearly strangles you every time you roll over?"

Casey vigorously shook his head. "I cannot be a party to this. No, sir! It is barbaric!"

"Come now, my man," Percy cajoled. "What harm is there in sleeping in the buff? Besides, tonight we have no choice."

"Oh, yes, we do." The valet's head still jiggled, as if he were possessed of a dreadful palsy. "We shall borrow from His Lordship."

Percy laughed. "My brother probably doesn't wear them either!"

"I am sure he does, sir." He stalked toward the door. "If he did not, *my* brother would not remain in his employ!"

"Well, go on then!" Percy irritably capitulated.

"But if you discover me dead from strangulation, it'll be on your head!"

"So be it! I shall never shrink from properly performing my duty!" The nose climbed to its full, awesome height. "And you, sir, would be well advised to learn that death itself is preferable to indecency!"

With that dire postulate, Godfrey Casey set out on his mission.

Chapter 15

It was early when Richard awoke the next morning, but the chambermaid had already set a low fire burning on the hearth to ward off the inevitable night's chill. He must have slept better than he'd anticipated, for he hadn't even heard her come and go. Dreading the thought of facing the day, he rolled over onto his side and gazed out the window.

The sun had not yet pierced the dawn's thick haze. Gray fog swirled softly at the casement, forming a misty buffer between the castle and the outside world. Delafield Hall seemed to stand in a universe of its own, effectively detached from the human race. Richard wished that were indeed the case, but it couldn't be. Society had penetrated the solid, stone walls, and he must answer to its members.

He flopped onto his back and looked up at the deep blue-velvet bed hangings. It was a grand bed, for a fine lord. It simply reeked of strength, power, and authority. From far back beyond anyone's memory, the Earls of Delafield had slept here. He wondered if their spirits, especially that of his father, were looking down on him with disappointment. What would the previous Lord Delafield advise him to do about this predicament? It was useless to speculate, for in his heart he knew that his sire would always want him to be a gentleman, even if it meant spending the rest of his life in misery.

But maybe it wouldn't be quite as bad as that. He and

Annabelle would have children, and he would treat them as informally as his father had done with himself and Percy. He would allow them to visit his room, and bounce on the bed, and wake him up on holiday mornings. He would teach them to ride and to shoot, to swim and to play in treehouses. They would make up for his shrewish countess.

He glanced toward the connecting door that led through a cozy sitting room to the now empty chamber of the future Lady Delafield. Smiling, he remembered how he and Percy had run back and forth between their parents' rooms, urging them to rise and hurry downstairs for Christmas or birthday gift opening. Annabelle would never permit such unrestrained childish intimacy.

Damaris would. He could picture her, her dark hair streaming across the pillow and starry-eyed children tugging at her arm. But there would have been one major difference between them and his parents. He and Damaris would have been together in one of the beds. Their children would have had no need to run from room to room.

A dull ache settled at the base of his breastbone. That happy scene would never occur. He would honorably wed the selfish, treacherous Annabelle, and Damaris would marry someone else. He fervently hoped that Damaris's husband would hail from the opposite end of England, so that they would live there, and he wouldn't be forced to see them together.

A light scratch at the door disrupted those bleak visions. The door edged open. Percy stuck his head around it.

"Dickon, are you awake?"

"Come in!" he tried to answer cheerfully. He would attempt to keep his own depressed mood from saddening his family. They were despondent enough without witnessing his suffering.

His brother slid around the door and closed it behind him. Percy looked awful. His eyes were darkly rimmed and slightly bloodshot. His hair was tousled as if he had just emerged from bed. He still wore his dressing robe.

"I couldn't wait another minute!" he burst out. "Dickon, this is all my fault!"

"For setting up the tournament?" Richard asked. "I scarcely think so. Though I would heartily like to blame someone, all accountability must rest on my head. I knew Annabelle was trying to trap me, and I let down my guard."

"No," he groaned, and mournfully spilled the story of the notes. "I wouldn't complain if you never wished to clap eyes on me again! I can't very well halt the tournament, but I'll leave as soon as it's over. I'll go to my own estate and never return," he swore.

Richard clenched his teeth. His body trembled with the impulse to leap from bed and throttle Percy, but he valiantly held his temper in check. He *had* let down his guard. It didn't matter that his brother had set up the situation. Percy was innocent of causing the disastrous results.

"I shall also confess to Mama," the young man miserably went on. "I had intended to inform the two of you together, but she sleeps late and . . ." He reached for the doorknob. "I'll remove myself from your sight."

"Hand me my robe." Richard slipped from between the sheets and swung over the edge of the bed, searching for his slippers.

"You don't want to toss me out?" Percy queried, fetching the dark blue brocade garment from across the back of a chair.

"You're my brother," he said, as if that explained it all. He donned the apparel and rang for Casey. "Let us have breakfast *en dishabille* in my sitting room. Most likely, none of our guests are up and about yet, anyway."

"You're certain that the sight of me will not disturb your appetite?"

"Balderdash, Percy!"

Richard entered his dressing room to perform his morning ablutions. Before he finished, his valet arrived with a tray bearing hot tea and a ewer of warm water.

"Good morning, sir."

"Good morning, Casey. Please see that breakfast is brought to the sitting room for me and my brother."

"Yes, sir." He began to assemble towels, cloths, and shaving equipage.

"Do it now, please. I'll dine as I am."

Casey gaped at this impossible man, by birth a gentleman, who intended to begin his day without being properly groomed and attired for it. He had expended such effort on Lord Delafield, and he was beginning to believe that the vexatious earl wasn't worth his marvelous skill. This was the final degradation. He would tender his resignation.

"Thank you, Casey," Richard prompted.

The valet flung down a towel and stalked away, his backbone very stiff and inflexible.

Richard fought the urge to laugh. No doubt his man was thinking of quitting. He would have to raise that already exorbitant salary. Ah well, he could afford it. Casey truly was worth his weight in gold. The *ton*'s emphasis on maintaining a fashionable appearance was just another example of how society held one in bondage. Hell! Had a man no freedom whatsoever?

By the time he had cleansed his face and teeth, and brushed his own hair, the breakfast arrived. He and Percy sat down at a small table in front of the sitting room window, which had been enlarged to accommodate the view. Glancing out, he saw that the sun had burned away the mist. His spirits rose. He plunged into the repast.

"Dickon, I've been thinking . . ."

"Perhaps that's not a wise thing to do, Percy," he quipped, hoping to lighten the grim atmosphere.

"Well, somebody has to!" his brother said determinedly. "You're just going to lie down and take it, without fighting back!"

Richard smiled faintly. "There is nothing else to do."

"Oh, yes, there is! You can refuse to marry Annabelle."

"Cut line, Percy! No matter how much we plot and scheme, I have no other choice. Let us try to look on the brighter side."

"There is none." He angrily jabbed his fork into a slice of ham.

"Certainly there is. For one thing, I'll have children to make up for it."

"That isn't enough. Dammit, Dickon! Tell the woman to go to hell! Inform the *ton* of the truth! Explain that you were going to meet Damaris, and that Annabelle threw herself at you."

"And drag Damaris into this sordid mess?" He firmly shook his head. "I love her too much for that."

"Talk with Damaris about it," Percy insisted. "She loves you, Dickon. She wouldn't be afraid of anything the *ton* might say or do! Answer me honestly. If Damaris was willing to face the scandal, would you agree to do so too?"

"Of course," he readily agreed. "Social life in London holds no fascination for me. As a matter of fact, I wouldn't care if I never saw another Season! But I have to think of what is best for Damaris."

"Once again, you are being arrogant and domineering," his brother warned. "You and Damaris are equals in this love. Shouldn't she be allowed an opinion in a matter which will affect both of your lives?"

Richard's heart gave a mad leap. If Damaris didn't care that he was the butt of censure ... But there were others involved, his family and hers.

"Mama and I would prefer complete exile to having Annabelle as your wife," Percy answered the unasked question.

"I wonder about the Graysons," he mused.

"Take the chance, Dickon. All you can do is try! You have nothing to lose. And you owe it to Damaris."

"All right," he decided. "I'll talk with her. If she'll see me! I doubt that she is in perfect charity with me, just now."

"She'll see you," Percy said smugly. "She'll have to. She's the Queen of the tournament."

"After what has happened, she may refuse to attend."

"Not Damaris! I've never known her to shrink from a challenge!" Percy laughed. "She will be present, and she'll marry you too, Dickon. Scandal or no scandal!"

He took a deep breath. "It's asking a lot of her."

"She is perfectly capable of handling this and much more!"

"Very well." Richard nodded. "I'll ride to Grayson Park this morning. If she declines to see me, I'll visit her father. I may be able to drop some hints in his direction. I've certainly done that many times in the past! Then I'll capture her attention at the tournament festivities. With Annabelle's injury, I shouldn't have to be concerned with her interference."

"You see?" Percy smiled with satisfaction. "Everything is working out. Now if only Missy would come to her senses!"

"You aren't going to lie down and take it without fighting for her, are you?" Richard paraphrased his brother's earlier attack.

"Oh, I'll fight," Percy said with deadly assurance. "I'll fight! Just you wait and see."

Damaris glanced out her window in time to see Richard Delafield depart the mansion. Tears sprang to her eyes. How dare he come here after what he had done! Angrily, she bit her lip. She hadn't been wrong. She had known that he would come here just to complete his mission of mortifying her beyond all belief. Thank God she had devised that bargain with her father. Refusing Richard entrance would keep him away from Grayson Park. Ignoring him at the tournament would rid her of him once and for all. It wouldn't be easy, but she could do it. Soon the whole, grievous business would be ended, and she could hide away to lick her wounds in privacy.

She watched him mount his horse. He didn't sit proudly as he usually did. There was an element of dejection in the carriage of his shoulders. With his great respect for Sir Osbert, he was probably rather cast down at the man's refusal to see him. Well, that was just too bad! Richard would learn that the Grayson family stuck together.

Damaris turned away from the window. He was gone and wouldn't be back that day. Of course, she would have to face him tonight at the banquet, but in the meantime, she had estate affairs to accomplish. She paused, unable to keep from looking back over her shoulder at Richard's retreating back. It was her downfall. Bursting into tears, she threw herself onto the bed and buried her head in the pillow.

When Delafield Hall had been a true castle, the Great Hall had taken up most of the ground floor. Over the years, the plan had been modified, with numerous rooms carved out from the original massive one. The only remaining reminder of that vast hub of medieval life was one huge space that the earls had always used as a ballroom. Located just off the entrance hall, it had been the scene of many rainy-day activities for Marston and Grayson children. The permissive Lady Delafield hadn't cared if they scuffed the floor or scratched the little gilt chairs that lined the walls.

Despite her reluctance to attend Percy's medieval banquet, Damaris was anxious to see what her old friend had done with the hall. Percy had kept his remodeling a secret, allowing only his mama, Uncle Vincent, and his workmen to enter. The doors were kept locked at all times. Not even a servant could gain admittance.

Damaris's heart pounded as the Grayson coach rolled to a stop in front of Delafield Hall. It was time to begin her performance, not only as Queen, but as a proud young woman who was strong enough to overcome the most shattering of mortifications. Smoothing the rich, ice-blue fabric of her gown, she slowly took three deep, consoling breaths and glanced at her father. Sir Osbert returned a firm nod of encouragement. Damaris lifted her chin.

Lady Grayson and Missy entered the castle first, followed by Damaris and her father in his Bath chair, wheeled along by a footman. With relief, she saw that the receiving line was rather lengthy. In that press, there would be no time at all to chat with hostess or hosts.

They passed through quickly, but even the brief touch of Richard's hand was enough to send sparks racing up and down her spine. Damaris took care to avoid meeting his eyes. Hurriedly, she murmured a greeting and fled.

It was easy to evade Richard in the milling crush of guests as they waited for dinner to be called. While Lady Grayson greeted friends and Missy flirted with Lord Hasbrook and her other beaux, Damaris stood by Sir Osbert, who was receiving a deluge of congratulations on his first public outing since the stroke. Unfortunately, however, Lady Kelford sat nearby, and it was inevitable that she enter the conversation.

"Here we are, two cripples!" the marchioness observed cheerfully. "Nonetheless, I am certain that we shall enjoy the events."

Cripples? Damaris stared at the beautiful woman. In her exquisite gown of mahogany velvet, shot through with gold thread, Annabelle surely gave no appearance of defect.

The widow took note of her curiosity and waved her slim hand toward the cane at her side. "Richard and I were walking through the woods, in the dark. I fell and hurt my ankle. Goodness! It happened so quickly that he was unable to catch me. The poor man was absolutely overset."

"It must have been most frightening," Damaris murmured politely.

"Indeed." Her eyes glittered with a brittle gleam. "But Richard was quite comforting."

"I hope that you have a speedy recovery, my lady," Sir Osbert said kindly.

"Oh, I am already much improved," she said airily.

"Unlike you, sir, I shall not remain a cripple all my life. How demoralizing! It is not surprising that people confined to chairs soon wither up and die."

Damaris bristled. An attack on herself was one thing. For Annabelle to flex her claws at Sir Osbert was quite another.

"Lady Kelford," she said, ice dripping from her voice. "I must oblige you to refrain from speaking on matters of which you know nothing. It is distasteful to my father, aside from being a most repulsive habit in general."

"You would *oblige* me?" Her nose rose a trifle higher, then she laughed frigidly. "Ah yes, you are the Queen. I suppose that we must play Percy's game and allow you to reign over us. Such a strange choice you are, Miss Grayson. One would think that Percy would have chosen a lady of some rank and beauty."

Damaris felt a flush rise to her cheeks. Try as she might, she could think of no scathing riposte. She was saved from the situation by the announcement of dinner.

As Queen, she should have been escorted to the Great Hall by the earl. But when Richard approached, he was captured by Annabelle, who helplessly seized his arm and begged him to assist her. In the ensuing confusion, Damaris entered without the support of a male arm, quietly walking beside her father's chair and being seated by Sir Osbert's footman after he had settled his master.

"I must apologize," Richard said unhappily as he sat down beside her at the center of the dais. "Lady Kelford . . ."

"You need not explain your preference to me. I am sufficiently aware of it," she murmured glacially and deliberately turned to Percy, who was seated on her other side. "What you have done here is marvelous."

The hall had been stripped of its plaster, revealing the sculpted stone walls underneath. Medieval weapons of war hung in place, relieving the austere gray. Behind the dais was a large, elaborate tapestry, intricately depicting a tournament scene from the Middle Ages.

"That is beautiful, Percy," Damaris admired, nodding toward the stitchery work of art.

"I am terribly proud of it." He beamed. "Mama gave it to me for Christmas. It is original . . . not a reproduction."

"I'm impressed." She continued her visual exploration of the hall.

The smooth ballroom flooring had been removed to expose the ancient stone flags, which Percy had covered with rushes. Trestle dining tables and benches extended in fingers from the dais. There were musicians in the gallery, playing a tinkling tune on lute, harp, and vièle. The guests themselves in their curious medieval attire rounded out the fantasy. Damaris smiled at her trencher made of hardened bread.

"I am more than impressed," she amended. "I am astonished. I feel as if I have stepped back in time."

"That is the greatest compliment anyone could ever give me." Percy glowed with pride. "Do you see those gentlemen over there? I hope they will be as approving as you are."

She followed his gaze, spying several darkly clad men unaccompanied by ladies.

"They are among the foremost scholars of medieval England. If my efforts pass their inspection, it will mean a great deal to my career."

"I shall hope for the very best!"

"Thank you. Damaris?" He lowered his voice. "You must speak with Dickon. He has a matter to discuss with you."

She straightened her shoulders. "I have nothing to discuss with him. Later I shall tell you why."

"I *know* why, but it isn't as you perceive. I will involve myself no further in this, except to tell you that you must let Dickon have his say."

"No," she said flatly, and stared fixedly ahead as footmen and maids clad in authentic apparel brought forth great platters of food and pitchers of wine.

The meal proceeded with scarcely a flaw. Some of the food was rather odd and some altogether too spicy for the modern palate, but there were so many selections that even the least adventuresome diner could sate his or her hunger. Wine flowed with reckless abandon, and many a toast was offered. The medieval banquet was a magnificent success. Damaris couldn't have been happier for her old friend.

"Now we must have dancing," Percy announced when the tables were cleared. "Dickon and Damaris must commence it."

"No, thank you," she demurred. "I have no knowledge of medieval dance."

"Didn't Missy teach you?" Percy asked.

"No. I had no idea that she knew."

"I taught her long ago." An expression of calculation crossed his brow.

"Come, Damaris." Richard took her hand. "We shall make something up."

"No!" She jerked away from him. "I do not wish to dance!"

Percy grinned connivingly. "We shall depart from tradition. Dickon, do you mind my taking your place, while you merely sit here with Damaris?"

"Of course not."

"Excellent!" Percy stood up from the table and left the dais, strolling to the trestle where Missy sat with Lord Hasbrook. He bowed elegantly.

Damaris smiled as she saw her sister gigglingly accept Percy's hand and walk with him to the center of the room.

"Sirs!" Percy shouted to the gallery. "Your dancing measure!"

Damaris's heart swelled with pride as she watched Missy gracefully perform the elegant movements. Furthermore, the girl seemed as though she was delighted with her partner. She tilted her head and smiled up at him, completely ignoring Lord Hasbrook, who had markedly stood up to better see the proceedings. Percy too was enchanted, gazing devotedly at her and guiding her with gentle charm. At the end, everyone, including the scholars, applauded.

"They were marvelous!" Damaris cried to Richard, forgetting her vow to ignore him.

"Yes, they were," he agreed, once again taking her hand. "Damaris, I . . ."

"I have nothing to say to you, my lord," she adamantly informed him, snatching it away. "Please direct your advances toward those who would be receptive of them."

"You must allow me to explain," he begged.

"I *must* do nothing of the sort!" Damaris snapped and turned her shoulder toward him, remaining silent and aloof for the rest of the interminable evening.

Chapter 16

Once more, Richard bore the strain of Casey's disapproval by taking breakfast in his sitting room and wearing his dressing robe. Beginning the day in the privacy of his rooms was worth the looks of thinly veiled contempt that his valet aimed at him. He intended to continue the practice until the guests were gone.

Munching on a bite of toast, he gazed out the window, surveying the tournament grounds in the meadow. Enterprising villagers were present already, setting up their stalls for the fair that would accompany the event. Colorful pennants were flying from the stands and from the knights' tents. Men were performing last-minute preparations to the field itself. The whole occasion was going to be quite a spectacle.

To the *ton*, the tournament might provide an intriguing novelty, but for the local economy, it offered a greatly profitable opportunity. Inns were packed and jammed for miles around. Every farmer and townsman who had a spare room rented it out at a vastly inflated rate. The county was overflowing with outsiders. Richard wondered if things would ever be normal again.

"Good morning, brother." Carrying a cup of tea and also clad in a robe, Percy dropped into a chair opposite him. "What do you think of all this?"

"Quite impressive," he allowed.

"Yes, it makes a splendid scene."

"Actually, I was referring to your power of organization." Richard shook his head. "Gad, Percy, I am astonished at what you've accomplished!"

"Oh, it's been months in the planning, and many people helped," he said modestly.

"Still, I can't keep from admiring you. This event will be remembered for decades." He picked up the teapot and refreshed his and his brother's brew. "Have you had breakfast? Shall I send for another plate?"

"Tell you the truth, Dickon, I'm rather too nervous to eat." He selected a piece of buttered toast. "This will be enough for me."

"I'll admit that I'm a bit anxious too," Richard confessed, "but not for the same reason. I had no luck whatsoever with Damaris last night."

"Don't worry so! You'll have all day with her. This evening too! She'll come around."

"I hope you're right."

"Of course I am! But just in case I am not, you should plan ahead. By nightfall, if she hasn't accepted your proposal, carry her off to the woods and compromise her. That sort of thing seems to work for you, Dickon."

Richard laughed. "Fine joke, Percy!"

His brother helped himself to a second piece of toast. "Truthfully, I was not jesting," he said in all seriousness.

"I can scarcely believe this! Have you anything but pulp between your ears?"

"Look at it this way." Intently, he leaned forward. "People should surmise that compromising Annabelle is rather questionable. She *is* a widow, so it isn't as if she had lost that priceless virtue. Furthermore, everyone knows that she has unmercifully pursued you, and that she has been shamelessly forward."

"So?"

"So if you compromised Damaris, the *ton* would look upon it quite differently!"

"As would her father," Richard said sardonically. "He'd probably shoot me."

"Well, you wouldn't actually have to . . . uh . . . *do* it. Just pretend that you did!" Percy picked up a rasher of crisp bacon and chewed thoughtfully. "If the two of you disappeared into the darkness for a suitable interval and returned with mussed hair and a button or two undone, people would draw their own conclusions. Damaris would have no choice but to marry you."

"This is too ridiculous for words!"

"No, it isn't. It would work," he insisted.

"Percy, be serious! I will not compromise Damaris!" he firmly declared. "She would despise me! And think of what it would do to my reputation!"

"Hell, Dickon, after all the didoes you've cut with Annabelle, it would probably be expected of you."

"Thank you for the compliment," Richard said dryly.

"Dammit it all, anyway! Here we are, two young, handsome, wealthy gentlemen. You even have a title. And we are having more trouble with ladies than anyone could ever imagine! I just don't understand it." Percy dragged the bowl of scrambled eggs toward him and began to eat them with the serving spoon.

Richard grimly watched his breakfast begin to disappear down his brother's throat. "Casey?" he called.

The valet appeared, took one look at Percy, and leaned, horrified, against the door frame.

"Please send for more food," Richard requested.

Casey was unable to do more than nod his head. His breath coming in small, short gasps, he quickly departed.

"More food?" asked Percy between mouthfuls. "Don't you ever worry about becoming fat?"

"It's the farthest thing from my mind." He sighed.

"You should give it some thought," his brother advised. "And another thing we should ponder is this situation with our valets. Mine acts as though he is finer than I am! I can't imagine why."

"Why, indeed?" Richard raised a sarcastic eyebrow. "Your manners and dress are perfect."

"If you're referring to those nightshirts, I'll have you know that I take off that garment of torture as soon as he leaves at night, and put it on before he arrives in the morning. It isn't always easy," Percy grumbled. "He almost caught me today."

"How troubling."

"Well, it is! Our valets are bullies! We shouldn't be forced to put up with it." Percy helped himself to three slices of bacon. "Are you going to eat that steak and kidney pie, Dickon?"

"No." Richard changed the subject. "It seemed as if you received a much warmer reception from Missy last night."

"Briefly, I did. She rather enjoyed being the center of attention during that dance, didn't she? But then she turned right back to Hasbrook! Perhaps I should compromise *her*." An unholy light dawned in his eyes. "Yes! I could . . ."

"Enough!" the earl ordered. "Neither of us will compromise any lady! That would bring about a far worse disaster than we face right now. You, Percy, should have your thoughts concentrated on your performance in the tournament."

"You're right, Dickon." He squared his shoulders. "I've a lot to accomplish today. I am going to knock Gerry Hasbrook from his horse and pound him into the dirt! Then we'll see which knight the fair lady prefers!"

"Yes," his brother said with amusement. "I'm sure that you will be a truly magnificent hero!"

Damaris dreaded this day much more than she had the previous evening's banquet. She must spend a large part of the morning and all of the afternoon with Richard, followed by the ball in the evening. At least the evening's festivities would not be as demanding as the day's. The ball, to be held on the lawn of Delafield, was open to everyone from the loftiest peer to the lowliest tenant. There would be such a great throng present that it would be easy to avoid Richard by becoming separated in the crush. Also, she could probably depend on Annabelle to ensnare him in her clutches.

"I hate Lady Kelford," Missy announced suddenly as they halted in front of the castle.

Damaris did not reply, waiting instead for the inevitable chiding Sir Osbert or Lady Grayson would levy upon their younger daughter. She was surprised when neither of them uttered a word.

"I abhor the way she has behaved toward Damaris," her sister continued loyally.

"She was rude to me as well," Sir Osbert pointed out.

Lady Grayson pursed her lips. "She behaves like a hussy."

"I cannot fathom Richard choosing her as his wife," the baronet marveled. "That is why there is something strange about that scene you witnessed in the grove, Damaris."

"I saw what I saw," she said quietly.

"Yes, but . . ."

"He chose the woman before," her mother interjected. "Annabelle Kelford is quite beautiful. It is not unusual for men to be blinded by such. He will discover his error eventually, but by then, of course, it will be too late."

"I just don't know . . ." Sir Osbert trailed off.

As they alighted from the carriage to join the crowd of guests outside Delafield Hall, Missy quickly drew Damaris aside.

"I am going to do something to spike the Kelfords' guns," she whispered. "Since my beaux will be participating in the tournament, I shall be unoccupied much of the time. I will divert Annabelle's pursuit of Richard, allowing you free rein to move in for the kill. Make good use of your time, Damaris. Oust her from his heart!"

"I will not . . ." Damaris began, but Missy had hurried away toward a group of young people who were waiting to parade to the tournament grounds.

She gazed unhappily after her sister. Missy's spontaneous loyalty was welcome. Her machinations were not. Moreover, she couldn't seem to get it through her head that Damaris was no longer interested in capturing Richard's heart. Had she no pride?

Damaris sighed. Perhaps she could find an opportunity to take the girl aside and warn her not to interfere, but she hesitated to do so. It would anger Missy and set back their current tenuous relationship.

A hand touched her elbow. "Damaris?"

She turned to look up into the handsome blue eyes of Richard Delafield. "How do you do, my lord?" she greeted him stiltedly.

"Not well, actually. This garb is as uncomfortable as it is absurd."

She flicked a glance over his attire and stifled a giggle. No wonder the earl was ill at ease. His hosiery was so scandalously tight that it must surely inhibit his circulation. Goodness, how it defined every muscle! She felt a flush warm her cheeks.

"Have you no pity for me?" He grinned devilishly.

"Certainly not! Your choice of costume is your own concern, my lord." She began to edge away.

"Damaris?" He caught her hand.

"I must see to my father."

"Your father is well tended. You see?" He nodded pointedly. "He is joining the march to the tournament field."

Damaris looked in the direction indicated. Sir Osbert was seated in a gaily embellished gig. Beside him was a pouting Annabelle Kelford.

"Oh, he will like *that*," she said sarcastically.

"The decoration?"

"His companion," she muttered. "She was terribly rude to him last night."

"I'm sorry. I had no idea . . ."

She jerked her hand away. "Lord Delafield, you would be well advised to keep Lady Kelford away from my family, and from me. We have no love for her." Glimpsing her mother, she stalked toward her.

"Damaris!"

Once more, he caught her arm. Once more, she pulled away. She glared at him.

"Please confine your attentions to those who desire them!" she snapped.

"It is time for us to lead the parade to the tournament grounds," he lamely informed her. "Please, Damaris, won't you be cooperative? For Percy's sake, if not for mine?"

"Very well." She regally lifted her chin and laid her hand on his arm, boldly staring into his eyes. "I shall do it for Percy's sake. For Percy's sake alone!"

Damaris sat in the position of honor in the centrally located stand and watched the procession of knights. It was unquestionably an imposing sight to behold. The horses, covered in richly adorned caparisons, pranced and tossed their heads, their bits jingling merrily. The bright sun glinting from their armor, Percy and his knights rode proudly around the arena to the wild applause of the bulging stands. Even if she was forced to bear Richard's company, Damaris was instantly glad that she had come. There would never be anything like this again.

She glanced back over her shoulder to see if Missy was as appreciative as she was. Her sister was sitting triumphantly, far to the rear, amid a group of elderly ladies. Beside her was the beautiful Lady Kelford, who was looking positively thunderous. Damaris wondered how Missy had maneuvered the widow into such a dreary location. Giggling inwardly, she returned her attention to the parade.

"Percy must be terribly pleased," she murmured excitedly, forgetting her vow to ignore His Lordship as much as possible.

"I would never have thought him capable of such a monumental task," he agreed. "I hope everything goes well, and no one is injured."

Damaris shivered. "I wasn't thinking of that, but you're right; this could be awfully dangerous."

"The weapons are designed to break easily. Let us hope that they do."

"Oh yes," she breathed, watching Richard's uncle line up against the young Earl of Winton for a joust. "Isn't Uncle Vincent a bit old for this?"

"Tell *him* that!"

The earl, mounted on a tall, restive thoroughbred, dashed forward, while Uncle Vincent proceeded more slowly, his ancient steed gasping along at a sluggish canter. The crowd laughed.

"Poor Uncle Vincent." Richard chuckled.

Due to the rate of speed, the young man met the elder well beyond the halfway mark. Metal clanged. Lord Winton toppled backward and fell to the ground. There was a sudden moment of shocked silence, then the audience broke forth with cheers and applause. The earl clambered to his feet and stared bewilderedly after the old gentleman as he rode forward to make a grand salute.

"I wonder how Winton likes being bested by an oldster?" Richard remarked. "He strikes me as being rather toplofty."

"I don't think he is very happy about it." Damaris watched the dejected young peer lead his horse away. "Perhaps he will comfort himself in knowing that Uncle Vincent has had years of practice."

"Yes." He paused, drawing an audible breath. "Damaris, I wish to explain . . ."

She stiffened, as the vision of Annabelle in his arms jarred through her mind.

"The other night," he began again, "I had no intention of—"

"It is not necessary to make explanation to me," Damaris interrupted heatedly. "In a sense, you have already done so. Please cease afflicting me with it."

"Dammit! Why won't you give me the chance to tell you what happened?"

"Lower your voice, my lord," she directed. "People are looking."

The threat of becoming a spectacle certainly had the power to hush him. Richard pressed his lips together, but the muscle quivering along his jaw betrayed his irritation. The Earl of Delafield was ready to explode.

The crowd roared, drawing Damaris's attention to the jousting. Two knights had just made their run at each other and missed their marks entirely. The vigor of their attempts had forced them off balance. Both fell to the dusty sand. Unlike Lord Winton, however, they got up laughing, waved to the audience, and clapped each other on the shoulder. Damaris smiled.

"This is pure stupidity," Richard muttered.

She ignored him.

"Let us take a walk," he suggested.

"No. I am performing my queenly duties. Besides, it is Percy's turn," she noted, seeing his brother line up against Lord Hasbrook.

Even from the distance, she could detect her friend's intensity by the tautness with which he sat his horse and the rigidity of his hold on the lance. The thoroughbred, champing the bit and half rearing, sensed it too. Percy smacked down the visor on his helmet with a fierce and audible clink.

Butterflies fluttered in Damaris's stomach. Percy was *too* impassioned. He was obviously determined to unseat his opponent. He might even mean to hurt him. Unconsciously, she laid her hand on the earl's arm.

"Richard, Percy is . . ."

The two knights flew at each other. As they neared the stand, Gerry Hasbrook's horse faltered. Throwing up its head, it stared with shock at the oncoming horse and rider, halted, and tried to spin around. Lord Hasbrook grimly held it and kicked its sides, but the gelding would not move forward. Knees and hocks trembling, it lay down while the triumphant

Percy galloped past, shouting a huzzah of victory. The onlookers erupted with laughter and catcalls.

"Thank God." Damaris exhaled her pent-up breath.

Richard clasped her hand. "I think I'll have a word with Percy. He's a bit too resolute in proving himself to your sister."

"Yes." Startled, she wished she could draw her hand away, but all resistance seemed to have left her.

"I shall return in a moment." With a final squeeze, he got up and left the stand.

Damaris glanced back at Missy. The girl was frowning severely, her gaze centered on the hapless Lord Hasbrook as he tried to get his horse back on its feet. Could Percy's success have had an effect on her sentiments? It was possible, even though his achievement had been one of default. Lately, one never knew about Missy's feelings.

Several more jousters had competed and an intermission had been called before Richard returned to the stand.

"Did you speak with him?" Damaris asked anxiously.

"Yes, but I don't know how much attention he paid. He was celebrating." Without hesitation, he took her hand. "Let's get something to eat."

"Very well." Agreeably, she rose. Dreading the tournament, she'd had little appetite for breakfast that morning, and now she was hungry. A meal, even though she must share it with Richard, was a welcome respite.

"There is a cold buffet at the castle, or we can get something at the fair."

"Oh, let us go to the fair! Do you mind?"

"Not at all." He settled her hand in the crook of his elbow and guided her toward the steps.

"Richard!" Annabelle hailed.

He continued on without a backward glance.

"Richard!" the widow repeated stridently.

Damaris tugged on his arm. "Lady Kelford is calling you."

"So?"

She curiously looked up at him. Richard hadn't changed his expression. Plainly he was pretending he hadn't heard the summons.

Damaris shrugged lightly. They must have had a lovers' quarrel. She snickered. How delightful that was! Annabelle must be furious! Richard was behaving indifferently toward her, and she couldn't chase after him because of her injured ankle. Damaris couldn't help giving his arm a small hug, just to irritate the woman further. She hoped Missy noticed the gesture. Her sister would love it!

Richard glanced down with surprise. He raised a questioning eyebrow. Damaris favored him with a brilliant smile.

"Do let us hurry, my lord. I am starving!"

"Then we must remedy the situation immediately." He drew her into the crowd.

With everyone striving to greet the earl, it took them quite a while to move through the crowd to a food stall, where Richard bought two meat pies and pints of ale.

"Let's get away from here." Without waiting for a reply, he led her to a shade tree some distance apart. While she held the food, he spread out his cape. After assisting her to the ground, he dropped down beside her.

"Damaris, we must talk," he said firmly.

"Oh, please do not bring up the subject again," she begged.

"I thought you seemed more receptive."

"No!" she snapped. "And if you persist in this, I shall get up and leave!"

"But you do not understand."

She started to get to her feet.

"All right," he said quickly. "You shall pick our topic of conversation."

Damaris bit into the spicy meat pie. "Um, this is delicious. Food always tastes better outside, doesn't it?"

He nodded. "Would you like to go on a picnic sometime?"

"No," she murmured.

What was he trying to do? Hurt her even more? What if she had said yes? Would he then have named possible guests, with Annabelle at the top of the list?

They finished the meal in awkward silence, then returned to the fair, browsing along the stalls. Damaris paused at a jewelry display. The merchandise was cheap, but one of the pieces, a tiny heart-shaped locket, was rather attractive. She picked it up.

"Permit me to buy it for you," Richard said.

"I couldn't. It wouldn't be proper." Reluctantly, she laid it down, wishing she had brought some money with her.

"Nonsense. It's only a trifle. You should have a remembrance of Percy's tournament."

And of you, she thought, her breast aching.

"I insist. This time you won't talk me out of it."

Before she could demur, he fastened the locket around her neck and paid the merchant.

"Thank you," she whispered, lowering her eyes to hide sudden, brimming tears.

"I wish it were gold."

Damaris shook her head. "I like it just as it is. You should buy something for yourself."

"No," he said quietly, "I don't know that I want to remember."

She bit her lip. His tiff with Annabelle must be very bad indeed, but didn't he realize that all would go well for him? The grasping widow would never let him go.

"We'd best go back," she told him, taking his arm. "I believe that the tournament is beginning again."

Chapter 17

Following intermission, the jousting continued. With their initial jitters eased by the experience of their first attempts, Percy's knights and their steeds improved their performances. Richard had to admit that several of the combatants executed the maneuvers quite well. He was thankful that his brother was among those who were successful.

He hadn't truly realized the depth of Percy's determination to be a champion jouster or, to be more specific, to degrade Gerry Hasbrook. Against his second opponent, Percy had been resolute, but he hadn't seemed nearly so impassioned. Richard doubted that Percy's attitude had changed merely because he had warned him against being so bloodthirsty. His brother exhibited more composure for the simple reason that he wasn't up against the viscount. Percy must believe that he could reclaim Missy's heart by humiliating Lord Hasbrook. Looking back, Richard could plainly remember the many hints to that effect. He just hadn't recognized the seriousness of those seemingly offhand comments.

All of it was perfectly ridiculous. If Damaris's sister was so featherbrained as to be influenced by feats of brawn and not by what was inside a man, she wasn't worth the winning. He was barely acquainted with the grown-up Missy, but she did seem rather shallow. Of course, she was very young, and therefore, impressionable. As she grew older, her incon-

221

sistency could change. Still, it was no wonder that she had captured Percy's heart. She was extremely pretty, though her youthful comeliness couldn't compare to the mature beauty of her elder sister.

He glanced surreptitiously at his companion. Damaris was absolutely breathtaking today. She wore a deep blue dress trimmed with gold, a costly looking costume that must have put a huge hole in the Grayson household account. He smiled, thinking of how much she had probably protested the expenditure, but he was shamefully pleased that Lady Grayson had won the skirmish. He was proud to be Damaris's escort, and the fine harvest the estate would achieve this fall would stand the bill.

Suddenly heavyhearted, he looked away. He was her escort now, and that was all he'd ever be, the Queen's escort at the Delafield Tournament. Damaris was not going to allow him to explain about the incident in the grove, let alone to make a marriage proposal. Her anger, or defensiveness, or whatever had caused this attitude, was just too strong. He wished he could accept the facts and give up gracefully, but he couldn't. Tonight, he must try again.

He caught her covertly studying him and grinned. She smiled faintly, but there was melancholy in her eyes. Dammit! If she weren't so stubborn, he could replace that sadness with sparkle!

"Would you like a glass of sherry?" he asked to cover the awkward moment.

"Yes, thank you," she consented.

He motioned to a costumed footman and gave the order.

The man knelt down to whisper. "Sir, it may be a moment. We've had to send to the castle for more wine."

Richard frowned. "Only the guests in this stand are to have this refreshment."

"Yes, m'lord, we know. Sir, them guests're drinkin' like fish."

Damaris tittered.

"Very well. Serve us when you can," he told the servant and turned to Damaris. "All I need is an entire house party of drunken *tonnish* guests."

"Oh, my lord, surely only the gentlemen!" she chortled.

A high-pitched, giddy, feminine laugh echoed from behind them.

"No," Richard stated irritably, "I am not so sure."

"Take courage." She giggled. "The tournament itself is almost over. You see? They are lining up for the melee. Your tipsy lady guests will soon return to the Hall, take naps, and be in fine fettle for the evening events."

The dizzy laughter rang out again. Richard turned around and groaned. The mirthful commotion had come from Annabelle. The marchioness had imbibed too freely and was in a high state of merriment. Seeing him looking at her, she lifted her glass in a mock toast and drained it, tossing it back over her shoulder. Missy, still seated next to her, frowned with disgust and moved her chair as far away as possible.

Damaris snickered. "Perhaps you should take control of your fiancée, my lord."

"She is *not* my fiancée!" he stormed.

"What?"

"She is . . ."

A roar from the crowd cut off his words. The melee, that free-for-all combat between all the knights at once, had begun. Percy had singled out Lord Hasbrook and now dealt him a mighty blow with the flat of his broadsword.

Damaris clutched his arm. "The weapons are supposed to break!"

Richard held his breath as Hasbrook returned the chop in kind.

"Do something!" she cried. "They're going to murder each other!"

"What the hell can I do?" he shouted over the din of the battle, moving to the edge of his chair and staring helplessly at the mass of milling horses and flashing steel.

Percy landed a hard wallop to Gerry Hasbrook's chest, upsetting the young man's balance, but the viscount righted himself and pressed on. He whacked Percy on the side of the head. Percy slid precariously to the right, and Hasbrook followed through with a smash to his side. Percy crashed to the ground and lay still.

"Percy!" Missy shrieked. "My darling!" Before anyone could stop her, she jumped up and dashed from the stand. Ducking through the barrier, she ran out onto the field.

"Richard!" Damaris screamed. "She'll be killed!"

"I'll get her!" He was already on his feet. Rushing after the girl, he leaped the railing and plunged into the melee.

Too frightened to weep, Damaris said a swift prayer and watched with horror as those two people she loved darted in and out among the horses' flying hooves and pivoting rumps, and the knights' swinging swords. They were going to die. At the very least, they would be terribly injured. The weapons weren't breaking as they should, and the men were too caught up in their game of war to take notice of the very real trouble in their midst. And there was nothing she could do about it.

Wildly she looked toward her parents, seated at the far end of the pavilion. Her mother had her head in her lap, her hands shielding her face. Her father, his complexion gray with fear, clutched the arms of his Bath chair and looked on in terror. Hastily, Damaris stood up and went to them.

"Richard will save her. I know he will!" she soothed.

"Oh, my baby, my baby!" Lady Grayson wailed. "She will be nothing but a bloody corpse when this day is done!"

"No, Mama, no!" Damaris clasped her quaking shoulders. "Richard will save her!"

Weeping copiously, Lady Delafield materialized beside them and slipped her arm through Lady Grayson's. The two mothers joined hands. Slowly, they rocked from side to side, moaning their children's names.

Damaris enveloped them both in her embrace and hazarded a look into the arena. Lord Hasbrook had perceived the danger. He tried to pick Missy up, but she batted him away. At that moment, Richard caught her around the waist and tried to toss her up onto the viscount's horse.

"Now it will be all right!" Damaris cried. "Missy, do as he says!"

But Missy turned on Richard, striking out in frenzy. Savagely, she struggled toward Percy's inert form while Lord Hasbrook bellowed and waved in an attempt to attract the attention of his fellow knights. The battle began to ebb.

"I think," Sir Osbert exclaimed hoarsely, "that they will survive!"

Missy wriggled out of Richard's arms and threw herself across the fallen hero. Knights circled the trio, protecting them from those of their number who were not yet aware of the disaster. Lord Hasbrook's horse, knees and hocks trembling, sank to the ground, blocking one side with its body and pinning the viscount's legs beneath it. The combat ceased.

Richard removed his brother's helm. Percy groggily shook his head and sat up. He gathered Missy into his arms.

"Look!" Damaris shouted to the two mothers. "All is well!"

"My child!" both shrilled simultaneously. Bounding to their feet, they ran from the stand and onto the field.

Sir Osbert sagged down in his chair. "Go after those fool women, Damaris," he gasped.

"Papa! Are you all right?" she asked, fearful that the stress had brought on another attack.

"I am fine," he grunted, "though I would be much better if I were not surrounded by peahens! Footman fetch my carriage! Damaris! See to your mama and sister!"

"Yes, sir." She hurried to the arena.

The crowd seemed to take the ladies' dash to the field as an invitation to join in the excitement. They surged from the stands, knocking down the barrier and jostling each other in an attempt to be the first on the scene. Damaris pushed through them, reaching Lord Hasbrook.

"Won't someone help me?" he begged woefully.

Damaris bit back a smile. She took the steed's rein and began to tug.

"Damned horse!" the viscount swore, smacking the animal's rump with the flat of his broadsword. "I'll send him to the knacker's!"

"There now," she placated, "you won't do that. He is much too fine."

"Just watch me! I am not in charity with anyone o

anything at this moment, Miss Grayson!" He glanced back over his shoulder as Missy unabashedly kissed Percy on the lips. "I have lost my self-esteem, and I have lost my lady!"

"Missy always belonged to Percy, my lord," she gently explained. "They have had an understanding for quite some time. Just recently, they had a quarrel, but everyone knew it would be short-lived."

"Well, I wish someone had told me that! No wonder that sapskull friend of mine has been in such high dudgeon! Gad, but I owe him an apology!"

Damaris sighed, gesturing to several burly men in the crowd. While she jerked the reins, they grabbed the animal's legs and tail and began to pull.

"Ouch!" cried Lord Hasbrook. "My leg is under there!"

"I hope it is not broken." She knelt beside him as he was freed.

"How could it be, encased as it is in this garb?" He grinned suddenly. "You know, Miss Grayson, you are rather pretty. Would you like to—"

"Thank you, my lord, but I am not interested." She helped him to his feet. "I daresay, however, that there are many young ladies here today who consider you a hero."

"D'you think so?"

She nodded gravely. "You have rescued Percy, Missy, and the Earl of Delafield."

"Well then ..." Proudly straightening his shoulders, he limped toward the stand.

Damaris smiled after him, then turned her attention to her mother and sister. "Papa is exhausted. He wishes to leave immediately and is having the carriage brought."

Percy looked longingly at Missy. "I shall see you tonight. I shall see Sir Osbert too. I have a very important question to ask him if ... if you are agreeable. Will you marry me, Missy?"

"Oh yes," whispered Missy. "Oh yes, I will!"

"Isn't it grand?" Lady Grayson beamed proudly as they walked across the arena. "Percy and Missy! They shall be wed! Ah, what a perfect result!"

"Yes, it is wonderful," Damaris concurred, glancing around for Richard. She must thank him for his part in rescuing her sister, and ... she was going to be very bold and ask him what he'd meant when he said that Lady Kelford was not his fiancée. She spotted him on the fringe of the crowd.

"Mama? Missy? Please join Papa. I shall be along in a moment." She hurried toward Richard.

As she broke through the throng, she saw that he was not alone. Annabelle was with him, her arm around his waist. Damaris stopped. Her heart lurched as Richard's arm encircled the beautiful widow's shoulders.

Whirling, Damaris stumbled after her family. Her heart might have received its final shattering, but two good things had come from today. Missy and Percy were to be wed, and she and her sister were definitely friends once more. That would be enough. It had to be.

Tents containing vast quantities of food and drink dotted the lawn of Delafield Hall. Great torches were spaced at suitable intervals to light the festivities as the evening progressed. Nobility, gentry, tradesmen, and tenants rubbed shoulders, all taking advantage of the earl's fine hospitality.

Richard stood watching, with Annabelle on his arm, as Sir Osbert announced the engagement of his daughter Melissa and the Honorable Percy Marston.

"Perhaps there should be another announcement as well," the widow purred, gazing up at him.

Richard studiously ignored her, watching hopefully for any gentleman who might be willing to take the lady off his hands. He was supposed to be escorting his Queen, but Annabelle had latched on to him as he'd left the castle and refused to relinquish her hold. Dammit all! As a gentleman, he couldn't simply walk away from her. She had sobered up from her overindulgence that afternoon and had quite recovered from drooping against him and passing out in the arena, but her injured ankle prevented her from standing safely without the cane that she had so *unfortunately* left inside.

"Richard?" Annabelle whispered. "Are you listening to me?"

"Shh."

His brother moved forward to speak to the assemblage.

"I know that we shall be the happiest couple," Percy stated proudly. "Missy is as fascinated by the Middle Ages as I am! In fact . . ." His eyes suddenly glowed with excitement. "By George, we'll re-create a medieval wedding! Would you care for that, my dear?"

Missy eyed him adoringly. "I would like it above all things!"

Pandemonium broke loose. Men huzzahed, women applauded, Percy's friends gave a mighty cheer, toasting the couple with their brimming mugs of ale. Richard groaned.

"Don't worry, darling." Annabelle patted his arm. "*Our* wedding shall be unremarkable."

He glanced across the crowd and met Damaris's eyes. Her smile faded as she peered at him steadily.

Lifting her chin, she turned and disappeared into the masses.

"Richard?" Annabelle tugged at his sleeve. "You are not paying me the slightest attention." She pouted.

"I'm sorry, my lady," he said stiffly. "That was not my intention. I attempt to make all of my guests feel welcome."

"*Guests?*" She snorted. "Surely you cannot consider me to be just one of your *guests!* Particularly after what has happened between us! And I specifically had this costume designed for your pleasure!"

He looked down at the jeweled bodice, which fit so tightly that its contents were in great danger of popping right out of the top.

"How could you have done that, madam?" he asked coolly. "You didn't even know that I was at home."

"I'd hoped that you would return for such a grand occasion! Really, Richard, can you not appreciate my efforts?" Two spots of red flamed on the points of her cheekbones. "I remember the time when this dress would have made you purr like a kitten!"

He set his jaw. "Those times have passed."

"No matter, we shall recapture them." She moved closer, pressing her breast against his side. "Darling, let us announce our engagement tonight."

He drew a deep breath. The time had come. In a moment there would be no going back. He was about to plunge himself into a tremendous scandal. The *ton* would never stop gossiping about the Earl of Delafield.

"No," he said flatly. "We shall not announce our engagement tonight. Not tonight, or any night. I will not marry you, Annabelle."

She gasped. "Richard! You must! You have ruined me!"

"You ruined yourself by chasing after me. If anything, you have ruined me. You did it before, and you are doing it again."

Once again, he surveyed the crowd. Where was Damaris? Had she been swept up by a group of friends? Perhaps she had gone into the castle. He must find her!

"Oh, Richard, Richard!" Annabelle cried. "How can you say these cruel things? When I have loved you all these years!"

"It is too late."

"Never!" Her grip on his arm increased. With her other hand, she smoothed the velvet of his sleeve. "Have you forgotten what we had together? You can't imagine how much I detested wedding stuffy old Kelford instead of you!"

"Then why did you?" he asked abruptly, looking her fully in the eye.

"My parents forced me," she stammered. "You knew that!"

"We could have eloped."

"It would have been impossible! They kept too close a watch on me. They were determined that I marry Kelford. I could never have escaped.

His mind drifted back to the kindly, rather elderly Lord and Lady Leigh. They had been indulgent with their only daughter. She'd had everything she ever wanted, from a vast wardrobe to her own personal phaeton, to . . . to a husband. She'd *wanted* Lord Kelford, a man old enough and so well settled in his title and wealth that he would spoil her as her father had. It hadn't been a case of her feeling sorry for the victim of the duel, or being repentant because she'd caused it all. She'd wanted Lord Kelford all along. Richard had merely been a toy for her diversion.

Something of his enlightenment must have reflected in his expression, for she clung to him more fiercely.

"It serves no purpose to dwell upon the past. Let us put it behind us, Richard!" she urged. "We can have a wonderful future. *Together!*"

How different things would have been if he had recognized the truth of the matter way back then. He would have had those years with his father. He would have learned how to manage the estates as well as the old earl had done. He would have watched Damaris grow into a lovely young woman. Damaris! Once more, he looked for her.

Far down in the meadow, he saw a flash of scarlet moving toward the woods. It was Damaris. She'd been wearing a magnificent red gown. He was certain of it! But what was she doing down there?

"Annabelle, we have no future." He gently removed her hand from his arm.

"But we can!" Her voice rose. "I shall prove it to you! This night, I shall come to you and . . ."

He shook his head. "No."

"It's that Grayson girl, isn't it? You think you love her!"

Heads were turning. Richard was acutely conscious of the curious stares of those nearby. Now Annabelle was placing Damaris in the midst of the scandal.

"Lower your voice!" he said roughly. "My God, can't we retain some measure of dignity?"

"But you are breaking my heart!"

"If so, I must apologize. I didn't think you had one." He beckoned to Gerry Hasbrook, who was eyeing them inquiringly. "Please assist Lady Kelford," he told the viscount. "I must be elsewhere."

"Richard!" Annabelle screeched.

He shoved the marchioness onto Hasbrook's arm and fled through the mob. Oh, why did everyone seem to want to stop him, to talk with him? Couldn't they see that he was in a hurry? Damaris was going to escape him once more. Where in the hell was she going?

Chapter 18

Damaris entered the woods. The soothing cool of the trees quickly dried the dew of perspiration that her vigorous walk in the heavy velvet gown had produced. Lady Grayson's idea of proper medieval fabric certainly did not fit in with exercise on a warm summer evening.

She paused within the fringe of the trees and took a deep breath of the lighter, fresher, forest air. She knew exactly where she was. Even though the path was slightly overgrown, she had spent too much of her childhood in the Delafield woodland to be mistaken. This was one of the back trails to Richard's treehouse. She and Percy had often used it when they'd mounted their sneak attacks on him. She wondered if anything remained of the lofty structure.

With a sigh, she leaned against a large oak tree, remembering those happy days of play. This might be the last time she could wander through these woods. When Annabelle married Richard, she doubted that she would be welcome to roam the Delafield property. Then too, it wouldn't be long before this forest rang with the laughter of another generation. If she came here, she would be a bothersome trespasser to their games.

Tears slid down her cheeks. Painful images of Annabelle in Richard's arms and Annabelle confidently standing beside him pounded through her mind. Damaris would have given him her whole heart to keep, but why should he want it? He had Annabelle, Annabelle whom he had always loved. She was nothing in comparison to the beautiful widow.

Wiping her eyes on her sleeve, she set off down the path. Though darkness was falling, she had to have time to compose herself before returning to Percy's party. She couldn't go on like this, not tonight or at any time thereafter. She must dispose of her love for Richard. She would force herself to remember only the times when he had been so angry with her, and when he had humiliated her. She would forget all else, most especially his kisses. She would make herself despise him.

Sniffling mightily, Damaris found herself under the spreading tree that had sheltered Richard's treehouse. What was this? The steps had been repaired! She gazed up into the leafy canopy. Even in the twilight, she could see that new boards had replaced the old. Someone had restored the treehouse! Old Asa? Surely not! His joints were much too stiff for such an enterprise. Percy? Impossible! He had been too busy with his tournament preparations. Richard? She sadly shook her head. He had probably forgotten that he'd even had a treehouse.

Damaris tugged at the bottom step. It was sturdy. The whole structure appeared to be very safe and solid.

A compelling desire whispered through her mind. Why not? There was no one here to witness her childish behavior. She removed her wide medieval headdress and laid it carefully on an exposed root. Hitching up her skirts, she began to climb.

It wasn't as easy as it had been when she was a child. She had lost some of that youthful agility, and the heavy, elaborate medieval costume was a nui-

sance. With much heaving and panting, she made it
to the top and seated herself on the platform, dan-
gling her legs over the edge.

How pleasant it was in the tree! She had forgotten
that sense of exhilaration she'd always experienced
when she was high above the world. It seemed as if
all of her problems had been left on the ground.

"Damaris! What are you doing up there?"

It was Richard! Hurriedly, she drew in her legs and
scrambled to her feet. She reached for the top step.

"No! Wait! I'm coming up!"

Blushing furiously, she realized that he could probably see straight up her skirt. It had always been the
rule that boys should turn their backs when girls descended, but he was ignoring it. He was climbing
right up! Hastily, she sat down, decorously arranging
her dress.

Richard alighted onto the platform. "Were you surprised to see the treehouse?"

"Yes! Did you have someone repair it?"

"I did it myself."

"*You?*" she asked incredulously.

"Yes, *me.* I remembered Asa's carpentry lessons."
He dropped down beside her. "Don't you think I did
well?"

"Yes, but . . ."

"But why?" he guessed.

She nodded.

"Fond memories, I suppose. I did the work in secret. People would think that the Earl of Delafield
had lost his wits if it was generally known. You
won't tattle on me, will you?"

"No," Damaris said slowly.

People. Was he particularly referring to Annabelle?
No, of course not. Anyone who loved him would de-

light in his little boyish idiosyncrasy. Most likely, Annabelle was somewhere below.

She peered over the edge to the forest floor. She hoped Lady Kelford was well out of sight. With her voluminous skirts, she would make an awkward descent, and she didn't want the future countess to behold it.

"What are you looking for?" Richard inquired.

"I . . . nothing," she stammered.

Of course he wouldn't want to betray the hiding place of his intended, and she wouldn't put him on the spot. She would leave quickly, and they could have their privacy. She started to get up, but he caught her arm.

"Don't go, Damaris. We have to have that talk. Now," he said quietly but determinedly. "About what happened in the grove. I . . ."

"It isn't necessary, Richard," she murmured. "I understand."

"You *do?*" he asked in disbelief.

"Yes." Her cheeks burned with remembered humiliation. "You wished to prove to me that your interests lie elsewhere. But why did you have to be so cruel about it?" she cried. "Couldn't you have simply told me?"

"Damaris, I came to the grove to meet *you!* Please believe me!"

"Oh, then you would have explained in person. Thank you, Richard. I hated believing that you deliberately set out to mortify me completely."

"No! You are wrong!" He slipped his arm across her shoulders and gave her a little shake. "Listen to me. When I received Percy's note—"

"Percy's note!" she interrupted. "I know nothing of Percy sending notes!"

"My brother was attempting a bit of matchmaking." He sighed. "I fear he made a tragic muddle of it."

"Oh no!" she gasped, suddenly realizing what the truth must be.

She had admitted to Percy that she loved his brother. In hopes of making her happy, he had set up the whole thing. Richard had nothing to do with it! He wasn't bent on humiliating her, but he didn't really love her either. He was meeting her to set the record straight. Annabelle must have followed him, and they'd hoped to indulge in a few moments' passion before she arrived.

"Percy meant well," Richard explained. "When matters went awry, he was terribly distraught."

Why hadn't Percy ascertained Richard's feelings for Annabelle before he had encouraged her? She would certainly give her friend a piece of her mind! Incensed, Damaris rose, but Richard clasped her around the waist and pulled her down.

"Dammit! Will you never let me explain? You are leading me off on such tangents that this whole thing makes no sense whatsoever!"

"I!" She tried to wriggle free. "Why don't you just tell me that you are in love with Annabelle, and be done with it?"

"Because I'm not!" he shouted. "I'm in love with you!"

Damaris half choked on her own gasp. She sat dead still. Mesmerized, she gazed into his eyes.

"I was coming to meet you in the grove because I loved you, and I thought you loved me too," he began patiently. "Annabelle followed me and threw herself at me. She has been in pursuit of me ever since she arrived at Delafield Hall. It's just as simple, and as complex, as that."

Her blood rushed wildly through her veins

Nerves danced in her stomach. She drew a long, slow breath.

"But, Richard, I saw you holding her today. At the tournament, after the accident."

He grinned. "She was foxed, you know. Somehow she made her way onto the field. As a gentleman, I couldn't let her fall on the ground, could I?"

"No-o-o-o."

"I have no feeling for Annabelle except, perhaps, anger." His smile faded. "She has destroyed a goodly portion of my life."

"That is past now." Her heart bursting with love for him, Damaris reached out to touch his cheek.

He caught her hand before she could caress him. "No, my love, it isn't."

"She cannot hurt you now! I shall not allow it!"

"Darling." He kissed her fingertips. "I fear you have no control over it."

"I shall scratch her eyes out!"

His smile returned, but it was one of bitterness, not pleasure. "Annabelle injured her ankle in the grove when I pushed her away and attempted to go after you. I was forced to carry her back to the Hall, thus providing evidence of a moonlit rendezvous. She considers herself to be compromised. Others do, as well."

"So?" Damaris shrugged.

"*So!*" In spite of his rancor, he laughed. "Love, you shall never convince me that you are so naive! If I do not marry Annabelle, I shall fall victim to the worst gossip, made even more malicious because of my previous scandal involving her."

"Ignore the wagging tongues!" she urged. "That woman would make your life a misery!"

"To be honorable . . ."

Damaris groaned. "Why must men set such an inflated value on honor? Oh, it is all well and good, in its place. But not to the ruination of one's life! Don't do it, Richard!" She squeezed his hand encouragingly. "Your friends and family will understand the truth, and that is all that matters!"

He nodded soberly. "I have decided that I do not care if I am accepted by the *ton*. I will not marry Annabelle. I told her so this evening. But Damaris . . . you and I . . . In the grove, I had intended to ask you to marry me, but now . . ."

"But now you will do so in the treehouse," she finished softly.

"You must realize that there would be censure by the *ton*."

"Because of the treehouse?" she asked innocently, trying not to giggle.

"Damaris! This is not a time for levity!"

"No. Certainly not. We must be serious while you propose and I accept."

"The *ton* . . ."

"I don't give a fig for the opinion of the *ton!*" She slipped her arms around his neck. "I love you, Richard."

"I love you." He drew her closer, his mouth claiming hers.

Damaris's heart soared as she gave herself up to his ardent embrace. He was hers. Her dream had come true. She must be the happiest woman on the face of the earth. What difference did anyone's attitude make? She would be the wife of the most wonderful man ever born!

Much later, she lifted her head, surprised to find Richard lying on his back on the treehouse platform and herself sprawled across his chest. Her long, dark hair streamed over their faces. Pushing it back, she

und, to her dismay, that some of the pins were
mpletely missing.

"Gracious! How did we get like this?"

He grinned lazily, stroking her back. "You always
ere a managing woman, my love."

"I didn't take the pins out of my hair," she
apped back, laughing. "What will people say when
ey see me?"

"I thought we weren't going to worry about that."

"Up to a point, my lord. I fear that this would even
ock our families."

"We'll tell them that we've been climbing trees," he
ggested with a chuckle.

Damaris kissed the tip of his nose. "I've climbed
any a tree, but I've never come down looking like
is."

She started to rise, but he drew her close once
ore. With a sigh, she nestled her head on his shoul-
r. It was so fitting to her dream to be up in the
eehouse with him.

"Aren't trees marvelous?" she whispered. "Let us
me here often."

"As you wish." Richard smoothed her hair.
'hough we must plan a speedy wedding, my love.
do not think I can go tree climbing with you again
ithout losing whatever shred of honor I have left."

"Yes." Tilting her head, she gazed longingly at his
os, then reluctantly sat up. "We had best return.
e've been gone a lengthy time."

They searched for her pins, finding most of them
attered about the platform. Richard awkwardly
lped her put her hair up. Both dreading to return
 the festivities, they clambered to the ground.

"I would be so very happy if we could only stay
re for the rest of the evening," Damaris said wist-
lly, replacing her headgear.

"So would I."

"Let's take the long way back!" she eagerly urged

"All right," he, very willingly, agreed.

Holding hands, they walked leisurely down th path.

Her hair glistened in the moonlight. So occupied i watching his lady, Richard could barely concentrat on where he was walking. She was his! Damari would be his wife! How could it ever have occurre to him to sacrifice this and marry Annabelle? He ha been a coward and a fool to be so terribly concerne with the opinion of the *ton*. Damaris was worth fa more than an absolute torrent of gossip.

She caught his eye. "Are you staring at me?" Sh smiled. "No doubt you are thinking that I look lik the personification of chaos."

"Actually, love, I believe that you are the mos beautiful woman I have ever had the privilege of see ing."

"Oh, Richard." Pausing, she gazed at him, her blu eyes soft with desire. "My darling."

He had to kiss her again, to taste the sweet honey of her mouth. *He* was her darling. Other than hi mother, there had never been a woman who ha called him darling and really meant it. Until now.

Damaris touched his cheek, breaking off the kiss "I would stand here and kiss you all night, but w truly must hurry back to the castle. Mama and Pap will miss me and begin to wonder."

A horrible thought assailed him. "Damaris! Yo may not care what the *ton* thinks of me, but wha about your parents? What if your father will no agree to the match?"

"He will. He likes you." She lifted her pert chin "Besides, didn't you call me a 'managing woman'?

He grinned sheepishly. "That was bad of me, wasn't it?"

"No." With her forefinger, she lovingly traced the line of his lips. "I *have* been rather autocratic, a trait I intend to change."

He kissed the palm of her hand, then tucked it into the crook of his elbow. They walked silently to the place where the path joined the main avenue to Delafield Hall. He hesitated, staring at the castle.

"Damaris, you are an excellent steward. You believe that a husband and wife should be equal partners in life. I . . . I agree with you."

"That was difficult to say, wasn't it, Richard?" she asked gently.

He smiled. "Well, it is a new concept to me, but your skill should not be wasted. I hope you will give me your advice. You love the land and you possess great talent in making it produce."

"Yes, I do love the land." She took a deep breath. "But I love you more, and I love you unconditionally. I shall advise you only if you are comfortable with it."

"You are making an enormous compromise," he marveled.

"Not really."

He held her close, once again possessing her mouth.

Footsteps, accompanied by a loud snicker, echoed on the drive. Richard sprang back. Damaris began to giggle.

"Asa!" she greeted. "And Hilda."

"Miss Damaris, m'lord. Just going home, we was, an' what a sight to see!" he cackled, nudging his tittering wife.

Richard felt heat surge up his neck, suffusing his face.

The old man beamed from ear to ear. "Well now, since Miss Damaris ain't the type to ... uh ... you know, I 'spect we'll soon be hearin' a fine announcement!"

"Yes, Asa, I expect you will," he managed.

"Glad you're seein' to yer health, m'lord. I was gettin' right worried about that gout! But I suppose you'll have enough ... uh ... you know ... to take care of it!"

Richard grinned self-consciously.

Asa's wife pushed at his back. "C'mon, you old fool! Let these young folks have peace."

"All right, all right!" He made an ungainly bow and started down the road. "Well! If that doesn't make me feel like a young fella!"

"Don't you go thinkin' like that! I get tired of yer puffin' and snortin'!" she caustically complained.

Richard quickly propelled the giggling Damaris toward Delafield Hall.

"What is 'uh ... you know'?" Damaris asked.

"I'll tell you later."

"When, Richard?"

"After we are married."

"People who love each other shouldn't have secrets," she said airily.

"I'll *show* you after we're married," he promised. "Now do you understand?"

"Not really," she mused. "Do you have the gout, Richard?"

"No!" he exclaimed.

"Then ..."

Her words were cut off by another passerby on the road. A gig driven by Richard's groom, Wesley, trotted smartly toward them and pulled up to a halt. Sitting stiffly inside were the Casey brothers.

"We are leaving," they announced. "We can no longer bear another moment."

Richard gaped. "Not even for a raise in salary?"

"My lord," the original Casey proclaimed with a sniff, "you cannot pay us enough to induce us to remain."

"I had hoped that employing both of you might ease matters."

"Only a slight amount. We have been forced to deal with this medieval frivolity, with lack of respect toward us by our inferiors, with impertinence of those inferiors toward you, their master . . ." He moaned. "And just look in the mirror, my lord. You and your brother are a discredit to our reputations!"

"Talk about impertinent servants!" Wesley cried. "I've a notion to set 'em down, m'lord, and let 'em walk! Hell with 'em! That's what I say!"

"Drive on!" barked Casey.

"I'll drive on! I'll drive on all right!" Wesley abruptly started the gig, nearly toppling the brothers backward.

"Who was that?" Damaris asked as they sped away, their voices raised in animosity.

"My former valet, and Percy's," he said dryly.

"What impudence! You are well off to be rid of them!" she stormed. "They must be blind. You have *always* been the most handsome man in the world. But you are also the most frustrating! I still do not understand what 'uh . . . you know' might be."

"Damaris, you may be brilliant at managing an estate, but you are particularly dense on some matters. I will *show* you on our wedding night."

She frowned slightly, then the lines on her forehead vanished as a light dawned. "Oh. *That's* it," she said, flushing.

"I do believe you understand." He grinned mischievously.

"Apparently Asa believes that a lot of . . ."

"Uh . . . you know?" he supplied.

"Yes," she said briskly. "He believes that it will prevent the gout.

"That is correct."

"Well then, you must hurry and speak with Papa, so that we may be wed as soon as possible. We must take precautionary measures." Damaris looked up at him, eyes twinkling. "After all, women do not wish to have the gout either!"

He speculatively studied her. "Do you intend to be managerial in this?"

She lifted her chin, tilting it merrily. "Oh no, my lord. In *this, you* shall be the authority!"

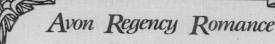

Avon Regency Romance

Kasey Michaels

THE CHAOTIC MISS CRISPINO
76300-1/$3.99 US/$4.99 Can

THE DUBIOUS MISS DALRYMPLE
89908-6/$2.95 US/$3.50 Can

THE HAUNTED MISS HAMPSHIRE
76301-X/$3.99 US/$4.99 Can

Loretta Chase

THE ENGLISH WITCH 70660-1/$2.95 US/$3.50 Can

ISABELLA 70597-4/$2.95 US/$3.95 Can

KNAVES' WAGER 71363-2/$3.95 US/$4.95 Can

THE SANDALWOOD PRINCESS
71455-8/$3.99 US/$4.99 Can

THE VISCOUNT VAGABOND
70836-1/$2.95 US/$3.50 Can

Jo Beverley

EMILY AND THE DARK ANGEL
71555-4/$3.99 US/$4.99 Can

THE FORTUNE HUNTER
71771-9/$3.99 US/$4.99 Can

THE STANFORTH SECRETS
71438-8/$3.99 US/$4.99 Can

Avon Romances—
the best in exceptional authors and unforgettable novels!

HEART OF THE WILD Donna Stephens
77014-8/$4.50 US/$5.50 Can

TRAITOR'S KISS Joy Tucker
76446-6/$4.50 US/$5.50 Can

SILVER AND SAPPHIRES Shelly Thacker
77034-2/$4.50 US/$5.50 Can

SCOUNDREL'S DESIRE Joann DeLazzari
76421-0/$4.50 US/$5.50 Can

MY LADY NOTORIOUS Jo Beverley
76785-6/$4.50 US/$5.50 Can

SURRENDER MY HEART Lois Greiman
77181-0/$4.50 US/$5.50 Can

MY REBELLIOUS HEART Samantha James
76937-9/$4.50 US/$5.50 Can

COME BE MY LOVE Patricia Watters
76909-3/$4.50 US/$5.50 Can

SUNSHINE AND SHADOW Kathleen Harrington
77058-X/$4.50 US/$5.50 Can

WILD CONQUEST Hannah Howell
77182-9/$4.50 US/$5.50 Can

Avon Romantic Treasures

*Unforgettable, enthralling love stories,
sparkling with passion and adventure
from Romance's bestselling authors*

MY WILD ROSE *by Deborah Camp*

76738-4/$4.50 US/$5.50 Can

MIDNIGHT AND MAGNOLIAS *by Rebecca Paisley*

76566-7/$4.50 US/$5.50 Can

THE MASTER'S BRIDE *by Suzannah Davis*

76821-6/$4.50 US/$5.50 Can

A ROSE AT MIDNIGHT *by Anne Stuart*

76740-6/$4.50 US/$5.50 Can

FORTUNE'S MISTRESS *by Judith E. French*

76864-X/$4.50 US/$5.50 Can

HIS MAGIC TOUCH *by Stella Cameron*

76607-8/$4.50 US/$5.50 Can

COMANCHE WIND *by Genell Dellin*

76717-1/$4.50 US/$5.50 Can

THEN CAME YOU *by Lisa Kleypas*

77013-X/$4.50 US/$5.50 Can